Squanto's Journey

THE STORY OF THE FIRST THANKSGIVING

Joseph Bruchac

ILLUSTRATED BY **Greg Shed**

SILVER WHISTLE · HARCOURT, INC.

SAN DIEGO   NEW YORK   LONDON   PRINTED IN THE UNITED STATES OF AMERICA

MY STORY IS BOTH STRANGE AND TRUE. I was born in the year the English call 1590. My family were leaders of the Patuxet people and I, too, was raised to lead. But in 1614 I was taken to Spain against my will. Now it is 1621 and I am again in my homeland. My name is Squanto. I would like to tell you my tale.

I look up and watch a heron flying overhead. It goes toward the falls that gave our people their name. We were the Patuxet, the People of the Falls. Our cleared fields were not empty of people then as they were when the English pilgrims landed in the Freezing Moon of 1620. Only six winters have passed, but so many things have changed.

I remember that day in 1614. White men had come often to fish in our bay and trade. They had brought us fine things in exchange for beaver and deerskins. This time—when their tall ships, with sails like the wings of giant birds, anchored offshore—this time was different.

John Smith was one of the English captains. He and his officer, Thomas Dermer, traded with us. I liked the way Dermer shook my hand. Smith had learned much from dealing with other Indians in the summer land of Virginia. He knew we valued honor.

The other captain was Thomas Hunt. After Smith left, Hunt landed at Patuxet. He told us he was Smith's friend. "Come to a feast on my ship," he said.

More than twenty of us went aboard to share food with friends. But Hunt was no friend. He set sail, taking us with him as captives. Left behind were our families, our homes, our people. Our lives were no longer our own.

Soon we were crossing the wide salt waters. The journey was long, but my spirit did not desert me. I remembered I was *pniese*, a man of courage. I told stories to my people and urged them to stay strong.

Hunt took us to Malaga in the land of Spain. There we were sold to be slaves. But men who serve the Creator lived there. It was they, who called themselves Brothers, who freed us from our chains.

I learned more of their language. I let them teach me about their ways of thanking the Great Mystery. I told them what I wanted most. I wanted to return home. With the Friars' help, I went to England. English ships often sailed toward the sunset. I realized that if I could be of use to the English, they might take me with them.

It took much work, but I learned the language well. In March of the year they call 1619, I sailed back to New England at the side of my friend Thomas Dermer, one of John Smith's officers. Our memories of each other were like the taste of good water. He told me that things were not well between my People of the First Light and the English. Englishmen and their ships were now being attacked when they came to shore. Perhaps if I accompanied the English, I could speak with the Indians and they could trade again in peace. My heart felt as if it were soaring on an eagle's wings as the ship cut through the waves. But I also feared what I might find.

"Where there were this many people," he said, telling me of great illness in New England brought on by white traders, "now only this many remain." He folded back all but two fingers.

It proved as he said. The sickness had come down upon Patuxet like the blow of a war club. Only a few of my people survived. My wife, my children, my parents, and all those closest to me were gone. I will not say their names now. I will speak them again when my own feet climb the highest mountain and I walk the Road of Stars to greet them.

Together, Thomas Dermer and I did our work. We made friendly contact with the Nemasket and Pokanoket. More than once, my words saved the life of my English friend. Peace seemed within our reach.

But Epanow, the powerful sachem of Capawack, viewed the English as one might a deadly serpent. Epanow, too, had been taken to England as a slave and brought back to act as a guide. He had escaped and vowed to always fight the white men. The deeds of other Englishmen convinced his people that he was right. In the summer of 1620, as Thomas Dermer and I talked of peace, an English captain invited a party of Indians on board their ship. Then suddenly, the white men shot them down.

When we reached the island of Capawack, Epanow and his warriors attacked us. Many English were killed. Thomas Dermer was wounded. With my help he was able to escape, but I was taken captive and given to the Pokanoket as a prisoner.

That November, when the *Mayflower* reached shore, the Pokanoket watched. They did not come close to the English. If the Pokanoket had been stronger, they might have attacked the white men—wiped them out or driven them away. But the Pokanoket were still weak from the great sickness. Where there had been thousands, now there were hundreds.

The strength of our people was so small now that the Narragansett to the south, untouched by the plague themselves, ordered the once-proud Pokanoket and Nemasket to pay them tribute.

I spoke to Massasoit, the sachem of the Pokanoket, as a *pniese* should, with respect and honor. "Befriend the English," I said. "Make them come to understand and support our people."

Massasoit did not listen at first. He watched silently through that winter.

Then Samoset came to visit. He was a sachem of the Pemaquid people, who lived farther up the coast. He had done much trading with the English. He knew some of their language.

"Let me talk with the Songlismoniak," he said to Massasoit, nodding to me as he spoke. Massasoit agreed.

The next day, March 16th of 1621, Samoset strode into the English settlement.

"Welcome, English," he said in their tongue. He showed them the two arrows in his hand. One had a flint arrowhead, the other had the arrowhead removed. The arrows symbolized what we offered them, either war or peace.

The English placed a coat about his shoulders to warm him. They invited him into one of their houses. They gave him small water, biscuits and butter, pudding and cheese.

"The food was so good," Samoset said to me later, laughing as he spoke, "I decided to spend the night."

When he left the next day, he promised to return with a friend who spoke their language well.

So it was that five days later, on the 22nd of March, I walked with Samoset back into my own village. Once Patuxet, now it was Plymouth. I looked around me. Though much was changed, I knew that I at last had returned to the land of my home.

"Perhaps these men can share our land as friends," I told my brother, at my side.

In the moons that followed, there was much work to do. The Pokanoket freed me to be a guide and interpreter for the English. Not only did I act as envoy between the English and our people, I also had many things to teach the white people about survival. They knew little of hunting and almost nothing of planting. It had always been the job of the Patuxet women to care for the crops while men such as myself hunted. But I had observed much in the years since my captivity. I had seen in Newfoundland how the English learned from our people how to grow corn.

"Use the small fish that wash up on our shores in great numbers," I told the English. "Bury those fish in the earth and they will feed the corn."

I showed them how to plant the seeds of corn and beans and squash together in hills. I told them when it was the Moon of Hoeing. They listened well and worked hard. I came to see that these pilgrims could be our friends and we theirs. Together we might make our home on this land given to us by the Creator of All Things.

A good harvest was brought in this fall. Some of their English crops have not done well. But the three sisters—the corn and beans and squash—have done well. As I look at the beans, growing up about the stalks of the corn, I think of how our two people have become entwined. I feel hope for our children in the seasons to come. With our help, the English have learned enough of hunting and fishing to provide the food for a great feast such as this one—this feast for all our people.

Now as we eat together, I give thanks. I have seen more in my life than most men, whether Indian or English. I have seen both death and life come to this land that gives itself to English and Indian alike. I pray that there will be many more such days to give thanks together in the years that follow.

I am Squanto. I am known to all those who gather here: English, Pokanoket, Nemasket, even a few of my own surviving Patuxets. I speak to you as a *pniese*, a man of honor. I will never leave this land. I give thanks for all of our people to the Creator of All Things.

Author's Note

The story of the Pilgrims and the first Thanksgiving Day is familiar to every child in America. However, the Native American side of that tale is seldom told. I've always been fascinated by the role played by Native Americans—and especially the man known as Tisquantum or Squanto—in helping that first New England colony survive.

Squanto's is a tale that I think is inspiring to both Native and non-Native readers alike. Not only did Squanto escape from slavery in Spain and make influential friends in England, but he was able to find his way back home. Even though his closest family and friends had died from a plague introduced by the English, he became the interpreter and guide for the Pilgrims. It is no exaggeration to say that without Squanto, the Plymouth colony might have failed. Squanto's journey is an incredible saga of both survival and acceptance. He was one of the first Native Americans to live successfully in the worlds of both the European and the Indian. As a person of Native American New England descent myself, Squanto's story has a special reverberation for me.

However, being Indian does not mean that you automatically know about all things Native American. Whenever I tell a story that comes from another Native nation, it is my responsibility to hear the living voices of those Native people. One of my first inspirations for this story was my late friend Nanepashemet, a Wampanoag scholar and historical interpreter, an academic and traditionalist respected in both worlds. Nanepashemet worked for many years at Plimoth Plantation, the living history museum of the original Massachussetts colony. The accuracy and relaxed, very Indian atmosphere of the Wampanoag village that now stands next to Plimoth Plantation is due to the integrity and commitment of such people as Nanepashemet. His own historical novel about Squanto is now being edited by Linda Coombs, another prominent Wampanoag scholar and defender of their nation's traditions. *Squanto's Journey* could not have been written without their work and the contributions of other contemporary Wampanoag people such as Russell Peters (Fast Turtle), the late John Peters (Slow Turtle), and many others who continue to stand and speak for the people. *Wliwini nidobak!* (Thank you, my friends.)

I also thank my sister Marge Bruchac for her extensive research into the true story of Tisquantum and the everyday lives of the Pilgrims and the Wampanoag people of the early seventeenth century. Virtually every telling of the first Thanksgiving story is marred by historical errors in the depictions of the event, from the food served at the feast to the clothing worn by the Pilgrims (not hats with buckles on them!). Whenever I write a story dealing with New England Native history, I always turn first to Marge, who has been consulted by numerous historical villages, museums, and Indian nations, including Old Sturbridge Village, the Mohegan Tribe, Historic Northampton, and Plimoth Plantation.

Then there is the land itself. Our Native people have always believed that the land talks to us when we listen. I have stood on the same ground where Squanto walked three centuries ago, feeling the sea breeze in my face and smelling the smoke from cooking fires, where the same foods he would have eaten were being cooked in the traditional way. As I stood there, I, too, heard the whisper of the earth, a song on the wind reminding me that those ancient voices will never be gone.

THE LABRADOR RETRIEVER

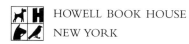

The Dog That Does It All

LISA WEISS & EMILY BIEGEL

HOWELL BOOK HOUSE

NEW YORK

Howell Book House
A Simon & Schuster Macmillan Company
1633 Broadway
New York, NY 10019-6785

Macmillan Publishing books may be purchased for business or sales promotional use. For information please write: Special Markets Department, Macmillan Publishing USA, 1633 Broadway, New York, NY 10019-6785.

Library of Congress Cataloging-in-Publication

    Weiss, Lisa
        The labrador retriever : the dog that does it all / Lisa Weiss and Emily Biegel.
          p. cm.
        Includes bibliographical references (p. 233).
        ISBN 0-87605-044-5
        1. Labrador Retriever. I. Biegel, Emily. II. Title.
        SF429.L3W45 1998
        636.752'7—dc21   98-38488
                                        CIP

Manufactured in the United States of America
10 9 8 7 6 5 4 3 2 1

Cover and book design by George J. McKeon

Dedication

This book is dedicated fondly to three pioneers of the modern Labrador Retriever: Joan Redmond Read, George Bragaw and Mary Swan. Their respective kennel names—Chidley, Shookstown and Chebacco—appear in the pedigrees of many famous Labradors. They were champions of the all-around dog, the Labrador that was correct in type and structure, stylish and smart.

Joan Read began breeding Labradors in the 1930s and exhibited at the very first Labrador national specialty show in 1933. She was a mentor to many present-day breed experts. When she passed away in 1995, she left a void that will never be filled. It was an honor to know her!

Left to right, three giants of the breed: Mary Swan, Joan Read and George Bragaw.

George Bragaw was as much at home in the duck blind as he was in the show ring. His early success as a breeder-exhibitor was followed by an illustrious judging career. George had very definite opinions, and loved to talk dogs with anyone and everyone. He generously shared his knowledge with so many of us. Sadly, George died in late 1997 and will be sorely missed by all who knew him.

The third musketeer, Mary Swan, can trace her involvement with Labradors to the 1940s. Mary is treasured as a breed historian and our link to the early years of Labradors.

Mary, Joan and George were the closest of friends for years. They shared many a wonderful goose dinner, provided by George, cooked by Mary, eaten at Joan's house!

Acknowledgments

FROM EMILY BIEGEL:

If it were not for a fortunate combination of circumstances that led me to the Guide Dog Foundation for the Blind, I'd have a different name and spotted dogs. Thanks, first and foremost, to my husband, John, for teaching me patience and giving me his unending love and support. To my daughters, Caroline and Amy, for putting up with dog hair in the food (once in a while) and a mom who always filled the house with four-legged friends. Although neither shows dogs, Caroline and Amy and their husbands, David Naluai and Jim Verschure, have their own Labradors now. Thanks to Mary Kras, my friend and colleague at the Guide Dog Foundation, for sharing her knowledge and excellent eye for a dog. And thanks to all of the Labrador people, who are as nice as their dogs!

FROM LISA WEISS:

A heartfelt thank you to my parents Lee and Jerry, and my family, who have always been there when I've needed them, and even when I haven't. My dad and I have had the rare opportunity to share a hobby that has allowed us to spend a great deal of quality time together throughout our lives. My mother's energy and intellect will never cease to amaze me. As we often joke, we are as different as night and day… she always reads the book and I always wait for it to be made into a movie! We enjoy doing so much together. My great ideas often get us into trouble, but usually her good sense prevails and bails us out. Hey, Ma, you wouldn't want life to be dull, now would you?!

Thanks to my three beautiful and talented children, Kyra Lee, a future Olympic gymnast; Bethany Jean, a future breeder-handler and Spice Girl; and my son Alexander Jacob, a future Pelé! They've all had their share of life with Labradors, toys that get chewed, sneakers that end up missing and birthday parties interrupted by litters being born. They're turning out wonderfully in spite of it all!

Thanks to my sister Patti Gibbons and Donna de Pasquale for their computer assistance and my sister Maggie Boba for all the baby-sitting.

Thanks to my friend Barry Rose who has the unique gift of 20/20 foresight in a world where most have 20/20 hindsight!

My sister Mollie Madden for taking many of the photos. And to Pam Setchell, Greg Goebel and Abby Kagan for their photo expertise.

Thank you to the Metz family who gave me Tawny, my first champion. Our families formed a friendship that has spanned more than 30 years.

To my dear friend Emily, "Auntie Em," for all the days and years of fun we've had together enjoying our Labradors.

To another dear friend of many years, Anne Nicodemus Carpenter, my sincere appreciation. Anne knew I really loved animals and she taught me how to understand them and what makes them tick. It's not something everyone knows, and it's not knowledge that's easy to impart. It's a gift I'll always treasure.

Emily, Kathy, Holly and I would like to thank all our Labrador friends who answered the call for pictures and information: Marianne Foote, Anna Clark, Kendall Herr, Nancy Martin, Ann and Randy McCall, Mary Swan, Mary Bragaw, Winnie Limbourne, Price and Sherry Jessup, Betty Graham, Marianne Cook, Sally Bell, Carl and Nancy Brandow, Emily Magnani, Canine Companions for Independence, The Guide Dog Foundation, Jean-Louis and Madeline Charest, Jennifer Stotts, Annie Cogo, Carol Heidl, Jan and Michael Harris, Lori Bentine, Mary Kras, Bob and Terri Shober, Patti Schultze-Weiss, Anne Jones, Marion Lyons, Virginia Campbell, Diane Pilbin, Pat Ross, Sue Willumsen and Jan Grannemann.

Contents

Foreword

It is with great pleasure that I present a brief introduction to this new book about Labrador Retrievers, written by Lisa Weiss and Emily Biegel.

I've know Lisa and her family since she was just a youngster in the late 1960s. We were part of a very congenial group of Labrador owners who attended the many dog shows in the Northeast/Mid-Atlantic States region. Lisa's dad, Jerry, has been a well-respected judge of Sporting dogs for many years, and Lisa is also a very popular dog show judge.

In 1981 Lisa took a job at the Guide Dog Foundation for the Blind, Inc., in Smithtown, N.Y., near her home. There she met Emily Biegel, director of the breeding program, and the two have been dear friends ever since.

Emily had gone to work at the foundation in 1977. She grew up with Dalmatians, and had shown them in the obedience and breed rings. Upon taking her job at the Foundation, she had her first experience with Labradors and discovered what wonderful dogs they are. Now there are several Labs at the Biegel house, and Emily is enjoying obedience work with them, as well as agility and retriever hunting tests. She is retired from the Foundation breeding program after 20 years.

One very special black puppy was born at the Foundation. He was named Lobuff's Bare Necessities, known to all as Baloo, and he brought a lot of fun and excitement to his breeder-owners, Lisa and Emily. He grew to be a handsome dog and a big winner. He was Best in Sweepstakes at the national specialty show in 1991, and with co-owners Beverly Shavlik and Sally Sasser, went on to be the number one Labrador in 1993 and 1994. He won many Best of Breed honors, including two at the Westminster Kennel Club show and four at various Labrador Retriever specialty shows. After a serious accident, he came home to Long Island to earn a CD and a JH title, and to enjoy the life of a stud dog. That's Baloo on the cover of this book, by the way.

Lisa and Emily have put together a comprehensive book that includes a history and a profile of the Labrador's characteristics; advice on finding, choosing and caring for a Lab; as well as chapters on breeding, dog shows, obedience trials and performance activities. From their days with the Guide Dogs, I know they have a very special empathy for the breed.

NANCY MARTIN
Ayr Labradors

Nancy Martin and friend.

Introduction

It is our hope that we have provided an interesting and informative look at our favorite breed. Someone once said that Labradors spoil you for any other breed, and we agree! We've tried to cover many aspects of the versatile Labrador, but there is always more to learn, so do use the Bibliography and List of Resources at the end of the book to broaden your Labrador horizons.

The Labrador Retriever is still an unspoiled breed, which is all the more remarkable in light of its popularity. Our love for Labradors compelled us to share our knowledge with you, the reader, to help ensure the future health and well-being of this wonderful breed—for you will be its future guardians!

This book has primarily been the work of Lisa Weiss and Emily Biegel. However, we wanted to make sure you get the best and most up-to-date information possible. That's why we turned to the experts to write some of the chapters.

The information in Chapters 6, 7 and 8 on health and basic care was written by Kathryn Sneider, DVM, who has been breeding and showing Labrador Retrievers under the kennel prefix Aquarius since 1975. She has bred several champions and has obtained obedience titles on some of her dogs, as well. She worked for many years as a microbiologist in a "human" hospital before returning to school to receive an undergraduate degree in Psychobiology (Animal Behavior). She graduated from the University of Pennsylvania School of Veterinary Medicine in 1995. She has been in practice since that date, and currently emphasizes reproduction and genetics. Her favorite patients are Labradors!

For Chapter 14 on Dogs and the Law, we brought in the lawyer. Holly D. F. Meister, Esq., received a Bachelor of Business Administration degree with honors from Hofstra University. She graduated from Hofstra University School of Law in 1991, where she was a member of the Law Review and served as research assistant to a law professor. She is admitted to the practice of law in New York and Pennsylvania, and currently works for the federal courts as a law clerk to a United States Bankruptcy Judge. A cat lover at heart, she and her Tonkinese cat, Merlin, *accidentally* own six Labrador Retrievers.

(Tetsu Yamazaki)

CHAPTER 1

What You Should Know About the Labrador Retriever

Before you get a Labrador Retriever, there's a lot you need to know about this wonderful breed. First of all, you need to understand what makes a Labrador tick. Understanding the essence of a breed is the key to knowing what sets that breed apart. Every breed has a look that is all its own, but along with the physical characteristics comes a set of specific personality traits.

Let's start with the physical. Every breed recognized by the American Kennel Club has an official breed standard, and we'll look at the Labrador standard in Chapter 3. A standard is a very detailed list of characteristics and physical specifications, along with a narrative of a dog considered to be a very good specimen. A standard is sort of a word picture, and after reading a well-written one, you should be able to visualize a well-balanced example of that breed. Breeders are always striving to breed the perfect dog, but we find perfection to be elusive. When you're dealing with animals, or any living creatures for that matter, the variables are numerous and unpredictable.

People do seem to prefer one color to another. Usually when someone sets out to buy a puppy, they have already decided on a specific sex and color. Breeders are always inundated with calls for yellow bitches. They've been number one in popularity for a long time. No matter what color or sex a person is looking for, chances are they are already convinced that one is better than all the others.

Does it matter what color your Lab is? Not at all! (Chuck Tatham)

I do not agree that you can link specific virtues or traits to either sex or any color, but there is no sense in arguing with someone who has their mind made up. It is my opinion that whether you get a Labrador in a black, yellow or brown *suit*, that Lab should and probably will be a bouncy bundle of fun and energy. My children always say that Lab puppies remind them of Tigger, the lovable bouncy tiger in the A. A. Milne *Winnie the Pooh* stories. As Tigger says, "His paws are made out of rubber and his tail is made out of springs."

THE LAB PERSONALITY

This brings us to the personality traits. Labradors are a very happy and even-tempered breed.

However, it is imperative that you establish yourself as the dominant figure in the relationship from day one. If you don't, you'll be fighting a long, uphill battle. Accomplish this task, and you should have many wonderful years together. I firmly believe that you can take a male or female of any of the three colors and make it a wonderful companion. Super dogs are made from well-bred, well-trained puppies.

The fact that Labs are so very willing to please and enjoy working for the praise of their masters is, I believe, why they are successful at just about anything they attempt. That is also why they usually become a very valued member of any family they join. I do say usually!

Because the Labrador is so clever, willing and able, it sometimes gets into trouble. It must be trained and given things to do and think about. If you don't give the dog a task, it will find something to keep itself busy. All too often, it is the busy work of a bright, energetic Labrador that causes a frustrated owner to give up on a basically nice dog.

Having just sung the Lab's praises loud and clear, it might seem as if I'm contradicting myself. However, the fact is that a well-bred Labrador is a very trainable dog. "Well-bred" and "training" are the key words. You should get a well-bred dog and properly train it if you want to enjoy all the benefits of this wonderful, smart, even-tempered breed.

Knowing how this breed evolved will help you understand its habits and idiosyncrasies. The history

Super dogs come from well-bred puppies. (Lisa Weiss)

In other words, you should only get a Labrador if you love to spend a lot of time with your dog. You must be willing to incorporate its exercise and training time into your daily routine. You have to provide a place where it can get ample exercise in a safe environment. Labradors are happiest when they are spending time with or performing tasks for their masters and families.

You should not get a Labrador if you are going to want a dog that is happy being left alone much of the time and needs very little exercise or attention. This is not a dog that should ever be left in the backyard, put out on a runner line or a stake, or tied to a tree. It is cruel and very frustrating for them. If you are working long hours you should plan to have someone come in and give the dog some exercise and attention. If you are busy with a newborn or young children and can't schedule enough time for obedience training and exercise

of the breed will be discussed in Chapter 2. In addition, you must understand that, tucked into these 55- to 95-pound packages (the approximate weight range from small female to large male) is a bit of Benjamin Franklin, Thomas Edison, the Bionic Man, Superwoman, Madame Curie and a stick of dynamite! All those brains, ingenuity, power and athletic ability have to be channeled in the right direction. If you don't give these dogs a way to exercise their brains and bodies, they'll find a way on their own. And you may not be happy with their choice of recreational activities.

Training is the key to success with a breed as smart as Labs. (Ed Katz)

It's important to understand that the Lab was developed as a sporting dog, and needs a job to engage its mind and use up its energy. (Corso Harris)

plant identification, and usually can't distinguish between the scrub oak you don't care about and the expensive ornamentals you just bought.

Garden ponds are more and more popular these days, and Labs love those lilies, but koi fishing is even more fun. Then there is what I call home improvement. This involves eating the deck or pulling the shingles and aluminum siding off the house. All this is done free of charge for you, the loving master. Your dog will hand you a shingle, look up at you with those adoring eyes and wag its tail as if to say, "Hey, aren't I great?"

You get the idea. We once left our first two Labs in the fenced backyard for about two hours. To my parents' shock

sessions, then perhaps a Labrador is not the right dog for you at this time.

THE LANDSCAPE ARTISTS

Don't be fooled into thinking that if you have a fenced yard your Labrador will be happy and safe when it is out by itself. It will be happy to be out in the fresh air while you are busy with other responsibilities, but it will be planning its own activities as well. Digging is always fun, whether it is right in the middle of the yard, through new sod or under a fence to escape and find new friends. Chewing on little trees and branches, which I call landscape architecture, is always fun when you have free time on your paws. Labs are just not good at

Left to its own devices, a Lab will always find plenty to do in the yard. (Bob & Emily Magnani)

and dismay, we came home to a yard full of foam rubber stuffing and wood bits that looked like they might have been our redwood patio furniture a few hours earlier. My sisters and I spent the afternoon cleaning up the mess. We thought my parents would surely call the breeder, Anne Carpenter, and ask her to take them back. Instead, my father built a dog run where Lobo and Buffy had to stay when unsupervised. It was equipped with a doghouse, and had lots of shade, toys and water. They were quite happy to spend a few hours at a time there. Soon after, we also enrolled in our first obedience class.

Your Lab wants and needs your guidance to be the well-trained pet you want it to be. (Chenil Chablais)

As many others do, we learned the hard way. The havoc those dogs caused from time to time was incredible, but they were the two most lovable rogues. Their wonderful traits always came shining through. There is no disputing the fact that Labradors are a great breed. They are so capable, so trainable and so eager to please, but they can't train themselves. They want and need your help and guidance.

A trained Labrador is a happy Labrador and a pleasure to live with. An untrained, bored Labrador can be destructive—unintentionally, but destructive just the same. An unruly, destructive dog of any kind quickly becomes unwanted and unwelcome. That is unfortunately why many Labs with lots of untapped potential end up in dog pounds, shelters or (for the luckier ones) in the hands of Labrador breed rescue. These are the luckier ones because dedicated rescue people often give these dogs some of the basic obedience training they need,

teach them some manners and then get them adopted into good homes where they get a second chance.

Work Wanted

Labradors are extremely versatile creatures. Their jovial and unflappable personalities make it easy for them to do so many jobs well. Their strong constitution and eagerness to please make them the number one choice of waterfowlers. Although all the retrieving breeds have keen noses, the Labrador seems to be the one who will go that extra mile when asked, and is willing to re-enter the icy water again and again. This is a trait the breed was prized for in its early stages of development.

Labradors are used as guide dogs for the blind more than any other breed. Because they love to

Labs have always been willing to go that extra mile, no matter what the task at hand. (Ed Katz)

fetch and carry just about everything, Labs are also very popular as service dogs. They serve not only as companions, but also as helpers to people who are wheelchair bound.

Police and government agencies that train dogs to sniff and search for drugs, explosives and arson accelerants use Labs almost exclusively. The Bureau of Alcohol, Tobacco and Firearms uses only Labradors, insisting that their noses are the keenest and that they are the most dependable workers.

HEALTHY AND HEARTY

Labradors have topped the popularity chart for quite a few years now. More Labs have been registered with the American Kennel Club for the past seven years than any other breed. Much of their popularity is due to the fact that they are touted as wonderful family dogs by many veterinarians, dog trainers and other dog experts. Two additional

reasons are that Labs are low maintenance as far as grooming goes and have far fewer inherent health problems than other breeds. (Specific disorders that can affect Labradors will be discussed by Dr. Kathryn Sneider in Chapter 6.)

There are breeds that seem to be plagued with heart problems, kidney problems and allergies of all kinds. There are other breeds where great numbers succumb to cancer. Some of the giant breeds are lucky to live 8 or 10 years, simply because larger dogs have naturally shorter life spans. A 10-year-old St. Bernard or Great Dane, for example, is considered ancient, but I've had many Labradors live to be 14 or 15. Although 13 or 14 seems to be about the average life span, I have known friends who have had 16- and 17-year-old Labs.

Those short coats mean Labs are low maintenance when it comes to grooming. (Greg Goebel)

Do Sex and Color Matter?

As I mentioned earlier, prospective puppy buyers sometimes have very definite opinions about color differences in Labs. But when I'm asked if one color or sex is better than another, my answer to both questions is, "No, not in my opinion." A well-bred Labrador (and of course, well-bred is the key), should be a delightful, trainable companion whether it is black, brown or yellow and whether it is a he or a she.

There are some obvious physical differences between the sexes. For the most part, the males are 10 to 20 pounds heavier or bulkier, and usually one to two inches taller than the females. If your preference is for a relatively smaller dog, then maybe a female is what you want. But in general, male or female characteristics that seem to be evident in other breeds are not seen in Labradors. People often say they must have a female because they want a dog that will not roam. My reply, to their surprise, is that most of the worst roamers and escape artists I have owned have been females.

A well-bred Lab makes a great companion, no matter what its color. (Ann & Randy McCall)

Yes, I've had some roguish males who roamed, but the fact is that the breed is prone to roaming in general. Labradors are just so friendly and inquisitive that they will often roam to find a playmate. Their noses simply lead them astray. They just have to see what they can smell and where it is coming from. It's definitely not a problem limited to males.

There are small differences in size, but you won't find much difference in character between males and females. (L.G. Pilbin)

It is not easy to train a Labrador to stay on your property. Many people turn to invisible fencing, but even that is not foolproof. I have good friends whose female Labrador, Phoebe, refused to stay on their property. Phoebe was about 11 months old, strong and stubborn. Of course, their next door neighbor, Frank, hated Phoebe because he kept his yard, gardens and garage absolutely immaculate. When Phoebe escaped she only wanted to visit his yard. She would dig up his plants and retrieve things from his garage.

Once Frank's door was open and Phoebe took a tour of his house and stole a bedroom slipper. Rick and Debbie, Phoebe's owners, were beside themselves and their unhappy neighbor was coming to the end of his rope. In desperation they called an invisible fence company to help take care of the problem. Little white flags were put all around the border of the property. Phoebe was fitted with the battery-powered collar that would first make a beeping sound as she approached the property line, and then give her a shock if she came to or crossed the property line. The fence company walked Phoebe around the property line, as did her owner, to show her the border.

At first it seemed this was going to solve the problem and everyone would be happy. However, Phoebe decided that the things in Frank's garage were worth the jolt and soon started leaving the property whenever she felt like it. The fence company came back. They told Rick and Debbie that they often were called back for Labradors. Phoebe was fitted with a second collar and battery pack. Both units beeped as she approached the property line and she got a double zap when she crossed the line. It did work. After the first couple of double zaps Phoebe decided that the grass was not so much greener at Frank's house. Phoebe was also enrolled

in, attended and graduated from obedience class. Now she is over two years of age and only wears one collar. She doesn't need the collar at all when someone in the family is working or playing in the yard. She has become a much loved and well-behaved family member, but it took a lot of work, time and effort. This story is typical of a Labrador, whether black, brown, yellow, male or female.

Another question people often ask is if one color sheds more than the others do. The answer is that shedding depends on the individual dog, its diet and how much time it spends out in cold weather. I think you do find that many yellow Labs don't have as harsh a coat as the blacks and chocolates (brown). They should, and breeders strive to breed yellows with tougher coats; but

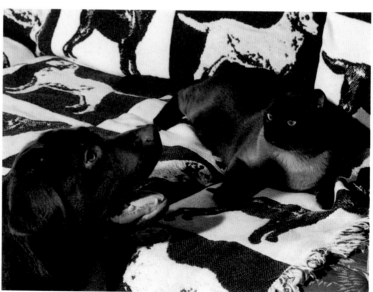

You can choose a color to fit in with your decor, or even to match your other pets! (Greg Goebel)

their top coats, for the most part, are softer and their under coats are a bit more downy. The shedding of that softer coat can seem more profuse. Because it is softer, it seems to stick to things. I don't want to exaggerate the problem, and I don't think it is such a huge difference that it should influence your choice of color.

Quite often people buy a Lab of a particular color so that its hair can blend in with their decor, rather than contrast. I love all three colors of Labradors, so I always decorate with lots of black, brown and tweed rugs and carpets. I never use solid red, white or blue.

TEMPERAMENT AND TRAINABILITY

Probably the two most important considerations for someone looking for a family dog are temperament and trainability. Unless you are specifically looking for a show dog, looks and appearance are probably secondary. While not every Labrador needs to look like a Best in Show winner, if you are going through the trouble of obtaining a good dog from a breeder, I think you will want one that looks the way a Labrador should look.

I believe Kendall Herr, a very respected long-time breeder and judge, best describes the Labrador. She says, "The Labrador has a unique stuffed animal look, which is obtained from the proper double coat, with a thick under coat to round out any angular look." In other words, the coat, which is a very distinctive feature of the breed, should make the Labrador look like a big, plush teddy bear.

The Lab's coat should make it look like a plush teddy bear. (Mollie Madden)

My children and I also have Cavalier King Charles Spaniels, and from time to time I have had other breeds. But if the dog warden knocked on my door tomorrow and said there was a law requiring homeowners to have only one dog, the dog for me would be a Labrador. The decision would be easy. I couldn't live without a Labrador. They are very special four-legged creatures, each with its unique personality, likes and dislikes. I find them to be so human—for example, most of them possess a wonderful sense of humor. I've had quite a few who were very funny characters, and we enjoyed each other's company endlessly.

Many Labs have a great sense of humor. (Ed Katz)

ONE OR TWO?

If you have the proper facilities, which I consider a house and a large fenced yard, having two Labs can be as easy as, and at times easier than, one. They do crave companionship. If you are really busy and not home all day, your Lab will be happier with another Lab or other dog. They can be left outside in most weather in a safe, secure area (such as a dog run), provided they have water, shade, shelter and some toys. The two will entertain each other and keep each other company. Another dog does

not replace human companionship, however, and both dogs will need individual attention and quality time.

I don't think it takes a lot more time to feed and care for two dogs as opposed to one. Ten dogs are a lot of work, but two are double the fun. I really believe the positives outweigh the negatives. It's an option you might want to consider.

However, I do not recommend taking on littermates or pups too close in age. Whenever I have seen families do this, the pups tend to bond to each other first and their personalities don't seem to develop the way they do when they are raised separately. If you are thinking about having two dogs, I believe you should get your first pup housebroken and trained, and make sure it has bonded to you before you take on a second pup. This takes about 12 months.

Because of their wonderful easygoing personalities, Labs will usually welcome a canine companion

If you're not home all day, your Lab will enjoy the company of another dog. (Greg Goebel)

Taking on a couple of littermates can prove to be a problem. It's better to make sure your first pup is trained and trustworthy before you get a second dog.

can bond with you and develop its own personality.

It is not a good idea to assume that the older dog will train the younger one. A parent would not let a two-year-old educate the new baby in the family. My daughters are 19 months apart. When they were about three-and-a-half and two years old, Kyra (the older one) helped Bethany cut and style her hair. It was a week before they were to be flower girls in my sister's wedding. Who was to blame? Only me. There have been similar times when I've been asleep at the helm and had an adult dog lead a younger one astray.

There was the time I decided to let two young dogs, uncrated, stay in the car while I ran into the supermarket for five

at just about any stage of their life. If they are pets and you have them spayed or neutered (which I advocate), it really doesn't matter if you have two of the same sex or one of each. There are many breeds, terriers for example, where you would not put males together, neutered or unneutered. You could be in for fighting and a lot of leg lifting. With Labradors, however, I would consider this unusual behavior.

If you are anxious to get a second Lab and your first dog is a puppy, I advise you to wait at least eight months, until the pup isn't quite so dependent on you. This is especially important if you plan to get another puppy (as opposed to an adult dog). This way you can make sure the second pup gets plenty of time alone with you so that it

Don't assume your older dog will teach the younger one how to behave. (Debbie Horan)

Once you have a Lab in your life, you're going to wonder how you ever lived without it. (Annie Cogo)

minutes. When I returned I was minus one back seat cushion. Whose fault was it? Mine! I counted to 30, really slowly, took some deep breaths and tried to look at the positive side. It wasn't a tire, the car was drivable—though somewhat less valuable. Those immortal words of Scarlet O'Hara flashed through my brain: "After all, tomorrow is another day."

If you are going to live with kids or dogs, or if you're going to live with both, I promise, there will be days that will truly test your strength and character. As my mother says, "You live through it, but the problem is that you are living through it." Most of the rules for living with Labradors are like the rules for raising children. First and foremost, you must love and want them. You must be consistent. Don't let them get away with something one day and scold them for it the next. Don't let your Lab play with an old shoe and then get upset if it eats

your $70 sneakers—you already said it was OK to play with shoes. These dogs are smart, but they can only live by the rules they are taught. Feed them good food, give them plenty of fresh air and exercise. Take precautions to keep them safe from cars, electric wires or outlets and other hazards. These basics will get you off to a good start.

LABS IN YOUR LIFE

This is a breed that, given a chance, will wangle its way under your skin and into your heart. I enjoy living with several Labs at a time and can't imagine living without one. People say they are wonderful with children, and that's true, but in fact they are wonderful with everyone. There are remarkable things about them at all the stages of their lives. They are active, responsive puppies. They are keen learners, even if somewhat over-enthusiastic adolescents. They are clever, fun-loving, devoted adults.

Of course they're good with children! (Harris)

Labs grow into faithful, dignified seniors. They can live 13 years or more.

They are intelligent, dignified and faithful senior citizens. If you are willing to put in the time, you'll be rewarded hundreds of times over.

The only problem is you'll create a creature that you'll find it hard to live without. Many Labs do live 15 or 16 years, but 13 years is about average, and that is just not long enough. I find once you have a Lab for that long, you won't live without one for very long again. The circle of life begins again when a breeder gets a phone call from you. There's a void in your life, and you're ready to start again with a new Lab puppy.

CHAPTER 2

The History of the Labrador Retriever

The Labrador Retriever is, comparatively speaking, a young breed. There are breeds today whose ancestry can be traced back to ancient times, such as Pharaoh Hounds and Afghan Hounds. But there are no reports of pictures of Labs on the walls of Egyptian tombs.

Labradors first came to the United States in the early 1900s. They had been used as gun dogs in Britain since the early 1800s, and were considered prized possessions among the sporting gentry, who sold or gave them as gifts to each other. When a fraternity of sporting gentlemen was established along the East Coast of the United States, those who enjoyed shooting waterfowl and upland game sang the praises of the Lab as the premier hunting dog.

How the Lab was named after an area of northeastern Canada, and yet ended up the hunting companion of the British aristocracy, is an interesting tale. Labradors were originally seen in Newfoundland, and not in Labrador, as their name would lead one to believe. There are several theories on the development of the breed we know today as the Labrador Retriever, and early names for the breed supply a few clues. Before they were officially dubbed Labrador Retrievers, these dogs were known as the St. John's Water Dog, the Little Newfoundlander and the Black Water Dog.

WHAT'S YOUR JOB?

Breeds of dogs were usually developed over a period of years to perform a certain task or do a specific job. Usually, the job defines the dog. For example, different Terrier breeds were developed to get rid of vermin. Terriers come in many shapes and sizes and have all different types of coats. Each Terrier breed was engineered with a very specific type of vermin in mind. Norfolk and Norwich Terriers are small, and were bred to keep barnyards and stables free of rats. They have to be small enough to get down in the rat holes, but strong enough to actually kill the rat they corner. They have very thick, coarse coats, which help protect them against a rat that might fight back. Airedales, on the other hand, are about two feet tall and weigh about 50 pounds. This breed was developed for hunting badger and fox.

The Labrador Retriever is a working dog, and should be equally adept on land and in the water. (Jan Grannemann)

The Labrador Retriever evolved as a working dog. The type of work it was needed for required it to be equally talented on land and in the water. A good Labrador can work in just about any weather and endure the coldest temperatures. It can work under the poorest of conditions and still be grateful for any food or treats thrown its way. One of the wonderful things about the Labrador is that it will wag its tail happily while doing almost anything that is asked.

IT STARTED IN NEWFOUNDLAND

In the book *The Dog,* written by James Dickie around 1935, he said of the Labrador Retriever, "There are a few people alive who must know the whole story—how interesting it would be if they could write it." Of course, those people are no longer alive.

The fishermen who settled in Newfoundland about 1500 were interested in developing a dog that could serve them and make their lives a bit easier. I am sure it never occurred to them that in the 20th century hundreds of thousands of people in many countries would own, train, show and love these dogs. What they knew was that they needed a powerful dog with a short, dense coat that was impervious to the cold water.

Exactly what breeds went into the pot that resulted in our modern-day Labrador is speculative and hypothetical. The fishermen off the coast of Newfoundland kept no breeding records. Many dedicated breed historians have spent countless hours researching the history of the breed. Will we ever know for sure? Probably not. Get a group of six or eight old-time Labrador breeders together and a red-hot debate will surely ensue. I believe no matter what breeds went into the making of the Labrador, the important thing to remember is why the breed was created. Always remembering this will give you a better understanding of the Labrador Retriever, or any other breed you want to learn about.

Some historians do believe the early Labradors were a combination of the New-foundland, Black Pointer and some of the water dogs that were brought to Canada by Portuguese fishermen. Although the Portuguese may not have actually settled or built shelters on shore, it is presumed that they explored the shore, and their dogs went back and forth from the shore to the boats with them. Some dogs may have strayed ashore, and were bred with the dogs that English fishermen had brought to Newfoundland a few years earlier.

While the Portuguese came and went on long fishing voyages, the English settled in the area and began fishing along the rocky coast. They needed a dog that was strong, but smaller than the giant Newfoundlands. The big black dogs, with their long coats, had advantages and disadvantages. Although Newfies could withstand the icy temperatures, the ice often got balled up in their coats, and this was a problem. However, it has been said that Newfies were great bed warmers!

THE RIGHT QUALITIES

The dog the fishermen wanted had to be a good retriever and be happy to receive very little in

Early Labs looked a lot like small Newfoundlands. (Courtesy of Pat Ross)

return—it had to be able to survive on fish and fish scraps. Other duties included pulling heavy loads and occasionally going out to hunt with the fishermen, who were sometimes able in this way to supplement their diet. The dogs were expected to pick up and bring back game birds that had been shot.

This was a niche that could only be filled by a dog with a specific body and coat type—an athletic dog with a keen desire to please and an extremely strong constitution. The dogs were often sent over the sides of the boats to retrieve fish that flopped out of the nets onto the ice or in the water. Because of the rocky terrain they had to negotiate along the coast, the breed had to have heavy bone as well. A fine-boned, fragile or delicate dog would have routinely broken its limbs.

These were tenacious little dogs, and I believe the name Little Newfoundland might have been a better one for the breed. We might not have the problems we have today with diversity in type if that name had stuck. "A small, short-coated Newfoundland" gives a clear picture of what this dog should look like.

My family had three Newfoundlands and many Labs when my sisters and I were young. Living with the two breeds, it was interesting to see how in many ways Labradors are still like Newfies in smaller, more compact packages. Newfies have the same gregarious temperament as their smaller descendants. They really are gentle giants, but they take up a bit more room in a house than a Labrador does, and they do slobber and drool. I love them and would like to have one again someday.

The Lab evolved to help fishermen, and still loves being in the water. (Clement Thibeault)

BY THE BOOK

The Labrador Dog, by Franklin B. Lord, (published privately by The Labrador Retriever Club, 1945) starts with an extract from *A History of the Skuykill Fishing Company* which, according to Lord, was the "oldest club in the world." The extract is a description of the Labrador, and Lord thought it quite fitting. "If you look to its antiquity, it is most ancient. If to its dignity, it is most honorable."

Lord then pointed his readers to another book, published in London in 1936: *The Labrador Dog, Its Home and History,* by Lord George Scott and Sir John Middleton. He quotes Scott as saying:

It appears that the aboriginal inhabitants of the island, the Beothucks, did not have any dogs. The English began to fish in Newfoundland in 1498; the Portuguese came in 1501; and the French in 1504. The English were the only fishermen who engaged in

shore fishery and made certain settlements about 1522. Most of the settlers came from Devon and were hunters. They wanted dogs for hunting and to retrieve their fish so they probably took the dogs that were then common in England over with them. There were references to a grey hound and a mastiff on the island as far back as 1611. These dogs brought by the men of Devon were the only canine population of Newfoundland and were bred and trained to meet the needs of their owners. From these various breeds of dogs bred over a period of 280 years under rigorous conditions there were evolved the Newfoundland dog and later on, the Labrador. They were the product of the environment and survival, and perhaps selection.

Scott and Middleton add, "The Labrador dog did not come from Labrador but from Newfoundland, mostly from the vicinity of St. James and White Bay. There were two kinds of dogs on Newfoundland, the big long-haired, black dog known as the Newfoundland, and the small short-haired dog known as the Labrador or St. John's breed."

As he decribes the two breeds, Scott quotes Colonel Hawker from his 1914 book *Advice To Young Sportsmen*:

> *Here we are a little in the dark. Every canine brute that is nearly as big as a jackass and as hairy as a bear, is denominated a fine Newfoundland dog. Very different, however…are the St. Johns breed of these animals.*
>
> *The other [the Labrador], by far the best for every kind of shooting, is oftener black than any other color…pretty deep in chest…has short or smooth hair; does not carry his tail so much curled as the other; and is extremely quick and active in running, swimming.*
>
> *Their sense of smelling is scarcely to be credited. Their discrimination of scent, in following a wounded pheasant through a whole covert full of game, or pinioned wild fowl through a furze brake or warren of rabbits, appears almost impossible.*

Lord further tells us, "The dogs were used by the fishermen…to haul in the winter's wood and to retrieve fish that had become unhooked. It seems that the fish which were taken at great depth often became unhooked near the surface and the dogs were sent overboard to retrieve them."

No one seems to know exactly when the first of these dogs arrived in England. Lord says it was the last decade of the 18th century or the first decade of the 19th century. Shooting journals of the Second Earl of Malmesbury (1778–1841) prove that he

had what he called a small Newfoundland dog in December 1809. Scott seems to think these "Newfoundland dogs" were the small dogs Peter Hawker described at about the same period.

Further, Lord says "the Third Earl of Malmesbury (1807–1889), who inherited the kennel, is quoted as saying, 'We always called mine Labrador dogs, and I have kept the breed as pure as I could from the first I had from Poole.'"

THE TRIP TO ENGLAND

Most historians of the breed agree that the sea route between Newfoundland and Poole Harbour, in Dorset, was well traveled. The fishermen went back and forth to sell their salted codfish. Their dogs often made the trip with them. Sometime around 1818, some of these dogs were seen in

Early English writers had nothing but praise for the Lab's good looks and superb hunting ability. (Courtesy of Pat Ross)

Poole and purchased. English waterfowlers were quick to appreciate these talented dogs. The Second Earl of Malmesbury was said to have purchased several from some of the ships' captains. The Third Earl of Malmesbury continued to import and breed the dogs.

Although the Third Earl said he kept his as pure as possible, it's likely that at some point the dogs were bred with local retrievers, in order to improve the local dogs. Some historians believe Colonel Hawker was the first to write about the dogs, and that he was actually the one to dub them Labradors; others disagree and believe that the early fishermen called them something that sounded like Labrador. The word *lavrador* means laborer in Portuguese language, as Janet Churchill points out in her book *The New Labrador Retriever*

The classic look we admire in Labs today was developed in England in the 1800s. (Judy Race)

(Howell Book House, 1995). Churchill also reminds us of the two very important features that are still hallmarks of the breed today: "coats that were water repellent and did not hold ice, and their swordlike tails (which we now call otter tails) that steered their stoutly made bodies through the rough ocean waves."

The Third Earl of Malmesbury gave some of his dogs to the Sixth Earl of Buccleuch, and it was he who actually started to keep good breeding records. Some of our American Labs can be traced back to the Earl of Buccleuch's dogs. From the 1820s on, Labradors became the waterfowler's dog of choice.

A SPLASH OF COLOR

Some of the early breed specimens did not look exactly like our Labradors of today, although they did bear a strong resemblance. Many early paintings show the dogs with somewhat longer coats, as you can see in the pictures on pages 17 and 19. Often you would see a black Lab with white on its feet or a large white spot on its chest.

These features still crop up occasionally. It is not all that unusual to have a pup of any of the three colors with white on its feet or a white patch on the chest. (White is harder to see on the yellows, unless it's a darker yellow.) Sometimes you get a black pup in a litter with tan markings on the legs, a yellow with black

From the 1820s on, the Labrador was the waterfowler's dog of choice.

little white on the bottom or back of the feet is nothing to be penalized for). Most would agree that those dogs aren't missing out on much.

IT'S OFFICIAL

In 1904 the Kennel Club in Britain listed Labradors as a separate breed. (Before that time, they were simply lumped into the broad category of Retriever, which covered all retrieving dogs.) Labs were gaining popularity by leaps and bounds, winning at field trials and in the show ring. In 1909 the Labrador Retriever Club was founded, and in 1916 the English standard was written. In 1932 and 1933 the famous Dual Champion Bramshaw Bob won Best in Show at the prestigious Crufts dog show in England. Dual Ch. Bramshaw Bob was owned by the Banchory Kennel, one of the breed's most famous early

markings or a chocolate with yellow markings on its legs or under its tail. Breeders refer to these puppies as *splashed.* They look like someone has splashed them with mud or paint.

I've often heard people ask, "Are they pure-bred?" The answer is, "Yes, absolutely." They possess the same wonderful Lab temperament, and still make great pets. In fact, the only thing they cannot do is enter the show ring (although a white spot on the chest is permissible on a show dog, and a

This "splashed" puppy is well-loved and makes a wonderful pet.

English kennels. The kennel belonged to the late Lorna Countess Howe, who is remembered for doing much to promote the breed.

Although the occasional yellow and livers (as chocolates were originally called) were seen, Labradors were primarily preferred in black. There were some early English breeders who liked the yellows, and made great efforts to breed and strengthen the color. Today we are able to appreciate the color we call yellow—it actually ranges from white or cream to fox red—because of their efforts. The late Veronica Wormald, of the Knaith Kennels, is credited with promoting yellow Labradors and encouraging others to do the same. She started the Yellow Labrador Retriever Club in England, and helped it gain acceptance. Mrs. Wormald bred and owned some of the top-winning yellow Labradors of her time.

It wasn't until some years later that chocolates also came into favor. They were finally accepted

Chocolate Labs have become quite popular today, as President Clinton and Buddy well know. (Courtesy of the White House)

as "true" Labradors, however, and are, of course, quite popular today. In fact, the First Dog of the United States of America is a chocolate Labrador Retriever named Buddy.

LABS IN AMERICA

Americans started importing Labrador Retrievers before World War I, and they became quite popular rather quickly. For classification purposes, the American Kennel Club grouped them together with the other retrievers that were actively being used for sport shooting.

The Labrador soon became the retriever of choice, particularly among the wealthy. These sportsmen, who lived primarily on Long Island, wanted to be like the English gentry. To accomplish this, they imported these marvelous dogs, as well as expert kennel men and gamekeepers from Scotland. Many of the Long Island Gold Coast families, as they were called, were involved in importing Labradors and regularly competed in the early bench and field events of the 1920s and 1930s. Their names will be familiar to many of you, and included the Phipps, the Marshall Fields, the Morgans, the Whitneys, the Belmonts and Wilton Lloyd Smith. J. P. Morgan had an English import named Banchory Snow who would bring him his slippers in the evening. Joan Read, the woman who started so many people in Labradors and was a champion of the breed, believes Snow was the first yellow Lab to come to this country.

Super Chief was a top winner for August Belmont. While the Belmont name may be more often associated with horse racing, August Belmont also served as president of the American Kennel Club.

In the late 1920s the AKC recognized the Labrador Retriever as a separate breed. In 1930 the Labrador Retriever Club of America was founded on Long Island, and the club charter is still held by New York State. Mrs. Marshall Field was the first president, and held the office from 1931 to 1935.

Mrs. Field brought Scotsman Douglas Marshall over as trainer and gamekeeper for her dogs. He was admired, respected and very good at his job. Douglas' children, Bob and Dolly Marshall, went on to be successful trainers for other kennel owners. Dolly became the first female professional trainer, and worked for Junius Morgan at the West Island Kennels.

Robert Goelet and Franklin B. Lord were co-vice presidents of the Lab club. Other prominent members included Paul G. Pennoyer, Charles Lawrence, William J. Hutchinson, Jay F. Carlisle, Alfred Ely, Benjamin Moore, August Belmont and W. Averell Harriman. During his lifetime, Harriman was governor of New York, a United

States ambassador, and a Labrador enthusiast. Another Scotsman who went on to make history in dogs, James Cowie, came to the United States to be the assistant gamekeeper to Tom Briggs (the first of the Scottish gamekeepers to emigrate) at Harriman's Arden estate in New York. Cowie went on to be a top-flight show handler, and piloted Ch. Earlsmoor Moor of Arden to many big wins. He later became a noted judge.

This was the heyday of the dual purpose dog—a dog that was equally competitive in field trials and the show ring. The pioneers of the breed were sporting gentlemen with great estates, and they seemed to enjoy bench and field competitions with great zest. These were the social events of their day and were really reserved for the upper crust of society. Joan Read recalled that in the

In the early days, Labs were owned by sporting gentlemen who always took their dogs in the field and the ring.

early days dog owners would not socialize with their trainers and handlers. There was a division between the people who cared for the dogs and those who owned them.

The dual-purpose dog eventually faded from the scene, as dog owners began to focus on one event or the other. Both areas of interest required a good bit of time, and the shows involved a lot of traveling, so competitors almost had to choose one or the other. Many years went by when there were

no dual champions at all in Labs. Now, happily, it is back in vogue to have a dual or even a triple purpose dog.

THE ALL-IMPORTANT KENNEL MANAGERS

Certainly, the dogs and the trainers who came to America in the 1930s or a little earlier to manage these great estates and kennels plotted the course the breed would follow for the next 20 years. Just importing the dogs was not enough to keep a breed going. The managers saw to the breeding programs, as well.

Jay F. Carlisle, owner of Wingan Kennels and president of the Labrador Retriever Club from 1935 to 1938, has been credited by the club as being the man most responsible for the rise in popularity of Labradors in the United States. But much of the credit must go to his kennel manager, David Elliot. Carlisle started his Wingan Kennels sometime between the first and second Labrador Club specialty shows (shows given for a single breed)—in 1933 and 1934. The late Percy Roberts (a famous handler and later an equally famous dog show judge) helped arrange for Elliot to come to Long Island. Elliot was another of the great gamekeepers training dogs in Scotland. He brought his own Lab bitch, Whitecairn Wendy, (which Carlisle purchased), with him, and became the manager and trainer at Wingan.

Carlisle had several other Labradors imported from England, including Drinkstone Pons, Drinkstone Mars, Banchory Trump of Wingan and Banchory Jetsam. Drinkstone Peg was imported

Early Lab Specialties were held mostly in and around New York, to accommodate the many Lab fanciers on Long Island. Helen Warwick is the judge here, and Ken Golden is handling Ch. Sam of Blaircourt. (Wm. Brown)

Helen and Jim Warwick's Lockerbie Kennels are behind many of today's great dogs.

after being bred to English Dual Ch. and Crufts winner Bramshaw Bob. She gave birth in Carlisle's kennel, and the resulting litter was full of winners: Ch. Bancstone Ben of Wingan, Ch. Bancstone Peggy of Wingan, Ch. Bancstone Lorna of Wingan, Ch. Bancstone Countess of Wingan, and Read's first champion, Ch. Bancstone Bob of Wingan.

Elliot and Carlisle got along very well. Carlisle credited his kennel manager with being responsible for some of the happiest days after he lost his wife, which was devastating to him. When Carlisle passed away, he left the Wingan name, the kennel, its equipment and most of the dogs to Dave Elliot, in appreciation. As Joan Read, who built her bloodlines from this kennel, has said, Elliot had the

finest bloodlines to work with, as well as the wonderful first-hand experience and knowledge he brought with him from Europe to use in building Carlisle's breeding program.

I grew up on Long Island, where most of the first Labradors were imported or bred. Much of the breed's history in this country traces to Long Island, and I've been able to meet many of the people who launched the Labrador in the United States. I heard many stories from my first mentor, retriever expert Anne Nicodemus Carpenter. I have spent countless hours discussing the history of this breed with dear friends, including the late Joan Read (Chidley Labradors), the late George Bragaw (Shookstown Labradors) and Mary Swan (Chebacco Labradors). I also spent lots of time with Janet Churchill (Spenrock Kennels), from whom my foundation bitch came.

Helen and Jim Warwick of the famous Lockerbie Kennels got their first champion from Joan Read. They went on to import many champions from the Sandylands Kennels in England, and also bred lots of their own.

Nancy Martin's Ayr Labradors and Janet Churchill's famous Spenrock dogs were offshoots of the Warwick's dogs (as were the Brainard's Briary dogs). Both Nancy and Janet imported lovely English dogs over the years from Ballyduff

Nancy Martin with Ayr's Mr. Lucky.

George Bragaw with two of the things he loved best: Labradors and the water. (Jessup)

and other kennels. George Bragaw also bred some of his bitches to the Warwick's dogs.

Lady Jacqueline Barlow lives in Canada, has had Labradors since the 1930s, and is also a wealth of information. She had dogs from the famous Banchory Kennels of Countess Lorna Howe in England, as well as from Her Majesty the Queen of England's Sandringham Kennels. The Sandringham dogs are used by the royal family for hunting, but the Queen has a keen interest in the breed and she is always on hand for Labrador judging at the Crufts show every March.

But despite being able to talk to all these people, and many other prominent breeders, I often wish I could have been born 35 years earlier so I could have been a part of this Labrador history.

MRS. READ

Joan Redmond Read was born to a prominent Long Island family. A biography of her life would fill many chapters and would be really interesting reading. Although she was truly a lady, she knew how to have a good time and I don't believe she ever let traditional rules or class divisions stand in her way. She enjoyed every aspect of the dog game, and socialized with whomever she liked, despite the conventions of her day. She admired the talents of many of the Scottish kennel managers, but especially Dave Elliot and Jim Cowie. She thought they were terrific handlers, teachers and trainers.

Until the day she died, Mrs. Read's house was the "home away from home" for dog and horse fanciers from all over the world. When you were invited to her home for dinner, you never knew who else you might be dining with, but you could be sure it was going to be a wonderful and most interesting evening.

During her lifetime Mrs. Read battled polio, cancer, the death of her youngest child and the loss of her husband. Through it all, the love of her family, friends and her dogs helped her carry on. Her Norfolk and Norwich Terriers, handled by Beth Sweigart and Peter Green, achieved great fame,

Joan Read, shown here with Chips, got a lot of people started in Labradors. (Percy Jones)

including Best in Show at Westminster and Montgomery County, the premier Terrier show.

She loved to judge Labradors and always got a huge entry—a testimony to her knowledge and love for the breed. Joan was a remarkable woman and helped many people get started in Labradors.

(Diane Pilbin)

CHAPTER 3

The Labrador Retriever Standard

The breed standard is the road map or guide to that breed, and every breed has to have one. A standard describes the ideal for just about every physical feature of the breed, from the tip of the nose to the tip of the tail, as well the breed's basic character. But most important, the standard gives the careful reader an understanding of breed type.

Type is a word we hear at dogs shows all the time. You might hear one breeder say to another, "That was a really typey dog that won today," or, "Oh, that dog today was totally lacking in type!" Newcomers to the breed sometimes have a hard time separating typey dogs from dogs that win the ribbons—and there is a big difference. Just because a dog wins at shows does not mean it is a typey dog or even, at times, a good specimen of the breed. Some dogs are just really flashy show dogs and make the most of themselves, but are actually rather mediocre, and other dogs that are excellent examples of type may be quite lackluster in the show ring. Only a judge who really knows the breed will be able to find the truly better Labrador. That's why so many people like to show under a breeder-judge—someone who has spent many years in the breed and knows it well.

THE IMPORTANCE OF TYPE

To me, type means quality. It is the essence of the breed. Type is what makes a breed a breed. It's what they look like and what makes them tick. As far as I am concerned, a dog can show like a movie star, have great conformation and move around the ring as sound as a dollar, but if it is lacking Labrador type, it should keep on moving right on out of the ring!

Why do I feel so strongly about this? Because type is what makes a Lab a Lab. You can go to a shelter and adopt a wonderful mixed-breed dog. It may be sound, move well and be able to learn lots of tricks, but no matter how much you love it or train it, you can't give it breed status. You can't dub it a Lab because it's black and loves to retrieve or a Dalmatian because it is white with black spots. It doesn't mean it's not a great dog—it's just not a particular breed. If that doesn't matter to you, just enjoy your pet. But if you are involved with purebred dogs, it's important to breed the best dogs you possibly can—dogs that are excellent examples of their breed.

Type is what makes a Lab a Lab. This is Ch. Tabatha's Windfall Abbey, JH, WCX. (Annie & Ron Cogo)

Dog shows developed from agricultural shows and fairs. At a show, the judge is really evaluating breeding stock. This is where the future of the breed lies, and why type is so important. So the next time you find yourself sitting ringside at a dog show, looking over the dogs, remember the words of the late Alva Rosenberg, a famous and well-respected judge: "Even a trolley can be sound; when you're judging, go for type."

THE STANDARD FOR STANDARDS

You'll find the current Labrador Retriever standard, along with some other Lab standards that have been used, in Appendix D. If you're interested in looking at the standards for other breeds, pick up a copy of the AKC's official book of standards, *The Complete Dog Book*. The standard and a brief history of every breed recognized by the AKC are in the book. New breeds are being admitted to the AKC registry almost every year, so make sure you get the most up-to-date edition.

THE TOTAL PICTURE

Labradors can't really be picked apart. In other words, when you're trying to decide if a Labrador is typey or not, you can't just add up the good and the bad, see which list is longer and decide if it's a good specimen of the breed or a bad one. When you look at a Labrador moving or standing, if the words "Labrador" or "type" aren't screaming through your head, then the dog probably has some real shortcomings.

When I look at a Labrador, first I take in the whole picture. I ask myself, "Is the dog basically balanced, not too long in body or too tall on leg?" Nor do I want a dog that is too short-backed or too short on leg. This is a dog that should have lots of substance and plenty of bone to carry that body. If you like word association games, the words "Mack truck" or "Sherman tank" should come to mind when you look at a Labrador, but never the words "wispy," "fine" or "elegant"!

MY FAVORITE STANDARD

The trend in recent years has been to make standards more and more detailed. But I think probably the less said the better—just the bare necessities. Once you've read a standard a few times, you've got to go out and start looking at dogs. Nothing beats hands-on experience. Quite simply, the Labrador Retriever standard could read:

A medium-size dog, about two feet high, two feet long, and about eight to ten inches wide. A dog that is very good at cleaning up any stray crumbs or food on the floor.

You must always look at the total picture when evaluating a Labrador. At eight years old, Am./Can. Ch. Boradors Significant Brother, CD, still shows why he is a multiple specialty winner.

Luftnase Hawley at Woodloch has beautiful eyes that are shaped like rounded diamonds, and an expression that melts your heart. She is sired by Ch. Dickendall Arnold.

Available in three beautiful colors, the Labrador has lots of thick black, brown or yellow hair that requires a good bit of vacuuming from your floors and furniture during shedding season. He has a powerful tail that is almost always wagging, and is very good at cleaning off coffee tables.

This dog is usually seen with a stick, Frisbee, or one (or better still, two) tennis ball in his mouth, and prefers being wet to being dry. He enjoys being with people and other animals and has been known to dig under, scale over or go through fences in search of them, dragging small trees or cement blocks that he's been tied to (though we don't recommend that), if he must!

Look at this expression! This is everything I'd want in a puppy. (Bob & Terrilyn Shober)

A standard gives you a clear idea of what a dog looks like, as well as its personality traits. After reading a well-written standard, you should be able to close your eyes and imagine how the dog looks and acts. So the description above would sum it up pretty well. But the American Kennel Club is a stickler for details, so the actual standard is a bit more technical.

In reviewing the ideal dog described by the Labrador Retriever standard, let's start at the head and work our way down to the tip of that otter tail. Because the standard is a written description of a visual image, a lot of specialized language has evolved to clarify the description. It's useful to learn these special terms, but I promise I'll define them as we go along.

THE HEAD

First, I like to see a sweet, warm expression that melts your heart. This usually comes across best when the eyes are a rounded diamond shape—not big round circles or almond slivers, and not too dark or too light. The expression is very important. It's hard to describe, because it's more than just the eyes or their shape—it's something from deep down inside the dog that leaps out at you through their eyes. I really think it comes from their souls.

Another feature that lends itself to expression is the stop, which is the place where the muzzle meets the head. The Lab should have a definite stop, so that the planes of the top of the skull and the muzzle are almost parallel. The back part of the

skull should be rather wide and not domed. I hate
to see big apple cheeks or snipey (pointy) muzzles.
The head should be more square than round or
long. The ears should be set on the skull smoothly,
not sticking up high or hanging down too far.
They should be in proportion to the size of the
head, never long and houndy.

They should have a scissors bite, where the
teeth intermesh in front, and a mouth with a full
set of teeth, but I don't get upset if an otherwise
wonderful dog has a level bite (where the teeth
meet in front but don't intermesh) or crooked
teeth. I've never had a Lab that had any trouble
eating or picking up anything I asked it to, no
matter what kind of bite it had.

THE NECK AND CHEST

The head should sit on a strong, powerful neck
that blends into well-angulated shoulders (that's the
slope of the shoulder blade). The breastbone should
be prominent, like the prow of a boat. The chest
should be barrel-shaped from well-sprung ribs.
(The spring is how much the ribs curve as they
come off the backbone. This greatly affects lung
capacity.)

As you look at the chest from the front, it
should be wide enough to place a flat, open hand
between the forelegs. Looking at the dog from
above, it should have substantial girth and not look
slabsided, or flat. The front feet should be directly
below the point of withers (the withers are just
behind the base of the neck, where the shoulder
blade meets the spine), coming down in a straight
line.

*Ch. Lobuff Seafaring Banner has a
lovely head and eyes. He's a grandson of
Ch. Sandylands Mark.*

*Toll House Texas Sonic Boom has nice
width of chest. You could easily get a
flat, open hand between those forelegs.
(Emily Biegel)*

Can. Ch. Ransom's Graycroft Quest, CD, JH, shows his thick "otter" tail. (Bill Clark)

down toward the end, almost cone shaped. It's the rudder that steers the boat. It should be thickly wrapped with hair and rather short, falling just above the hock (the joint on the hind leg that sticks out between the thigh and the feet).

The tail should be carried right off the back when the dog moves, wagging happily as it goes along. The tail can never be carried high over the back like a hound (or out of aggression). It should also never hang limp or be tucked under the body in fear.

THE BACK AND TAIL

Moving down, the back should be straight and strong, with no dips in the topline. (I'm talking about a two- to five-year-old dog in prime condition; you'd have to forgive a little here for an older dog or a bitch that's had a few litters.) There should really be a straight line from the withers to the tip of the tail.

The tail should be set on right at the top of the croup (the muscular area right at the end of the back). If the dog has a croup that slopes away from its back (we call that a steep croup), with the tail set on lower down the croup, that ruins the picture, especially when the dog is moving.

We say the Labrador Retriever has an "otter" tail. It should be very thick at the base, tapering

THE HINDQUARTERS

The hindquarters must be very strong and should look wide, from the side and from the back. They must also be well muscled. The stifles should be well angulated, or well bent. (The stifle is the knee joint, and is formed where the upper and lower thighs meet.)

If a dog is well angulated in the shoulders but is straight behind, it may reach out with its front legs when it moves, but won't cover a lot of ground because the rear won't have the power to drive the dog forward. If its front is straight and it has an angulated rear, the rear will push the dog along but the front legs won't go far enough fast enough, and the dog will look as if it can't get out of its own way. A Lab will only move along smoothly and effortlessly if it's well-angulated front and back.

When I am looking at the way the dog is made, it's almost like looking with X-ray vision. Unfortunately, I'm not Superwoman, so I have to imagine the skeleton inside the dog and think about how the bones are positioned and how they move as the dog moves. It takes some doing, but the whole thing will make more sense if you do.

THE COAT

Just as the clothes make the man or woman, we come to the Lab's clothes, the very important double coat. This is a very distinguishing feature. The coat gives the Labrador that lovely plush look. Although it *looks* plush and soft, a proper coat really should feel quite harsh. A good coat usually does not lie flat, so I believe a bit of a wave is fine and actually denotes a good coat. A coat can only lie perfectly flat if it is a slick single coat, which is not correct.

PERSONALITY COUNTS, TOO

When you are judging, if a good typey Labrador is standing in front of you, the dog won't let you ignore it. As you start to go over the dog, its tail wagging happily as it looks up at its handler for a little treat, something starts to happen. You're suddenly aware that the dog is quite enjoying your attention, even though it doesn't know you at all.

You sense this because it exudes a certain friendliness that really can't be contained. That essence of Labrador oozes out, and you can't help but find yourself smiling—or at least I do. Whether the dog is black, yellow or brown makes no difference. I firmly believe that a good Labrador can't be a bad color. But one color per dog, please (although a little white on the chest or on the bottom of the feet is OK—it adds character).

FAULTS AND WHAT THEY MEAN

Standards do contain faults. They warn us about undesirable traits that may crop up in a breed from time to time. But one thing you should not do is judge a dog by its faults. As I mentioned earlier, it's the total picture that counts.

A standard may list faults pertaining to height, weight, temperament, color, dentition or any other

A Lab can be black, chocolate or yellow, but yellow comes in a variety of shades. This is Balrion Reddy for Anything, an English dog in an unusual shade called fox red. (Glenda Crook)

The Lab's double coat protects it in the water. (Jan Grannemann)

characteristic it describes. Sometimes it asks judges to simply consider this undesirable characteristic to be a flaw, and judge the dog accordingly. Sometimes the standard will say a particular fault results in a disqualification, which means the dog should not win in the show ring.

The Labrador Retriever standard lists faults associated with the dog's bite and dentition, improper elbow structure, incorrect feet, structural defects in the hocks, poor movement, aggressiveness and shyness. It also lists five faults that can result in disqualification: any deviation of more than half an inch from the height prescribed in the standard (22½ to 24½ inches at the withers for a dog, 21½ to 23½ inches for a bitch); a thoroughly pink nose or one lacking in any pigment; eye rims without pigment; docking or otherwise altering the length or natural carriage of the tail; and any other color or combination of colors other than black, yellow or chocolate. I strongly objected to the addition of these disqualifiers to the standard.

If you've been in the breed for any length of time, you know that these disqualifications—especially the one for height—have been very controversial. People who primarily breed dogs intended for fieldwork believe the height is necessary for the dog to physically perform its duties, bounding through tall grass and over varied terrain. They believe the other disqualifications will help keep the breed looking as they think a true Labrador should.

There are many other people in the breed (including myself) who believe that there is no wrong size for a sound, typey Labrador. If a Labrador is otherwise balanced, its height, or lack of it, should not make any difference. Field and show people disagree about what a true Labrador has historically looked like. In addition, the trend in recent years has been to have fewer disqualifications in a breed standard, and the standard that was in force for Labs until 1994 didn't have any. Pigment and coat color were covered by simply describing what was acceptable and what wasn't. And docking the tail is illegal under AKC rules anyway.

The result of this controversial change to the standard has been interesting. While it was supported by many people who breed Labs for competition in the field, those dogs are not judged on their appearance, but solely on their performance. And because it was not supported by many people who primarily show their dogs in conformation, many show judges have not really enforced the new disqualifications.

These four lovely dogs in all three colors have accomplished plenty in the show ring and in the field. (Chuck Tatham)

WHO MAKES THE STANDARD?

A standard is drawn up—and changed—by the parent club of a breed. The parent club is a national group that has been recognized by the American Kennel Club as the guardian of the breed. The AKC does set the format for standards, and approve all changes, but it is the parent club that really controls what is said.

If it is deemed necessary for a breed standard to be changed, the parent club appoints a standard committee, composed of club members who are breed experts, to write up a proposal. The proposed changes are put to a vote of the membership—which should be made up of people all over the country who are involved with all facets of the breed. If the members pass the revision, it is sent to the AKC's Board of Directors (who, for the most part, are or have been breeders, and care deeply about their breed). If the Board agrees that the changes are reasonable, necessary and for the good of the breed, they are approved.

All changes made to any standard are sent to every AKC-approved judge for that breed and are

Good temperament is a very important consideration in any breed. This is Phoebe with Leah and Jared.

published in the club's monthly magazine, *AKC Gazette.*

Why would a club decide to change a standard? If some of the wording in a standard is vague or difficult to understand, revising it would make it clearer. For example, if a standard says, "ears of medium length that hang down, but not too far," the wording might be considered vague or ambiguous. One person might take "medium" to mean three inches, while another person might think it means six inches. If the length of the ear is an important feature (and it is in most breeds because it affects the look of the head and the expression), it might be better if the sentence read, "The ears should be approximately five inches long, not hanging down below the jaw bone." Then the required size is clear.

Another reason for making changes to a standard might be if a temperament problem arises in a breed where there had not been one before. The parent club might consider the problem to be serious and feel a need to make judges aware of the problem. They might feel that for the good of the

All Labrador owners share their love for the breed. (Michael Harris)

breed, if a judge comes across an overly shy or nasty dog, they should disqualify this animal from competition.

The AKC's rules say a dog with three disqualifications because of a physical defect noted in the standard is barred from competition permanently. A dog that bites a judge or someone else in the ring can and should be disqualified permanently on the spot. A dog that bites a judge might also bite a child at ringside, another exhibitor or another dog. Hopefully, no matter how beautiful that dog is, if the standard insists on a good, even, steady temperament, breeders are not going to breed to a dog that has been disqualified for a temperament fault. It wouldn't be in the best interest of the breed.

Ultimately, the breed is helped if the bad seeds are not given the chance to reproduce. Inserting something to protect the future of a breed would be an important enough reason to change a standard.

But politics sometimes also plays a role. While all Labrador Retriever owners are united by their love of the breed, they don't always agree on what's best for it. That's why a change in the standard doesn't always represent a consensus in the breed. It's my opinion that the changes in the Labrador standard were not in the best interests of the breed.

(Gail Vernali)

CHAPTER 4

Finding the Right Dog for You

With Labrador Retrievers currently the most popular breed in numbers of American Kennel Club registrations, every local newspaper is filled with "puppies for sale" ads. It's confusing for the prospective buyer. Who should you call? The ads may say very different things and mention widely varying prices. How can you tell where to buy a puppy that will be the right addition to your family?

The first rule is to be patient. Most of us don't go out to buy a house, a car or other major investment on the spur of the moment. We research, talk to people and make an informed decision. The purchase of a pet, which will become part of the family for a decade or more, is just as important a decision and shouldn't be hurried. Doing a little research now will pay off for years to come.

In the not too distant past, almost every town had a pet shop with a front window filled with adorable, mixed-breed pups. These puppies were usually the result of accidental breedings and were sold for a nominal sum. Today, more people are neutering their pets and keeping them in secure areas, so these shops have given way to larger, more sophisticated marketing operations, where purebred dogs command big dollars. Maintaining a steady supply has given rise to commercial breeding farms, where purebred dogs are mass produced to fill the demand. There has been a lot of publicity in the past few years

It pays to wait for just the right dog. Charter boat captain Tim Ainley enjoys his life in the Caribbean with his Lab, who came from a reputable breeder.

All puppies are cute, but what they grow up to be depends largely on their genetic makeup. Don't be misled by the terms "AKC" or "purebred" or the fact that the puppy has registration papers. The American Kennel Club is a registry, and its only job is to verify that a dog comes from two parents of the same breed. There is no quality assurance implied.

GOOD BREEDERS ARE BEST

The best place to buy a puppy is from a breeder, but not just any breeder. Let's look first at backyard breeders—people who own a pet or two, which they breed to someone else's pet, solely for the purpose of producing puppies to sell. These largely well-meaning folks usually don't have the appropriate hip and eye clearances for their dogs, and often don't know that they ought to! They tend to place their puppies when they are very young, which can result in lifelong behavioral problems. They are not usually a resource for information on health and behavior questions that might arise later. Finally, they are not usually able to take back a puppy, if that should ever be necessary.

Backyard breeders can sell their puppies for less than a serious breeder can. If my neighbor breeds his Labrador female to his own male and sells the puppies at six weeks old, there is not much invested in the litter. On the other hand, my dogs all have hip and elbow X-rays and yearly ophthalmological exams. When planning a breeding, I consider only which dog is the most compatible with my female, whether that requires shipping her

regarding these kinds of operations and the often shocking conditions under which the dogs are housed and maintained. That's a whole other story. For our purposes, let's simply consider that these puppies are produced without regard for inherited physical and temperament problems.

All puppies are cute, but their genetics will determine much of what they grow up to be.

WHY PRICE SHOULD NOT BE AN ISSUE

I sometimes hear people say that they don't want a "show dog," just a pet, so they decide to economize by finding the lowest-priced puppy possible. That's a false economy. I recently had a conversation with a woman whose six-month-old puppy had crippling hip dysplasia, a malformation of the joint that can cause extreme pain. Her veterinarian had advised total hip replacement surgery for both hips, at a cost of about $3,000. She and her family loved the dog dearly and were willing to make great financial sacrifices to relieve its pain. It turned out the puppy she bought was "on sale," because

to a stud dog across the country or using chilled semen, which involves ovulation timing (a veterinary expense), airport trips to collect the shipments and artificial inseminations (another veterinary expense). There is a great deal of time and money invested in a litter before it is even born!

Although Labradors are quite hardy, there are some genetic problems that the typical backyard breeder isn't usually aware of. Hereditary eye diseases, seizure disorders and orthopedic abnormalities are lurking in the gene pool, waiting to appear and cause an owner heartbreak. Although it is possible for such problems to occur in a serious breeder's stock, it is *far* less likely.

Reputable breeders sell both pet-quality and show-quality dogs, and they'll know which are which. (Lee Weiss)

it was past three months old. She told me that she had snapped up this bargain because she couldn't afford to buy from a private breeder. You're probably asking, as I did, "Can you afford *this*?"

Reputable breeders also sell pets. In fact, a reputable breeder isn't going to sell you a show-quality puppy—those are reserved for serious exhibitors. What a reputable breeder *will* sell you is a pet puppy with the same genes for good health and temperament that the show puppy has.

FINDING A REPUTABLE BREEDER

Now that you know where you should buy your puppy, how do you go about finding reputable breeders? Chances are they're not advertising in the newspaper. Quality pets are usually sold through word of mouth. Do your homework: Talk to Labrador owners you meet, talk to several local veterinarians, go to dog shows where you can see lots of Labradors and meet the breeders.

The American Kennel Club maintains a breeder's directory, but it only includes those breeders who pay to be listed. It's not a bad jumping off spot, though, so consider this avenue if you're having trouble locating a breeder. You can visit their website at www.akc.org. Don't be put off by the prospect of traveling out of your immediate area to find a good puppy; serious breeders may live a distance from you.

When you call a breeder, you may be lucky enough to find out that a pet puppy is available, or will be in the near future. But puppies are not like cans of soup on the supermarket shelf—most likely, you'll have to wait to buy one. Breeders can't control when their bitches come into season and can be bred. Then there are the unforeseen disappointments, such as missed breedings and small litters. When someone tells me that they *must* have a puppy for their child's birthday on October 15 or for Christmas (and no serious breeder would allow a puppy to be a Christmas surprise!) or during their summer vacation, I know that this person doesn't understand the nuances of Mother Nature. This is the person who will go to a pet shop or pick up the local paper to find someone who will satisfy their need *that day*. Serious breeders are more interested in placing

Dog shows are a good place to meet serious breeders. Some even bring young dogs to the show, either for sweepstakes competition or simply to socialize the pups.

puppies with families that want a quality puppy, whenever it's ready. And serious dog owners are willing to wait.

WHAT BREEDERS LOOK FOR

Serious breeders screen potential buyers. I want to know that there is a secure fence around the dog's new home, that someone will be at home with the puppy at least part of the day and that the buyer understands the responsibilities of owning a Labrador. I sell all of my pet puppies with AKC Limited Registration, which makes them ineligible for dog show competition and breeding, although they can compete in obedience and other performance activities. This is also the time to discuss neutering pet puppies of both sexes.

It's important for children to understand how to handle puppies and that a dog is not a toy. (Bethany Agresta)

Mother Nature doesn't always provide puppies when and where you want them, but they're definitely worth the wait.

The idea behind Limited Registration is that it is a tool used to protect the breed. A purebred dog breeder loves their breed, and wants to see its good qualities preserved in future generations. Therefore, breeders prefer to discourage breeding a particular dog until it has been checked for genetic diseases, and until you can see that its temperament is sound and that it is a fairly good specimen of the breed. A Limited Registration can help address these concerns. And it can be reversed later by the breeder, if the dog turns out to be good enough to breed.

Limited Registration also discourages breeding just to make money, without

I always invite buyers to come and meet my puppies and adult dogs before they make their decision. (Mary Ellen Forestieri)

strive for, and what health clearances my dogs have. I invite them to come and visit, not only to see puppies, but to meet and handle my adult dogs. When families visit us, I observe how the children behave and relate to the dogs. Although some children are a little reserved at first, I am more concerned about children who are overly rough with the dogs. No matter how good-natured Labradors are, I don't want my puppy in a home where the dog is a toy for the children, expected to tolerate tail-pulling or other inappropriate handling.

Parents also need to consider whether they are buying a puppy with the thought that the children will be responsible for its daily care. All breeders know that the whole family must be excited by the prospect of a puppy because usually the adults will end up with most of the responsibilities—no matter what promises your kids made!

I am always interested in the welfare of my dogs and make sure that buyers know they can call me at any time to discuss problems or concerns. My interest in the dog extends beyond the initial sale, and I am prepared to take the dog back *at any time during its life* if circumstances require it.

WHAT BUYERS SHOULD LOOK FOR

What should you expect when you visit a breeder? First of all, be sure to set up an appointment and honor it. Entering the home, observe whether it is clean and neat and whether there is any objectionable odor. Although a litter requires constant care, the puppies should be clean and free of odor. They

regard to health or temperament, because the puppies from a dog with Limited Registration can't be AKC-registered. Puppies without registration papers can't be sold for as much money, so there is much less motivation to breed.

I tell buyers about my breeding activities, what kind of temperament and personality I

should look a little plump, robust and clear-eyed and should exude good health. Runny eyes, potbellies, long toenails and dull coats indicate a lack of care—buyer beware! The puppies should be well socialized and confident, but not aggressive. An experienced breeder knows their puppies' individual personalities well and can suggest which puppy will best fit into your family.

When you visit, be sure to see and handle the adult dogs, especially the pups' mother. Don't let someone tell you that the dog is protective of her litter and can't be seen. Typical Labrador mothers are benevolent and proud to show visitors their family. The sire may or may not be

Puppies need lots of sleep and quiet time.

An experienced breeder will help you choose a puppy that will fit in with your activities and your lifestyle. (Susan Willumsen)

present, but the breeder can show you pictures and tell you about the dog chosen to sire the litter.

When you purchase a puppy, you should receive a pedigree, a registration application, guidelines for diet and training, and veterinary records for the puppy, including vaccinations given, a schedule for the remaining vaccinations needed, and a veterinarian's certificate indicating that the puppy is healthy. You may receive copies of hip and eye clearances for the parents, as well. Some breeders use written contracts to spell out any guarantees they offer, while others simply offer verbal confirmation. If you feel confident with the breeder's reputation and manner, a verbal agreement may be sufficient. (For more on puppy contracts, see Chapter 14.)

COME ON HOME!

Now you're on your way home with your little furry bundle of joy! When you get home, give the

An adult dog can make a very special companion.

puppy a chance to adjust to its new life away from its littermates. Expect some crying during the first night or two, although Chapter 5 will discuss how to minimize the upset. Remember that a small puppy is just like a small baby, needing lots of sleep and quiet time. Keep visitors to a minimum until the puppy is settled. Plan to have your veterinarian examine the puppy within the first few days, and bring its records with you.

Now you're ready to embark on an adventure. The work you do with your puppy in the next six months to a year will shape its personality and behavior as an adult.

CONSIDER AN OLDER DOG

If your lifestyle won't accommodate the amount of care a puppy needs, perhaps you should consider an adolescent or an adult. Breeders sometimes have dogs that are retired from active showing or breeding, or older pups that have not fulfilled their early promise as show prospects. Although you won't be involved in actually molding this animal's personality, Labradors are very adaptable and can assimilate very easily into your home.

WHY NOT RESCUE A LAB IN NEED?

And, on the subject of adult dogs, the many Labrador Retriever rescue organizations do a fine job of screening and placing dogs in new homes. You may want to contact a local rescue group to find out if a suitable dog may be available. Rescue dogs come from pounds, shelters and owners who

give them up. They are veterinarian-checked and neutered, and many have been put through a basic training course.

Rescue organizations require an adoption fee that helps to defray their costs. But the fee is generally lower than the purchase price of a puppy from a reputable breeder. Plus, you have the satisfaction of knowing that you took in a dog greatly in need of a home. Just remember that a rescue dog (or any other adult) comes with a history, which you probably won't know about. Be prepared to be patient until the new family member settles into your home and your way of life.

Should you get a youngster or an adult? There are advantages to both. (Emily Biegel)

Living With a Labrador

Labrador Retrievers are delightful creatures with huge hearts and a unique ability to adapt to many different circumstances. They are instinctively gentle with children and older folks, and they want very much to please. Most Labradors have no neuroses or complicated emotional makeups—they are not afraid, but are confident and outgoing. Sound like your dream dog? Wait! There are some Labrador qualities you need to know about.

WORK FIRST

First and foremost, a Lab was bred to be a working dog. Think about it: This dog was designed to work side by side with humans, taking direction to perform its job. Unlike the herding breeds, which work more independently, a Lab is bred to sit at a hunter's side, wait for the instruction to retrieve a downed bird and deliver it to hand, uncrushed and fit for the table. The dog's remarkable courage allows it to enter any sort of water or brush to complete the job. It has been said that Labradors are "genetic Privates," not wanting to be top dog, but preferring to take orders from people.

When a Lab doesn't get any direction, the resulting frustration can bring on destructive behavior. We often say that a Labrador needs a job. Every Labrador likes to work, and its jobs can range from delivering the TV remote, to fetching the morning newspaper, to helping carry in the groceries to doing tricks like catching a cookie balanced on its nose. Labs enjoy doing these simple tasks and are very proud and

You'll find your Lab is an accommodating dog with a sense of humor. (Emily Biegel)

pleased when they receive your praise. Start early, teaching your puppy ways to work with you, and you won't have a bored, frustrated dog that expresses itself by chewing the shingles off your house.

CHAMPION CHEWERS

And speaking of chewing, remember that Labradors were bred to retrieve and carry objects. Every puppy of every breed goes through an oral stage when it chews everything it can find, but Labradors are even more intent than the average dog on learning about their environment by picking up and chewing anything and everything. Provide safe, acceptable toys such as hard bones and balls to satisfy your puppy's need to chew. Don't give the puppy old shoes, socks or clothes. How is the pup to know the difference between

what's old and what's new—which socks can be chewed and which can't?

We don't advise rawhide toys for two reasons: Rawhide is leather, after all, so you're encouraging a taste for your shoes and gloves. Labradors are also voracious eaters (more about this later), and will devour large chunks of rawhide in record time, possibly leading to intestinal blockage. Also avoid rope toys, which Labradors can destroy and devour quite readily, and tug-of-war toys, which can encourage aggressive play. Stick to nylon and hard rubber toys, latex toys (very soft and harder to tear into) and real sterilized bones. You have to monitor your puppy's play; if the pup really tears into even these durable toys, the items should be taken away when you're not there to supervise.

Nylon, rubber and latex make good puppy toys. Lexy is trying to decide whether to eat this ball, or save it for later.

Whether it's retrieving a duck from the water or your TV remote from the couch, a Lab wants a job to do. (Ed Katz)

SOCIABLE FELLOWS

Labradors are amateurs at digging holes compared to some other breeds, but this activity also arises from boredom and loneliness. The Labrador was bred to be your companion and working partner; it doesn't want to be left alone out in the yard and will express this unhappiness by performing the home and landscape "improvement" tasks we mentioned in Chapter 1. In the dog's eyes, even the company of another dog doesn't make up for the relationship it wants with you.

This is part of the enormous sociability of this breed. Labs love people, especially children, other dogs, cats and life in general. They should never be left outside unless securely fenced, since the passing child on a bike or jogging neighbor will attract your dog's attention and it will want to join the fun. Even if your yard is secure, never leave a Labrador outside unattended while you are not at home because it will happily go off with a stranger if the opportunity arises. Dognapping does occur, and purebreds are especially vulnerable.

FOOD, GLORIOUS FOOD

Labs love—and I do mean *love*—to eat. This trait seems to be universal in the breed, and can lead to fat dogs, sick dogs and even poisoned dogs. Monitor your dog's food intake carefully, watch the snacks and resist those melting eyes that are trying to tell you, "I'm starving, feed me!"

Keep the garbage in a cabinet or up off the floor, and scout your yard regularly for anything your Lab might find appealing (that would be just about anything!). Easter baskets laden with chocolate, dead varmints at the beach, steak bones and everything in between are fair game for the ever-hungry Labrador.

PROTECTION WHEN NEEDED

Don't encourage protectiveness in your Labrador. A Labrador already has a finely-tuned, intuitive sense of protectiveness, which is only displayed when absolutely necessary. Lab owners often say their dog would welcome burglars into the house

Labs love to chew, and have no idea what is and isn't appropriate. That's why it's your job to make sure they never have access to things you don't want them to devour.

and show them where the silverware is hidden. I disagree! A Labrador is friendly and safe when greeting your visitors, but possesses a sixth sense that tells the dog when protection is called for. I always feel safe traveling at night or being home alone with my Labradors on duty. I have no doubt that they would protect me if the need arose.

BASIC HOUSETRAINING

General training for Labs is quite easy. This is a breed that seeks to please you, but you have to be consistent and patient to get the desired response. Let's talk first about housebreaking. From the time a litter is very young, the pups will leave their sleeping area to relieve themselves away from "the nest." When you bring your puppy home, you can capitalize on this behavior by providing a sleeping place (such as a crate), which your puppy will try hard to keep clean.

Notice I said "try." A puppy, like a human infant, has to develop the ability to control its urges to relieve itself. In the beginning, you help the process along by providing frequent trips outdoors.

When you bring your puppy home, start its housebreaking lessons by taking it directly outside. Although you might think that paper training is a good idea, remember you are only prolonging the process by introducing an unnecessary step. Your message is "outside is for relieving yourself." But using paper tells the pup "first we'll teach you to relieve yourself in the house, and then we'll teach you that outside is really the right place." It's confusing for the puppy.

A crate will really help your puppy make it through the night. Keeping the crate in your bedroom for a few nights, where your presence helps to comfort the puppy in its first time away from its littermates, helps it settle down. You can also hear crying or barking if the puppy needs to go out during the night, but don't let this turn into playtime or you'll be up every night thereafter! If the

Your puppy will naturally try to keep its pen or crate clean. You can capitalize on this instinct by skipping the papers and taking the pup outside often. (Greg Goebel)

During the day, limit the puppy to one or two rooms of the house, preferably with washable floors, and watch it closely. When it needs to relieve itself, it will start to circle, sniff and sometimes whine. That is your cue to pick the puppy up, go outside to the *same spot every time* and use a phrase such as "get busy." When the puppy performs, give it extravagant praise and head back to the house. Gradually, the phrase "get busy" (or whatever you choose) will remind the puppy just what you want it to do. This comes in very handy when you're traveling with your dog!

Never spank or shout at your puppy if it has an accident in the house or crate. And *never* rub a puppy's nose into its mess. The pup will have no idea what it is being punished for. Just take the puppy outside, clean up the mess and remember to watch more closely the next time. Be consistent, keep your sense of humor and remember that eventually even the most recalcitrant puppies get the point!

Eventually, your dog will learn to tell you when it needs to go out, but for now you have to take it upon yourself to schedule the puppy's breaks. I wouldn't say that Labradors are the easiest breed to housebreak. But once a Lab learns something, it remembers it very well, so the time you spend now will pay off handsomely in the future.

puppy needs to go out during the night, get up, pick it up and carry it to a designated spot outdoors. Encourage the pup to relieve itself, praise it when it does, and then carry it back indoors and tuck it back into the crate. Turn off the lights and get into bed yourself.

A WORD
ABOUT CRATES

Feeding your dog in its crate gives it an added incentive to keep the crate clean. Does this make you feel uneasy? It shouldn't—your dog feels fine about it. A wire or fiberglass dog crate represents a den to your dog. It is the dog's own space, where it can eat and sleep undisturbed.

If you think of it as a cage, a cruel place to put a dog, come to my house where we have the Labrador version of musical chairs. Every time a crate is vacated, another dog gets into it and curls up to nap. These are adults and even senior citizens. They haven't been crated in years, but they still like the security the little den offers.

You don't need a huge crate, but get one that has enough room for your dog to stand up and turn around in comfortably. Most of the dog's crate time will be spent asleep, so a big crate isn't necessary. In fact, you may have to initially decrease the crate's size by blockading it with a cardboard box turned upside down or a plastic milk crate if your puppy is having frequent accidents in the crate.

Labs love to eat, which is why it's important to give them plenty of exercise and watch their food intake. But you can also use their hearty appetite to encourage them to learn tricks.

Once the puppy is consistently keeping its crate clean, you can put a bath mat or other washable cushion inside, but if the puppy chews it, just leave the crate unlined. Don't line the crate with newspaper, since the puppy is probably accustomed to relieving itself on newspaper. Always provide a special chew toy for crate time, which will reinforce the idea that this is a good place to be.

THE LAST WORD

The character of a Labrador is sterling. This breed can provide you with many years of love and companionship. Your Lab will love to be with you whatever you are doing—walking on the beach, riding in the car, trekking city sidewalks. Wherever you go, you'll have a willing and enjoyable companion. Just remember what the breed's origins were, and be prepared to spend some time teaching your Labrador how to be a good companion and family member.

Please don't leave your Lab alone in the yard, where it may end up taking a swim and a nap at the same time. All your dog really wants is to be with you.

Lab puppies are active and inquisitive. That's why it's your job to make sure they can't get into trouble. (Emily Magnani)

CHAPTER 6

Basic Labrador Care

The Labrador Retriever is one of the easiest breeds to care for. Breeders and owners will sometimes call them "carefree" dogs, but that's not entirely accurate. Anyone who owns a Labrador knows there is some routine care every Lab needs. With a little persistence and patience, most owners can learn how to perform these tasks themselves—persistence to keep trying even when you don't think you can do it, and patience because your dog is learning the task at the same time you are!

Whether it is bathing, cleaning ears or trimming nails, don't expect your dog to know what to do the first time out. You must teach your dog how to behave during routine care. Keep each learning session short and sweet, and always end on a positive note. For example, it may take you five or ten minutes to coax your dog into a position where you can trim one nail, but you must tell it what a good dog it is as soon as you trim the nail, and end the session there. The next day try again, and maybe you can trim two nails at the same time. Each day both of you will get better and better at it.

EXERCISE AND THE ATHLETIC LAB

Labrador Retrievers are athletic, strong dogs with a zest for life. They are not meant to lie on the sofa all day—although when they are in the house, this does seem to be a favorite pastime of adult Labs. A young Labrador Retriever needs a large amount of exercise. This doesn't mean a Labrador can't be raised in a city environment, but as an urban Lab owner you will have to be committed to long walks several times a day, strolls in the park and frequent trips to the beach or a country house.

New procedures, like nail trimming and bathing, can scare your puppy. Take it nice and slow.

Exercising a Labrador can be fun for both you and the dog. Games of fetch with a ball, a stick or a bumper are great exercise. Labradors are natural retrievers, so the only part of these games you will have to teach your dog is to give the object back to you once it is fetched. Remember to use good judgment about when it is time to rest, and enforce those rest periods, because most Labrador Retrievers (especially puppies) will keep retrieving to the point of exhaustion.

You also need to use your judgment about the conditions under which you are exercising your dog. Remember that in hot weather, too much exercise can lead to heat exhaustion. Be sure to limit the exercise as conditions warrant, and to bring plenty of fresh, cool water with you whenever you take your dog out for exercise.

Swimming

Labradors love swimming, and this is another great way to exercise your dog, especially in hot weather (although with their double coat, which gives them extra insulation and keeps the skin dry, Labs do quite well in the water even when it's cool). You can start water games early in the puppy's life by using a small baby pool filled from the hose in the yard.

Beaches, rivers, creeks and lakes are great places for exercise, but you need to beware of strong currents, sharp rocks or pieces of glass and other hazards. During the summer months, many of these areas may not permit dogs, although they may sometimes be used after the park officially closes in the evening.

If you have access to a swimming pool, that can be a great alternative. Just be aware that the chlorine in a swimming pool may bleach out your Labrador's coat, which will be most obvious in the chocolate Labs. You'll need to remember a few things here, as well. You will get fur in the filter, which may need to be cleaned more frequently, and your dog's nails can tear a vinyl liner if the pool has one.

More important, though, are some safety considerations for your dog. A dog allowed to swim in a pool should be taught right away how to get out of it. Even a dog that swims as well as a Lab can become exhausted and drown if it can't get out of a pool. Take the time to show your dog the steps or stairs, and be sure it knows how to use them. I have seen Labrador Retrievers who've been taught to use the vertical metal stairs to get out of an in-ground pool!

Running

Jogging or running is obviously good exercise, provided your dog has been conditioned by gradually increasing the time and distance. Don't expect your Labrador Retriever to accompany you on a 10k race one weekend if you haven't built up its endurance. A dog should be trained just as you would be—begin with short distances and build up gradually. Puppies under one year of age should never be asked to jog or run any farther than a short sprint, because the pounding of their body weight on growing bones can be detrimental to their health.

Once your adult Labrador Retriever has been trained to go the distance with you, you'll have a great running partner. Remember to check the pads on the bottom of its paws on occasion, since

Labs love to retrieve, and will fetch a stick or a bumper until your arm falls off. (Jan Grannemann)

dogs can get blisters and abrasions, too. And bring along plenty of fresh water or balanced electrolyte solution, for both you and your dog. Long walks are less strenuous, and can also be good exercise.

If you can't or don't want to exercise that much with your energetic puppy, try using a laser pointer. This is often sold as a cat toy, but puppies like to chase it, too. You point it on the floor or the ground, where it projects a bright red dot. Most dogs will chase the dot as you move the pointer.

Your Labrador will thoroughly enjoy almost any activity that you and your family enjoy. Picnics (a special favorite, for obvious reasons), soccer games, hiking and biking are all ways for the Labrador Retriever to be involved with its family and to get exercise—something all Labs need and expect.

FEEDING A HUNGRY LAB

Nutrition is extremely important in keeping your dog healthy and in good condition. Although I

Your pup may exercise to the point of exhaustion. That's why it's up to you to put a stop to the games and enforce rest periods.

have owned one or two finicky eaters over the years, most Labrador Retrievers are notorious for their ability (and desire) to eat too much and for their deep appreciation of just about any food. Many of the dogs I see in my veterinary hospital are approaching obesity. Just as it does in people, obesity will shorten the life of your Labrador.

Choosing a Food

There are many good foods available today. In general, unless your dog has a specific health problem that calls for a special diet, dry foods are better than canned or moist foods. Canned foods vary widely in their ingredients, from almost all cereal grains in some to pure meat in others. Since canned food is predominantly water, it is more

expensive to use—you end up paying more to get the same amount of nutrition you'd get in a smaller portion of dry food. In addition, canned food does nothing to keep your dog's teeth clean, whereas chewing dry, crunchy food does help. And finally, moist foods are loaded with sugar, salt and red dyes. For all these reasons, I don't recommend them.

Dry food is the most economical, although you will find a wide price range for different brands of dry dog food. The price generally reflects the quality and digestibility of the ingredients used in making the food, which means the more expensive foods are definitely the better choice—and can even be more economical in the long run. For example, the less expensive foods may be 70 percent digestible, which means 30 percent of what you feed is not digestible and will come out the other end as waste. The more expensive foods can be 85 percent digestible, and therefore only 15 percent ends up in the backyard. Feeding a higher quality food therefore has two big advantages: You need to feed less of it, and you also have less waste to clean up. This is especially helpful when housebreaking a puppy.

The better quality foods have little or no dyes in them, since these do nothing to enhance food quality and may even be harmful. The more expensive foods are sometimes called "premium" pet foods, and are sold only through pet stores or large distributors. The less expensive foods are often sold in the supermarkets.

Get in the habit of taking your dog with you on all kinds of outings. Your dog will get the exercise it needs, and you'll have your best friend at your side. (Susan Willumsen)

Which brand of food to use can be a difficult decision because there are so many brands available. I prefer to use a high-quality premium food from a reputable manufacturer. Dog food is a big business, and there are many small companies making dog food. But not all of them can afford to do the extensive testing that the larger companies do. Look on the label and make sure the food you choose meets AAFCO (Association of American Feed Control Officers) testing standards, preferably through feeding trials rather than solely by analysis of the food.

Once you choose the food and your dog is eating well, time will tell if it's the right food. Dogs are individuals, and they don't all do best on the same diet. When you try a new brand, wait at least eight weeks to see the results. After several months on a new diet a dog's coat should be shiny, its eyes bright and clear, and its skin soft and supple. Its bowel movements should be formed but not hard, and it should not have much flatulence (gas). If you are not happy with your dog's condition, try another brand. Switch food gradually by mixing the new with the old in increasing amounts over a week's time. You need to switch it slowly so that your dog will not develop intestinal upset.

How Much Food Should a Puppy Eat?

Another current and controversial question is what to feed a growing puppy. Years ago, no one thought twice about feeding a specifically formulated puppy food to a puppy for the first year of its life.

Feeding a high-quality food is especially important for a high-energy dog like a Lab. (Greg Goebel)

S H O U L D Y O U A V O I D P R E S E R V A T I V E S ?

Some breeders and owners believe it's important to buy food free of preservatives, or only use foods that are naturally preserved. Ethoxyquin is a preservative that came under attack several years ago when it was found on a Food and Drug Administration list of potential carcinogens (agents that may cause cancer) for humans. Many dog food manufacturers, including those that make premium foods, use ethoxyquin as a preservative.

The manufacturers say they need to use only very small amounts to preserve large quantities of food, and therefore it is safe. And the FDA continues to allow ethoxyquin as a preservative in food for both animals and humans. Another point to consider is that our dogs only live 10 to 15 years, not 70 or 80 as we do, so their lifetime consumption is significantly less than ours would be.

Dog owners will have to decide for themselves what they feel is best for their dog, but finding out which foods contain ethoxyquin and which have other preservatives is not always easy. If the manufacturer adds ethoxyquin, it must be listed in the ingredients. But if the manufacturer buys meat already preserved with ethoxyquin and never adds more, it does not have to be listed as an ingredient. Calling the manufacturer to ask what preservatives are used in its foods may be helpful.

However, some people in the veterinary community now believe the higher protein and mineral levels found in puppy food may increase the pup's growth rate to a point where it can cause orthopedic problems, particularly in the larger breeds, which grow more quickly. There is some evidence to support this, and when taken off puppy food and given adult maintenance food instead, affected puppies seem to improve.

Some companies have now reformulated their puppy foods and even have different foods for breeds of different sizes. Meanwhile, some breeders recommend puppy food for only the first six months of life, while others switch to adult food as early as three months of age. No one knows for certain how long a puppy should be on puppy food. At this time, it is probably best to keep puppies on puppy food until at least nine months of age, while their bones are still growing.

However, it is very important to control how much puppies eat and not allow them to become too chunky. Watch your puppy as it grows. You should be able to feel the ribs with your fingers when you press gently, but not be able to see them. When viewed from above (when you are looking down on your puppy's back), you should see an hourglass shape with a gentle indentation right behind the rib cage. This is also a good way to check an adult dog's weight.

Your breeder can tell you how much food to begin feeding your puppy. Most puppies need to eat three meals a day until about five months of age, simply because their stomachs cannot hold all the food they need for proper growth in one or

Puppies definitely need to start out on a special growth diet, but we're not sure how long they should stay on it. (Kendall Herr)

Feeding an Adult

A fully grown adult Labrador eats about four cups of food a day, but this is a very broad generalization; there are many differences among individuals and among brands of food. An active, young dog that works in the field is going to require more calories than an older, sedentary dog. A dog that spends a lot of time outdoors in the winter will require more food than that same dog would require if it spent most of the day in the house. If your dog requires more than four cups of food a day, it is probably best to feed two meals a day so as not to overload the stomach. Many breeders recommend two meals a day, in any case, to help keep your dog's energy level consistent.

two meals. The amount of food fed to a growing pup should be gradually increased to keep up with its needs, as gauged by its body condition. If the puppy is finishing its food quickly at every meal, it probably needs a little more. If it is leaving food over every time, you're probably feeding too much.

When the puppy reaches approximately five months of age, you can try cutting back to two meals a day, but that does not mean cutting down the amount of food. Feed your puppy just as much, but divide it into two meals instead of three.

Somewhere between 12 and 18 months, the puppy's growth rate decreases significantly and its metabolism slows down. You'll have to decrease the amount of food as well, or your dog will soon be overweight.

When viewed from above, a healthy young dog of the right weight shouldn't look too round. (Kathy Sneider)

Given the hearty appetite of most Lab puppies, it's important to control their food intake so they don't become chunky. (Emily Magnani)

Free feeding is another way of feeding dogs. It means the dog has food available at all times, and the theory is that a dog will not overeat if it knows there is an unlimited supply of food always available. This method is often inappropriate in households with more than one dog, because competition for food is now added to the equation. In homes with a single dog, however, free feeding your dog may or may not work—it really depends on the dog. Some dogs will overeat and some will not. Since Labradors take pride in being poster dogs for low-calorie food advertisements, I have my doubts that free feeding works well for this breed!

Whichever feeding schedule and food you choose, remember to do two things: Measure the amount of food you feed in a day so you can make adjustments as needed, and check your dog's condition by feeling the ribs and looking critically at its body.

Supplements: Should You or Shouldn't You?

Dietary supplements are not generally needed if you are feeding a good quality food, and may even do more harm than good. Some breeders recommend adding vitamin C to a puppy's diet because they believe it may reduce the risk of hip dysplasia. Although the theory has not been proven, the addition of vitamin C is probably harmless, since any excess is excreted in the urine. But other supplements, such as vitamins A, D, E and K, and minerals such as calcium and phosphorus, are not excreted. Instead, whatever is not needed is stored in the body. If given in excess they may accumulate to high levels, leading to disaster. Many orthopedic problems have been proven to be related to imbalances or excesses in calcium and phosphorus.

Adjust your dog's portions according to its lifestyle. Dogs that spend a lot of time outside in the winter, for example, will need more food. (Sue Willumsen)

Food manufacturers have spent a lot of time and effort to ensure their food is balanced and nutritious. Adding supplements can throw off carefully planned ratios of nutrients. This is not to say you can't give your Labrador some treats from your dinner plate on occasion. Pizza crust is a particular favorite in my house. But if you do give "human" food treats, remember that they are only a treat, and should not constitute any significant percentage of the dog's daily diet—which should be a high-quality dog food. As for other vitamins and minerals, nothing should be added without consulting your breeder and veterinarian.

A new niche in the pet industry is nutraceuticals, which are food supplements that do not fall into the category of pharmaceuticals as regulated by the Food and Drug Administration. The market is currently being flooded with these products, in powders, pills and capsules.

Glucosamines and chondroitin sulfates, perhaps the most widely used of these nutraceuticals, are promoted to ease the pain of arthritis or other orthopedic problems. These substances act as synthetic joint lubricants, and at least one brand has been proven in a scientific study to retard the progression of arthritis. Some formulations add other ingredients purported to help ease arthritis pain. Many veterinarians are now prescribing these products for their geriatric patients with arthritis. Some are actually telling clients to put their puppies on them as a way to prevent orthopedic problems, but this kind of use has not been adequately studied and I wouldn't recommend it at this time.

Other nutraceuticals are touted to cure anything from runny eyes to poor coats, bad skin and

Some breeders swear by supplements for everything from sound joints to a healthy, shiny coat. What do scientists say? The jury is still out. (Ann and Randy McCall)

constipation. These usually contain vitamins, minerals and fatty acids that the manufacturer claims are missing in processed foods. They also contain fiber, beneficial bacteria and enzymes to improve digestion, and phytochemicals to fight disease.

The truth is, I find these products intriguing and I am keeping an open mind about them. Theoretically, they seem to make sense, but whether they are really necessary is another question that requires further research—and therein lies the problem. Since these products are not regulated by the FDA, no scientific testing is required before they are marketed to the public. Are the ingredients truly beneficial to dogs? Can a dog digest and therefore "use" the product, or will it just pass through the system? Is there any harm in these supplements? Again, only time will tell, but I do find myself tempted to try some of them. Check with your veterinarian or breeder if you are interested in a nutraceutical for your Labrador.

ROUTINE CARE

Labradors are easy to care for, but it will benefit you and your dog to have a regular schedule of routine maintenance just as you do for yourself, your children and even your car. Eyes, ears, teeth and nails are the areas that require the most attention.

Eyes

The only regular eye care needed is to routinely check for abnormalities. The best way to know what is abnormal is to know what normal is for your dog. If you are used to looking at your dog's eyes carefully, you will notice when and if something changes. This way you can detect potential problems early, and problems that are found early are more easily treated and cured.

Some nutraceuticals do benefit the joints, and they can help ease arthritis in older dogs. However, I wouldn't recommend them for the youngsters. (Jorge Butteri)

Discharges from the eyes can be watery or mucoid, and have a yellowish or greenish tint. Either type can indicate a medical problem. Watery discharges occur with any irritation to the eye, such as dust, dirt, pollen, eyelashes or foreign bodies. Examine the eye for the source of the irritation and try rinsing it with an ophthalmic saline solution. If you can't find anything in the eye and the problem persists, contact your veterinarian.

A mucoid, yellowish or greenish discharge usually indicates a more serious problem. Occasionally, especially in older dogs, the tear ducts stop producing enough tears, and in order to moisten the as well. Conjunctivitis is a bacterial or viral infection of the conjunctiva (the white part of the eye), caused by any sort of irritation to the eye. The conjunctiva becomes pink or red and the dog appears to be uncomfortable. Topical ophthalmic ointments are needed to treat both of these conditions, so a visit to your veterinarian is needed without delay.

Since Labrador Retrievers are very active outdoor dogs, bushes, trees, brush and even cats can cause cuts and abrasions on the cornea (the outer covering of the eyeball). If your Lab is keeping its eyelids shut or has a discharge, check for foreign bodies and flush the eye with sterile saline. If there is no improvement, the dog needs to go to the vet promptly to be checked for a corneal ulcer. Ulcers can become very serious very quickly, so if you notice any eye problem that doesn't clear up quickly, make a veterinary appointment right away.

Get in the habit of looking closely at all your dog's features. Then you'll be able to spot any problems before they become serious. (Greg Goebel)

Check your dog's eyes regularly. They should be clear and bright. (Chenil Chablais)

eye the mucous glands begin to produce more mucous. This syndrome, called keratoconjunctivitis sicca (KCS), or dry eye, is very irritating to the eye, and affected dogs often develop conjunctivitis

Ears

Healthy ears are light pink and clean of any discharge or odor. Routine care of the ears includes checking them often for abnormalities or discharges. Weekly cleaning with an ear cleaner purchased either at a pet supply store or from your veterinarian can help prevent dirt from sitting in the ear canal and causing an infection.

Begin by holding the ear flap up above the dog's head and filling the ear canal with the cleaner. Externally massage the ear canal, which runs along the back of the jaw bone, to loosen any dirt and debris. Wipe out the cleaner with a cotton ball, and allow your dog to shake its head to get rid of the excess. Do *not* use swabs with cotton tips to try to remove debris and wax, because you can actually push the wax deeper into the ear canal.

If you notice any odor or discharge coming from your dog's ear and cleaning the ear does not solve the problem, you will need to visit your veterinarian.

Ear mites are probably the most common infections in very young puppies. If you bought your puppy from a reputable breeder you probably have nothing to worry about, since ear mites are acquired from other animals with ear mites or in less than clean environments. The discharge associated with ear mites is reddish brown, and your pup will scratch its ears and shake its head.

Ear mites can only be seen with a microscope, so they must be diagnosed by your veterinarian. If your dog has them, you will need medication made specifically to kill ear mites. Sometimes the ears also need to be flushed to remove all of the dirt and

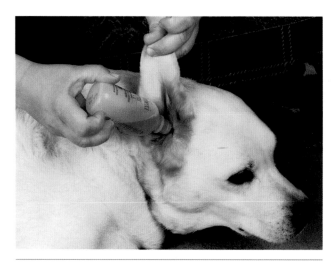

Regular ear cleaning can help prevent many problems. (Greg Goebel)

debris deep inside the ear canal. Your vet will do this if it is necessary.

Bacterial and yeast infections are also fairly common, and cause a discharge with a foul smell. These will need medication from your veterinarian. If your Lab spends a lot of time in the water, you may want to check your local pet supply shop or ask your veterinarian for an ear drying solution that can be used after the dog swims. This can greatly reduce the incidence of ear infections.

If your Lab spends a lot of time outdoors, check its ears for dirt, foreign materials and ticks when it comes in. Ticks seem to especially like the head and neck area.

If your dog has chronic irritations and infections in its ears, it will probably shake its head a lot. This can cause the dog to break a blood vessel in the ear flap, which creates a hematoma (blood blister). Consult your veterinarian if you see any kind of red lump or bump in your dog's ears.

One last thing about ears: Although it is rare, I have seen dogs with chronic ear infections develop permanent head tilts because an inflammation of the ear canal has impinged on nerves in the brain. So keep a close eye on those ears!

Teeth

If you want your dog to have a healthy mouth throughout its life and not knock you over with its breath by the time it's six years old, you need to clean its teeth. Part of the job can be done by feeding dry dog food and dog biscuits. Chew toys such as nylon bones, natural sterilized bones, gummy bones or toys specifically made to clean teeth are also available at pet supply stores. Just be careful when you give new chew toys to your Labrador, because the breed has extremely powerful jaws that will destroy even products labeled "virtually indestructible." Ingesting pieces of toys that are not digestible can cause gastrointestinal blockages.

Even with these toys, however, our pets still don't get the intense chewing activity that their ancestors got in the wild. They also live a lot longer than wolves and wild dogs, and for both these reasons we need to clean their teeth to help preserve them for as long as they're needed. Toothbrushes designed for dogs and toothpaste with beef or poultry flavor are readily available and should be

If your dog spends a lot of time outdoors, check it regularly for ticks. (Sue Willumsen)

used once a week. I even know a Lab that lets his owners use an electric toothbrush to clean his teeth! (He has his own toothbrush head, of course.)

Another appliance looks like a toothbrush, but instead of bristles it has a nylon scrub pad on the end. I tried it, and thought it worked even better than a toothbrush. Chlorhexidine gel is also good for brushing teeth. Whichever method you use, you must begin training your dog to have this done as a young puppy. And never use toothpaste designed for humans, since dogs cannot rinse and spit as we do.

While brushing your dog's teeth, check the gums for any redness (a sign of gingivitis), swelling (tooth root abscesses or growths) and cracked or chipped teeth. If you see any of these problems, a visit to your veterinarian is in order to see if any further treatment is necessary.

If you still find that despite your brushing regime, tartar (a hard, yellowish or tan material) is building up on your Lab's teeth, you can use a dental scaler to remove it. A dental scaler should be available at larger pet supply stores. However, it has very sharp edges and should be used carefully. Place the scaler at the gum line and push it *away* from the gums to scrape off the tartar. Never push the scaler toward the gums, as it can cut the gums easily if you slip. And never use a scaler on a dog that cannot sit still for this kind of attention, as the sharp tool can be dangerous. If all this fails and your dog still has tartar buildup or bad gingivitis, it will need a full dental cleaning and polishing under anesthesia at your vet's office.

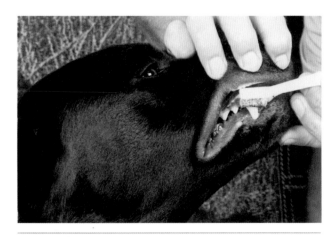

Special toothbrushes and toothpaste make the job of cleaning your dog's teeth easier. Regular brushing will keep its mouth healthy and its breath sweet. (Greg Goebel)

One last word: If you ever find that your dog is refusing to eat (a rare occurrence in most Labradors), check its mouth. If something is wrong with its teeth or gums, eating may be painful. Have the oral problem seen to right away.

Nails

A dog's nails constantly grow, just as ours do, and they require routine trimming. If they are not kept short, the nails can deform the feet and spread the toes, causing the dog pain. Untrimmed nails can actually grow so long that they curl around and grow into the pads, which is very serious.

Like us, the dog's nails are made of layers of keratin, and have no feeling when they are cut. Down the center of the nail, however, is the quick—the blood vessel and the nerve—and if you cut this the dog will yelp and the nail will bleed. Your dog will also be hesitant to let you do its nails again. Fortunately, the quick ends before the end of the nail (you can see it in a light-colored nail), and you can safely cut up to the quick without causing your dog any discomfort. Unfortunately, as the nail grows, so does the quick. This means if you haven't trimmed your dog's nails in a long time, you won't be able to trim them as short as you should without hurting your dog.

If your dog's nails are already long, you need to trim them a little (about an eighth of an inch) every three or four days. In most dogs the quick will gradually recede. Eventually, you will get the nails short, but it may take some time. The best thing to do, therefore, is not to let them get long in the first place. Dogs that spend a lot of time walking on concrete will wear their nails down naturally and may not need as much trimming as a house dog or one that runs on softer surfaces. My own rule is that when I hear my dogs' nails click on the hardwood floors, it's time for a trim.

There are two kinds of nail clippers big enough and strong enough for a Lab: the guillotine type and the scissors type. The scissors type comes in small and large, and both are effective, but I prefer the large because they cut large nails easily. The type and size of clipper you use is not really important. What matters is that you and your dog get used to routine nail trimming.

To trim your dog's nails, begin training as a puppy—as early as eight weeks of age. Get your Lab to sit, lie down or stand in a comfortable position. I find I have more control if I make the dog lie down on its back or side on the floor. Yellow Labs have easier nails to trim than black or chocolate Labs because you can see the pink quick through the nail covering. If you have a yellow dog and you can see the quick, cut the nail close to, but not through, the quick. If you can't see the quick, cut the nail at the point where the tip curves downward.

Ask your veterinarian or breeder to show you how to make a fast cut. Practice by only cutting a little bit at a time, and you will eventually get a feel for it. Don't panic if you accidentally cut the quick and the nail begins to bleed. Styptic powder

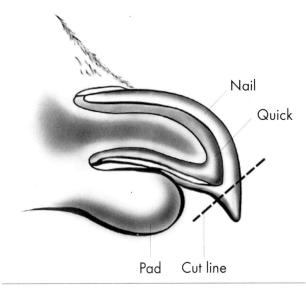

When you hear your dog's nails clicking on the floor, it's time for a trim.

works very well to stop the bleeding, and you should always have some on hand while trimming nails. It is available at most pet supply stores. If you don't have any styptic powder and you cut a nail too short, try rubbing the nail in a bar of soap. If this doesn't work, placing a dry compress on the nail tip and holding it for three to five minutes will usually work.

Don't give up trying to trim nails if you make a mistake; here's where perseverance comes in. It will pay off in the end, knowing your dog can walk comfortably, and your floors will be less scratched.

CHAPTER 7

Taking Care of Your Lab's Coat

One of the most important things to remember about any animal is that a good coat begins from the inside out. In other words, good nutrition is necessary to provide the building blocks of healthy skin and coat. Veterinarians sometimes say that the skin is the window to the body. We see this when dogs are ill or have poor nutrition; their skin and coat look poor. A healthy dog, however, will usually have a beautiful coat.

The Labrador has a dual coat. The hair you see when you look at your dog is called the topcoat. It is longer hair, with a slightly harsh feel to it and natural oils that give it a shine. The oil serves the same function as wax on your car—it makes water bead up and run off—but the dog shouldn't feel or look oily. The second part of the coat is a layer of duller, shorter and softer hair underneath the topcoat, called the undercoat. The undercoat is very dense and protects the dog's skin from the cold. This is why Labrador Retrievers are able to swim in cold water without getting chilled. The next time you take your Lab to the beach, examine its coat after it comes out of the water. You will see how the water runs off the dog like it would off a duck. When you separate the topcoat, you will see that the undercoat and skin are dry.

Your dog's oily topcoat and dense undercoat keep it warm and dry, even in the water.

that although the Lab has a short coat, your dog will shed and will require some regular brushing to keep the coat healthy and reduce the amount of hair in your home. How much hair your Labrador will shed may depend on several things. First, Labs that are kept indoors in moderate to warm temperatures will have less coat than Labs that spend a great deal of time outdoors. An outdoor dog requires a heavier coat to maintain its body temperature in the cold and, luckily, nature provides it.

Shedding is also seasonal. All Labs seem to shed the heaviest in the spring, when they lose whatever winter coat they have grown. This is especially true of dogs that spend a lot of time outdoors, since they are most responsive to the seasons. House dogs, although they actually have less coat, tend to shed a bit year-round (but again, most heavily in the spring).

Not all Labs have the same coat, and the color of the coat often affects the texture and quality. The blacks and chocolates tend to have a slightly harsher feel to their coats, and have a little more oil that makes their coats more shiny. Yellow Labs tend to have a softer, less shiny coat. But the differences are small, and color is often more a matter of preference than of grooming requirements. Since Labs do shed, I generally tell people who are undecided about color to match their carpeting!

As I mentioned in Chapter 6, the Labrador Retriever is a low-maintenance dog and does not require a lot of grooming to keep it in good condition. That being said, it is important to remember

Shedding is seasonal, and tends to be heavier in the spring. (Lisa Weiss)

Blacks and chocolates tend to have shinier, harder coats. (Charles L. Smith)

Finally, shedding can be influenced by hormones. Unspayed bitches probably have the most variation in their coat, due to their hormonal cycles. They get great coats during their heat cycle and pregnancy, and tend to shed excessively—sometimes going almost bald—right after these times. Just ask anyone who shows dogs, and they'll tell you that when the show is right and the judge is perfect, their bitch will usually be out of coat!

Dogs that spend most of their time indoors during winter, where the heat is very dry, tend to develop flaky, dry skin that sheds a little more than normal. This can be particularly evident on a black Lab. If you notice flaking on your dog but otherwise the skin looks healthy and the dog is not scratching excessively, it probably only needs a little extra oil added to its diet. Years ago I used to recommend corn oil, but now we know that the components of the oil needed to maintain healthy skin and coat are the Omega 3 and 6 fatty acids. You can purchase supplements that contain only these fatty acids, and many dog food manufacturers are now adding them to their list of ingredients.

PREPARING TO GROOM

All Labradors should be taught from an *early* age to accept basic grooming and handling. If a puppy is never taught to allow someone to touch its feet, open its mouth or stand still for a bath, it will be much harder to try to do these things when the dog is older. Remember that it should be *your* choice, not the puppy's, as to how much grooming can be done. Be persistent with training, and if it starts to become a battle during a bath, nail clipping or ear cleaning, try to end on a positive note.

If you and your dog are struggling over a nail trim, for example, you may feel like just letting the dog go. But what that teaches a puppy is that it doesn't matter if you insist—the pup can still win and make you stop! Instead, your goal should be to gently continue the chore until the dog allows you to clip one nail (or look in its ear or stand still for a bath for 15 to 30 seconds), and *then* stop. This

way, the training session ends with you winning
and with the dog momentarily having given in to
the procedure.

Some Labrador breeders prefer to train their
dogs to be groomed when standing on a grooming
table. While I can see the benefits of this type of
training, I have never owned a grooming table. My
grooming is usually done with my Labs sitting or
lying on the floor, or on the picnic table in the
backyard. It doesn't really matter where, or in what
position, you groom—as long as you do it.
Whatever works for you and your dog is fine.

BRUSHING

A weekly brushing with a wire slicker brush is
usually all that's needed to keep a Labrador's coat
clean. This kind of brush has thin, bent wire pins
set in a flexible pad. A slicker brush is good for

*A shedding blade will remove dead hairs from your dog's
top coat. (Greg Goebel)*

lifting out the loose undercoat, as well as any loose
topcoat hairs. Some people prefer to use what is
called a shedding blade, which is a serrated metal
strip mounted in a loop, but this will only remove
topcoat, not undercoat.

If your Labrador gets wet or muddy, a good
toweling with a terry-cloth towel or a chamois
will work well to clean the dog right up. If any
dirt remains after the dog dries, it can be brushed
out easily.

BATHING

Bathing is often not necessary, and probably only
needs to be done two or three times a year. Bathing
a Labrador with soap removes the natural oils from
its coat and makes it less resistant to weather and
dirt. In fact, you will often hear British show judges
complain that Americans bathe their Labradors too
frequently, making the coats too soft.

*Your grooming tools. Right to left are a slicker brush, a flea
comb, a shedding blade and a groomer's mitt. (Greg Goebel)*

Sometimes, especially during the hot summer months, a good outdoor bath with the garden hose, finished by drying with a towel, is all that's needed to spruce up the coat. But if the coat is really dirty, especially the undercoat, you may need to use a shampoo. In general, do *not* use your own shampoo on your dog. Your shampoo is made for hair, not the *fur* of your Lab. Pet shampoos are specially formulated to work better on fur.

Dog shampoos can be made either for general use or for special purposes or coat colors. A general dog shampoo can be used on all three Labrador colors, and some of them will give your dog's coat a pleasant smell for several weeks. Alternatively, there are shampoos made specifically for black, yellow or chocolate dogs. Shampoos for the black coat tend to highlight the shine and deepen the black color. The chocolate or brown shampoos bring out the richness of the color and, again, highlight the shine. The yellow shampoos are usually the same ones used for white coats, and tend to bring out the white by adding bluing (also an ingredient in laundry detergent) to the shampoo. I had a yellow Lab that I bathed once with a shampoo for white dogs and once with a shampoo for bronze dogs. There was a very noticeable difference. The white shampoo brought out the white and made the dog appear lighter in color; the bronze shampoo high-lighted the yellow and made the dog appear slightly darker.

Whichever shampoo you choose, you may find it difficult at first to wet down your Lab for its

Bathing your dog can be an adventure. Fortunately, you don't have to do it too often. (Greg Goebel)

bath. Remember, your dog has a dual coat that is meant to repel water like a duck, so you may have to really use your fingers to separate the topcoat to

Different types of shampoos suit different color coats. (Chuck Tatham)

get the water and shampoo down to the under-coat. Always make sure to rinse the shampoo out well because dried shampoo on a dark dog will look like flaky, white dandruff.

If you are so inclined, Labs can be bathed as often as you wish, provided you do not need to maintain the oily coat for any reason (such as showing in a conformation show). A little trick known to most dog exhibitors is that a cold rinse will help retain as much coat as possible after a bath, whereas a warm or hot rinse will remove as much hair as possible. If a Lab begins to shed heavily, it is probably best to give a warm or hot bath, to get out as much coat as possible and to let the new coat begin to grow in.

In lieu of a bath, there are a few dry shampoos available. These are usually foams or powders that can be applied to the coat and brushed or toweled off. These are good for cleaning up spots of dirt, but don't do a very thorough job of deep cleaning.

After a bath, you may need to do extra brushing to remove the remaining loose hair from your Lab. It always seems that after a bath, they shed more for the next one to three days. Your slicker brush is great for removing this loose hair.

CLIPPING

In general, the Lab's coat does not require any clipping or scissoring. You may find that some breeders and show exhibitors like to tidy up the outline of the dog by clipping some of the feathers (longer fur)

on the back of the hind legs, the flank or the tail, but this has largely gone out of fashion. You may still see a few Labs in the show ring that have had their whiskers cut off to give a cleaner look to the muzzle, but this is by no means a necessity. For the average Labrador pet owner, my advice is don't buy any scissors or clippers because you won't need them!

ANAL GLANDS

Since most Labradors will never need to see the inside of a pet grooming salon, there are a few things a groomer would do regularly when a dog comes in for its bath and trim that you will have to keep up with yourself. These include checking the eyes and ears for any signs of problems,

That nice short coat doesn't need any clipping. (Greg Goebel)

A nice swim is often all a Lab needs to stay neat and clean. (Jan Grannemann)

clipping the nails and, in some dogs, checking the anal sacs. Care of the eyes, ears and nails was discussed in Chapter 6. As for the anal sacs, I have not found them to be a problem in Labs. But they can occasionally cause trouble, and you should know what to do if that happens.

All dogs have two anal sacs (or anal glands) positioned under the skin around the anus at about five o'clock and seven o'clock. These glands have ducts that exit into the rectum, and expel their contents as stool passes by and puts pressure on them. The glandular secretion is *very* odoriferous, smelling like fish that are not fresh. Many people believe the purpose of the potent odor is to mark stool with the dog's scent which, in turn, marks the dog's territory.

On occasion, these glands can fail to empty properly, and the full glands can become uncomfortable for the dog. The most common sign of impacted anal glands is that the dog will scoot its rear end on the ground. If you see this happening frequently, you can try emptying the anal glands yourself. First, make sure you cover the anus with a tissue or paper towel because if you are successful in emptying the glands, you will mark yourself with the potent odor for the rest of the day!

To empty the sacs, you apply pressure with your thumb and forefinger, about three quarters of an inch to one inch away from the anus (on the outside), with your fingers at five o'clock and seven o'clock, and squeeze. If you're successful, the contents of the glands will be expelled. If you can't empty the glands and your dog continues to scoot, a visit to the veterinarian is in order, since the glands can abscess if they don't empty. Having said all that, I want to reiterate that Labs, in general, don't often have serious problems with this area.

All in all, the Labrador is truly a wash-and wear-breed, and often a swim in a lake or in the bay keeps them just as clean and neat as they will ever need to be.

(Lisa Sheperd)

CHAPTER 8

Keeping Your Dog Healthy

We could just as well call this chapter "An Ounce of Prevention is Worth a Pound of Cure." Good preventive care starts right when you are choosing your puppy, and you should be sure to follow the guidelines in Chapter 4 about health clearances when searching for your puppy or adult dog. Once you take your healthy puppy home, you can keep it healthy with preventive health care.

CHOOSING A VETERINARIAN

Establishing a good working relationship with your veterinarian is important, since he or she can answer any questions you may have as your Labrador Retriever grows, and can help set guidelines and schedules for preventive health care. Often, your dog's breeder can refer you to a veterinarian who is familiar with Labs and whom you can work with easily. If not, ask neighbors and friends whose opinion you value for a recommendation.

Sometimes, your breeder may recommend a particular vaccination schedule or a specific diet for your puppy. Your vet may suggest something different. If this happens, ask them both to explain their reasons, and then choose what you feel is right. If your veterinarian doesn't want to explain, but insists on his or her way, perhaps you should consult with a veterinarian who is more willing to share his or her thoughts.

Once you bring your puppy home, your first order of business is to make a vet appointment so your puppy can have a thorough physical examination. Even if your puppy already had a physical exam from the breeder's veterinarian, it's still a good idea to have the puppy examined by your own vet within 48 to

72 hours of bringing it home, just to make sure your new pal is healthy. In addition, some state laws mandate that you have the right to return the puppy and receive a refund if it is not healthy. Those laws usually require you to take your puppy to the vet shortly after you get it, in order to protect your rights. So make that appointment! Be sure to bring a stool sample to be checked for parasites, which I'll discuss later in this chapter.

VACCINATIONS

Your puppy may or may not need a vaccination on the first visit to the vet, depending on what the breeder has already had done. In many areas, state law requires a breeder to give you a health record that shows what treatments a puppy has had. Then, you and your vet can discuss which vaccinations

It's always a good idea to bring your new puppy in for a check-up within the first three days. (Winnie Limbourne)

and what vaccine schedule are best for your area, since certain diseases may be more common in some areas of the country than in others.

The proper use of vaccines is a somewhat controversial issue in veterinary medicine today. Some researchers have suggested that using too many vaccines may cause diseases of the immune system in dogs and cats, which seem to be on the rise. Their suggestion is to reduce the number of vaccines we give to our pets and/or to reduce the number of vaccines we give at one time.

Unfortunately, no one knows for sure how long a vaccine truly protects against a specific disease. These questions are currently being studied, and we should know more information in the next few years. In the meantime, it's probably best to tell your veterinarian you'd like to use a vaccine protocol that minimizes the use of vaccines but will still protect your puppy against serious diseases that are common in your area.

The basic puppy vaccine your new Labrador will need is a distemper, adenovirus, parainfluenza and parvo virus inoculation (DA2PPv or DHPPv). If the parvo virus portion of the vaccine is one of the newer "super parvo" vaccines, your puppy will get one every three to four weeks until it is at least 12 weeks old. Many veterinarians, including myself, are hesitant to stop vaccinating this young, and will suggest that your puppy be vaccinated until at least 15 to 18 weeks of age. I'll explain why a little later in the chapter.

AN INTERNET CAVEAT

The Internet is filled with discussions on vaccines, so feel free to research all of these subjects on your own. Just remember that a lot of the information on the Internet may be strictly somebody's opinion, and may or may not be based upon sound scientific testing or evidence. Always carefully consider the source of the information when you evaluate it.

There are several other vaccines available, but in view of the current controversy, I consider them all optional. A leptospirosis vaccine is often combined with the DA2PPv. But there are over 200 types, or serovars, of leptospirosis, and the serovars used in vaccines are not always the ones that most commonly cause illness in dogs. Also, the immunity provided by the vaccines only lasts a short time—perhaps just three to six months.

A vaccine against corona virus is also commonly added to the basic vaccine. I have chosen not to use this vaccine, since corona virus is not as deadly as parvo virus and is not usually fatal in adult dogs at all. I would rather risk my dogs contracting corona virus and having some diarrhea and stomach upset for a few days than give them yet another vaccine.

Tracheobronchitis, commonly called kennel cough, is another disease for which a vaccine is available, but you will probably not need it unless your dog is exposed to large populations of other dogs, such as at dog shows or boarding kennels. Kennel cough is caused by many combinations of viruses and a bacteria, and the vaccine probably protects only against the bacterial portion, known as *Bordatella bronchiseptica.* For this reason, the vaccine doesn't fully prevent kennel cough, although it may reduce its severity. It can be given either by injection or by drops in the nose.

Another optional vaccine counters Lyme disease. Once again, there are two types of vaccine on the market and much controversy over which, if either, to use. The first vaccine is called a *bacterin,* which means it contains the bacteria that causes Lyme disease but has been processed so that it can no longer cause the disease. In most dogs this vaccine seems to work well to provide immunity, but there were some reports from researchers suggesting a link to kidney and neurological problems. These problems seemed to occur mostly in Labrador Retrievers and Golden Retrievers.

The newer Lyme vaccine contains only a small portion of the bacteria and seems to provide adequate immunity with no side effects reported so far. Only time will tell if this is a better vaccine or not.

Finally, I must mention rabies vaccines. In most states, it is mandatory to vaccinate all dogs and cats against rabies. How often you must vaccinate varies, and is usually determined by how common rabies is in a particular state. Although a rabies vaccine is not given when a puppy is very young, all puppies should be vaccinated by six months of age, and then again a year later. Some states then require an annual booster vaccination, but others accept a vaccine every three years. Check with your vet or local animal control officer for the requirements in your state.

The best way to decide which vaccines to use is to discuss them with your veterinarian, since he or she can tell you which diseases your dog is at risk of contracting in your area. Despite the lively discussion about which, how often and how many vaccines a young puppy needs, most people agree that an annual booster vaccination is currently recommended.

How Do Vaccines Work?

There is one very important point about puppy vaccinations that should be emphasized: Your

Immunity from mother's milk can last up to 18 weeks, which is why puppies need a series of vaccines to make sure they are fully immunized. (Lisa Weiss)

puppy is not fully protected against diseases until its last vaccine, at 15 to 18 weeks of age. To understand why that's true, you'll need to understand the basics of what a vaccine actually is and what it does in the body.

A vaccine is a bacteria or virus that can cause a particular disease. It has been rendered inactive or killed, so that it cannot produce that disease. When injected into an animal, the vaccine stimulates the body's immune system to make antibodies to fight it. When a puppy is born, it receives temporary antibodies from its mother's milk that will protect the puppy until it's old enough to make its own antibodies, at about 15 to 18 weeks. At some point during those 15 to 18 weeks, the temporary antibodies fade away. This happens at different ages in different puppies, and you can never be sure exactly when they are gone. If mom's antibodies are still present when a puppy is given a vaccine, they attack the vaccine and render it ineffective. But when mom's antibodies fade away, giving the vaccine to the puppy will stimulate the puppy's body to produce its own antibodies. Because you are not sure exactly when her antibodies are gone, and because you don't want the puppy to be without any antibodies at all, either from mom or from the vaccine, you need to give a vaccine every three to four weeks until you can be sure mom's antibodies are gone and the puppy will make its own.

Immunity vs. Socialization

This brings me to one final point about puppy vaccines. Since your puppy is not fully protected until it receives its final vaccine at 15 to 18 weeks, you should be very careful about where you bring your puppy and what you expose it to before then. In fact, from a purely medical point of view, probably the safest thing you can do is keep your puppy in your own home and yard, and not let it go anywhere else until it's had its last shot. You may even find some vets who will suggest that.

The problem with that approach, however, is that dogs do some of their best learning at a very early age. Exposing a puppy to a variety of new situations and people, in a positive way, during this period is important to the puppy's behavioral development. For example, I live on a main road with lots of traffic and occasional accidents, construction, car backfires and sirens. I also live near a small airport. While the noisy yard is not always great for backyard barbecues, it is wonderful for raising puppies. On the Fourth of July, when other owners are busy tranquilizing their dogs, my dogs sit back and watch (and hear) the fireworks with me. I believe you need to achieve a balance between keeping your puppy physically healthy and exposing it to as many different and new situations and people as possible.

I always recommend to new puppy owners that they do not take their puppies to parks, beaches, ball fields or out for neighborhood strolls, since there is a higher risk of stray, unvaccinated and potentially unhealthy dogs having passed through these areas. But it is a good idea to take them to your relative's and friend's homes, and allow them to visit

new places and see new dog friends that are healthy and vaccinated, and take them for rides in the car.

SPAYING AND NEUTERING

The next step in protecting the health of your new Lab puppy is to have it neutered or spayed. There are strong medical, behavioral and social benefits to be derived from this simple operation.

For example, once a male dog is neutered there is absolutely no risk of testicular cancer, and there is a much lower risk of prostate disease when your dog gets older. Behaviorally, it reduces your male's dominance tendencies and his urge to roam. Males can be neutered any time during their first

A puppy cannot be kept in isolation. You must balance the need for socialization with your concerns about the pup's immunization schedule. (Kathy Sneider)

year of life, although they hardly seem to be affected by the surgery when it is done at around six months of age.

Females should be spayed before they come into their first heat, since this almost eliminates the possibility of breast cancer. Spaying before the second heat still reduces the risk of breast cancer, but not quite as much. By the time a bitch goes through her fourth heat, she no longer derives any benefit in terms of breast cancer risk, but spaying at any age will still reduce the risk of ovarian cancer and pyometra. Pyometra is a potentially life-threatening infection of the uterus in predominantly older, unspayed females.

Spaying or neutering greatly reduces your dog's health risks and in no way diminishes its energy level or desire to work and play.

prevent unwanted litters and future heartbreaks by spaying or neutering your Lab.

Remember, the body has other sources of testosterone and estrogen—your boy will still grow up to be a man even if he's neutered, and your girl will still be a girl, even if she's spayed!

HEARTWORM

Your new Labrador Retriever will be put on heartworm prevention medicine by your veterinarian somewhere around 12 weeks of age, and then will require a blood test for heartworm either every year or every other year. How many months of the year you need to give your dog this medication depends on

Behaviorally, spaying your puppy bitch will avoid the male Romeos who will be forever at your door and in your yard while your little girl is in heat.

Society benefits from neutering and spaying, also, as it helps in pet population control. Sadly, pets are destroyed every day in shelters just because there are not enough good homes for all the pets born every year. You can do your part to

how prevalent heartworm is in your area. Many veterinarians on the East Coast are currently recommending heartworm treatment year-round. Since heartworm is transmitted by mosquitoes, anyone living in an area that does not have a hard frost during the winter should keep their dog on treatments year-round.

Although the drug is given once a month, it does *not* last in your dog's system for a full month.

Within one or two days it simply kills any heartworm parasites that your dog has picked up through mosquito bites in the previous 30 days.

Many heartworm medications are now combined with parasiticides to prevent intestinal parasites, as well. One of the newer products even contains a flea growth regulator to eliminate flea infestations. (More on fleas later in this chapter.)

INTERNAL PARASITES

You should have a sample of your puppy's stool checked for internal parasites. These include hookworms and roundworms, which are very common in puppies. It can also include tapeworms, which are transmitted mostly by fleas, and whipworms, which are found in the soil. Coccidia and giardia are both single-celled parasites that are seen more often in puppies that have grown up with many other puppies, such as in puppy mills, breeding farms, shelters and some pet shops.

Although very rare, some of these parasites are transmissible to humans, particularly young children or adults with compromised immune systems, so your veterinarian may choose to deworm your puppy even though the stool sample was negative for parasites. Internal parasite eggs live in cycles, and a negative stool sample doesn't always mean that your dog does not have any parasites. As I've already mentioned, most monthly heartworm preventives have a dewormer combined with them, so the monthly dose will

routinely deworm your dog of most, but not all, of these parasites.

LICE AND MITES

External parasites that affect puppies and dogs include fleas, ticks, mites and lice. Lice are the least common. They are visible to the naked eye, and can be easily treated with any insecticidal dip. However, you must be careful when applying dips to puppies because some are too potent for youngsters and can cause serious illness. Consult your veterinarian if you think your puppy or adult dog has lice.

I've been asked many times if the lice the children brought home from school are a danger to the family dog or cat. The answer is no. Lice are a

Heartworm is transmitted by mosquitoes. Labs, which so love to swim, are therefore at risk. (Ed Katz)

host-specific parasite, which means dog lice will not infect humans, and vice versa.

Mites are not as common as fleas and ticks, but can be a problem on occasion. There are three types of mites found on dogs and puppies: demodex, sarcoptes and chyletiella. Chyletiella mites are commonly called "walking dandruff," since they look like flakes of dandruff that move on the dog's coat. Both chyletiella and sarcoptes are contagious to humans and to other pets in the house.

As with lice, dogs and puppies can be treated with an insecticidal preparation but, once again, be sure to read the label carefully or consult with your veterinarian when using these products on young puppies. More recently, ivermectin, a medicine taken internally, has been used safely in even young puppies.

Sarcoptic mites cause canine scabies (or mange), which is highly contagious between animals of different species as well as humans. Ten to 50 percent of people in contact with canine scabies develop a slight rash that is extremely itchy. Most cases disappear quickly, since the mite does not prefer to live on us, but I have seen a few cases where the pet owner had to see a dermatologist. The most common sign of this type of mange is dry, crusty patches, usually first seen on the edges of the ear flaps, the elbows and the hocks. Hair is usually thin or missing, and the dog itches intensely. Some dogs are so itchy that they can't eat or sleep, and begin losing weight.

Your veterinarian will need to do a skin scraping to try to find the mite causing the problem. Treatment for these mites used to involve dipping the dog in a very messy and smelly

lime sulfur, but today the treatment of choice is ivermectin.

Demodectic mites cause demodectic mange, which can be seen in two forms: localized and generalized. Localized demodectic mange appears as small, usually hairless areas that the dog bites or scratches. These are most common on the head and legs, but can occur anywhere on the body. Once again, your dog will need a skin scraping to try to find the mite causing the problem. Treatment is usually a matter of applying a cream regularly for months to the affected areas. If the problem is too widespread for that, your vet may prescribe a different treatment.

The generalized form of the disease is much more serious, and often involves the entire body. The predisposition to develop this disease seems to run in families, and to occur more often in certain breeds—luckily, the Labrador Retriever is *not* one of them. Treatment options vary, and you should discuss them with your vet.

FLEAS

Fleas are tiny black insects that move very quickly. You can see them on your Lab when you part the fur. Of course, it's easier to spot them on yellow Labs than it is on black or chocolate Labs! Fleas are the most common external parasites that plague dogs. Luckily, medicine has made great strides in the past two or three years in new treatments for eliminating fleas on our pets.

Look around your dog's head, ears, armpits, groin and the base of the tail to spot these little insects. If you don't find any, look for tiny black specks in your dog's coat, which can be flea "dirt," a combination of flea feces, digested blood and flea eggs. If you find these black specks and still are not sure if it's really flea dirt, comb some specks onto a white paper towel and wet it with tap water. If it's flea dirt, it will leave red streaks on the paper from the digested blood.

Remember that it's much easier to prevent fleas in the first place than it is to try to get rid of them. With that in mind, several years ago a monthly tablet called lufenuron was introduced. The product stops fleas from reproducing. Lufenuron is available from your veterinarian and is sold alone or in combination with a monthly heartworm medication. Most pet owners are very happy with its effects, and most now purchase the combination tablet so they only have to give their dog one tablet a month to prevent heartworm, internal parasites and fleas.

Lufenuron works very well to prevent infestations, but does not kill the adult flea. And the flea still has to bite the dog to get the lufenuron. Therefore, lufenuron is great if your dog is occasionally exposed to fleas, but if you live in an area where your dog is constantly exposed to large numbers of fleas, it may not be the right choice.

Two other products have recently been introduced. These are both topical liquids that are applied to the dog's skin in one or two places, and over the next 48 hours they are absorbed into the fat layer of the skin and stored in the hair follicles all over the dog's body. These products kill adult fleas when they simply come in contact with the dog. In other words, the fleas don't need to bite the dog in order to be dispatched. This is great

Just about every dog is susceptible to flea infestations. But fortunately, many new products fight fleas more effectively and are less toxic than the old collars and dips. (Ann McCall)

news for dogs that are allergic to flea saliva (which is more common than you would think!).

The first of these products is called imidacloprid, and only kills fleas. The second is called fipronil, and kills both fleas and ticks. Both are available from your veterinarian.

The other products that have been on the market for years are insecticides—many of them in the organophosphate group, which can be harmful to your pet and to wildlife if not used properly. Read labels carefully if you choose to use these products. Also, remember that these products will only kill the existing adults, and you should always treat the dog again in two to three weeks to kill the new adults hatching from the eggs.

Flea collars and electronic mechanisms do not prevent or kill fleas. Flea collars are also very dangerous if your puppy should get the collar off and eat it. The new products, although expensive, are a much better choice, and will cost less money than an exterminator!

If your dog does get fleas, it will often become infested with tapeworms, as well. When the flea bites the dog, the dog bites and sometimes eats the flea, which contains tapeworm larvae. Now your dog has tapeworms. Two common signs of tapeworms are a dull coat and small pieces of tapeworm segments, which look like pieces of rice, in your dog's stool or on its coat around the anus. See your veterinarian for medication if you see these segments.

If your puppy has fleas and it's less than 12 weeks old, many of the flea products available are too strong and some shouldn't be used at all. Probably your best defense against fleas on a very young Lab puppy is a flea comb. A flea comb is a special comb with very closely spaced teeth. Combing the coat with it will comb out the fleas—you will see them on the comb. Put the fleas in alcohol to kill them, or into a deep paper bag so you can discard them. Make sure the bag is deep enough to keep the fleas from jumping out.

Some people believe garlic and brewer's yeast given in their dog's food helps them repel fleas. While there's no scientific proof of this, it may help in a few cases and there's no harm in feeding it. I'm doubtful, however, that it would be a good defense against a large number of fleas.

TICKS

Ticks are probably the second most common external parasites that affect dogs. Ticks are particularly dangerous because they can transmit serious illnesses to dogs (and people!). They carry tick paralysis, Rocky Mountain spotted fever, Ehrlichia, Babesia and Lyme disease. All these diseases are found in ticks in the northeastern United States. Other parts of the country may have one or more of these diseases present in the local tick population.

Ticks don't bite the dog the way a flea does. Rather, they burrow and embed their heads into the skin and begin to suck blood. Since it's generally thought that it takes the tick up to 24 hours to embed itself and pass on the disease organisms it may be carrying, it is extremely important to check your dog daily for any ticks, especially during active tick season (which varies in different parts of the country). Be especially watchful if your dog has been in the woods, or running through tall grasses and bushes. Removing the ticks as soon as possible will help prevent disease.

To remove a tick, grasp it as close to the dog's skin as you can with a pair of tweezers, and pull slowly but firmly. This will help to remove the head of the tick, which you should not leave embedded in the dog's skin. Don't pull ticks out with your bare hands, since the diseases a tick can carry are dangerous to humans, as well. For the same reason, don't squish the tick between your fingers. After removal, put the tick in alcohol to kill it. Don't throw it in the toilet or wash it down the sink, since this won't kill ticks, and they may even multiply in there!

As far as tick prevention goes, other than keeping your dog away from areas of high risk, there are only a few products available that can actually

Any dog that spends time in woods or fields should be thoroughly checked for ticks as soon as it gets home. (Annie & Ron Cogo)

reduce the number of ticks your dog gets. One of these is a collar with the chemical amitraz. It works well to repel and kill ticks.

Another product is fipronil, a topical liquid, which is also used to kill fleas. Fipronil will kill ticks in contact with it within 24 to 48 hours. Since ticks can transmit a disease to your dog in 24 hours, it's still a good practice to examine your dog daily and remove them as soon as possible.

PROBLEMS THAT AFFECT LABS

Every breed has its own list of potential disorders, and the Labrador Retriever is no exception. Reputable breeders will ensure that their breeding stock is free from inheritable diseases to the greatest extent possible, but just as in life, there are no guarantees. For example, two dogs with eyes that have passed all the standard tests and have been given the proper clearances may still occasionally produce a puppy that turns out to have an eye disease. This is not the breeder's fault; it is simply genetics at work.

Labradors, like all breeds, have certain genes in their gene pool that cause them to inherit a disease or have a predisposition to a disease. When gene mapping is completed for the dog, we may move closer to eliminating some of these diseases. Already, a blood test has been perfected to detect carriers of an eye disease in Irish Setters, and we hope a blood test for Labradors with this same disease will be available soon. When it is, breeders will be able to select breeding stock based on this test, and therefore eliminate this disease from the breed.

Obesity and Hypothyroidism

Although obesity is not usually classified as a disease in animals, Labs have a very strong desire for food and an ability to make their owners feel like they're not feeding them enough. A large number of Labs I see are obese, and it's usually the owner's fault. Any self-respecting Labrador never refuses food, so it's your job to ration it out!

A few cases of obesity may be caused by a thyroid gland that's functioning at a low level. This condition is called hypothyroidism. If you believe you do not overfeed your Lab, but it is still obese, your veterinarian can run simple blood tests to diagnose hypothyroidism. It can be treated easily with daily medication.

If your Lab doesn't have hypothyroidism and is obese, the answer is the same as it would be for you: more exercise and less food!

Obesity is of particular concern in young, growing Labs, and again in old age. Excess weight on a puppy can lead to extra stress on the bones and joints, which may cause orthopedic problems such as hip dysplasia. You should adjust your puppy's food intake by observing its body. You want to feel its ribs easily with slight pressure from your fingers, but not be able to see individual ribs.

When your Lab is a senior citizen, its joints will not work as well as they did when it was younger. It may even develop some arthritis. Keeping a dog at a good weight will help it get around easier and live a happier, more active and longer life.

Having said all that, I will tell you that people who've bought puppies from me call me after a visit to their veterinarian because the vet said the puppy was too fat. I always ask to see the puppy myself, and many times the pup is just fine. The problem is that the vet is not familiar with Labradors who come from good show lines. These pups have well-arched ribs and will look much different than Labradors from good field lines or from poor quality lines. Just remember, the true test is done with your fingers on your dog's ribs.

Hip Dysplasia

Hip dysplasia is a relatively common problem in almost all of the large breeds. Current thinking is that it can be caused by many factors, including genetics, growth rate, environment and nutrition. No one knows for sure how much each factor contributes to the disease.

Hip dysplasia was once thought to be caused by a malformation of the ball and socket joint of the hip. That is, the head of the long bone of the leg (the femur) does not fit properly into the socket of the pelvis (which is called the acetabulum). More recently, we've learned that even hips that are formed normally may be at increased risk of developing dysplasia if there is excess looseness,

It's especially important to make sure your senior citizen does not become obese. (Greg Goebel)

or laxity, in the hip joint. The problem with laxity is that it allows excessive motion within the joint. So there seem to be several reasons why dogs develop hip dysplasia.

Hip dysplasia can range from mild to severe. The best way to diagnose the problem is by X-ray. But as we were taught in vet school, "dogs don't walk on their X-rays." In other words, a dog that on X-ray has mild dysplasia may be severely crippled, while a dog with severe dysplasia on X-ray may get along fine most of the time.

Not all hip dysplasia needs to be aggressively treated with surgery. If your dog is affected, the type of treatment recommended will range from giving your dog an occasional aspirin when needed to total hip replacement. The decision is based on your dog's X-rays, its symptoms and its age.

Since hip dysplasia does have a genetic component, it's important to eliminate dysplastic dogs from any breeding program. The most common way to certify that a dog's hips are clear of hip dysplasia is to have an X-ray done and sent to the Orthopedic Foundation for Animals (OFA) for evaluation. The OFA will have several board-certified veterinary radiologists review the X-rays and grade the hips as excellent, good, fair or, if dysplastic, mild, moderate or severe. Although the OFA will evaluate X-rays on dogs less than two years old, they will not issue a permanent clearance or a number until the dog is 24 months old.

The PennHip method of evaluating hips is catching on, but is still not as widely used as OFA—which is a shame. PennHip measures joint laxity, which can be measured as young as 16

There's just no reason to breed a dog that does not have sound hips. If we all breed only the dogs with the tightest hips, hip dysplasia will eventually be eliminated from the breed. (Ed Katz)

weeks of age, since it doesn't change as the dog ages. Any Lab X-rayed for PennHip measurements is compared only to other Labradors, not to other breeds. Your dog then receives a joint laxity distraction index (DI) number. PennHip suggests that only dogs in the top half for their breed (in other words, those with the tightest joints) be used for breeding. Those dogs who fall into the lower half, or the loosest hips, have a greater chance of developing hip dysplasia in the future.

Theoretically, if we bred only dogs with the tightest hips, we could eventually consistently breed Labs with tight hips and thereby reduce the incidence of hip dysplasia. Wouldn't that be great?

Panosteitis

Often called simply pano, this is a bone disease of young, rapidly growing dogs. It is caused by inflammation of the interior canal of the long bones. Some people equate it with the growing pains sometimes seen in children.

Often, more than one bone is involved and the dog can exhibit shifting leg lameness. If you press firmly on the affected bone, the dog usually shows signs of pain. Puppies may be depressed and have reduced appetites.

Pano can occur at any time from six to eighteen months of age. Some puppies have mild bouts that only last a week or two, while others can be plagued for several months. Aspirin, carprofen and prednisone are often used to relieve the pain. Affected puppies should have restricted activity. Luckily, puppies do outgrow this problem.

Elbow Dysplasia

Elbow dysplasia is a general term used to describe several problems of the elbow joint. It includes ununited anconeal process, fragmented coronoid process, incomplete ossification of the humeral condyle and elbow luxation—quite a mouthful! The first sign is usually sudden onset of lameness, most often at around four to eight months of age.

Some affected puppies will need surgery and others will do fine with rest, aspirin and the new joint lubricants (polyglycosaminoglycans, glucosamine and chondroitin sulfate). You and your veterinarian will have to make the decision whether or not to do surgery, based on the severity of the disease (as seen on X-rays) and the severity of signs your dog is exhibiting. If you still can't decide, seek another veterinarian's opinion.

One thing to remember is that whatever treatment you choose, your pet will probably develop arthritis in that elbow later in life.

Osteochondrosis

Osteochondrosis is a disease of the cartilage covering the ends of the bones. For some reason,

Pano mostly affects young, growing dogs. Fortunately, most of them grow out of it. (Greg Goebel)

perhaps related to nutrition, growth rate or heredity, the developing cartilage does not form properly and becomes thickened. This abnormal cartilage is more prone to trauma, leading to flaps of cartilage, either attached or floating free in the joint. This condition is osteochondritis dissecans (OCD).

Signs of lameness and pain in the joint occur suddenly when the osteochondrosis turns into OCD. Again, this disease occurs in young dogs between five and eighteen months, and males are more commonly affected than females. The joints most commonly affected in Labradors are the shoulder, stifle and hock.

Treatment is controversial, and the choices are surgery or conservative treatment with rest, pain medication and the new joint lubricants. Arthritis is also very possible after this trauma to the joint. Some veterinarians believe it is better to do the surgery quickly to prevent too much trauma to the joint, and hopefully reduce the risk of arthritis. Others feel conservative treatment works just as well. What we do know is that some dogs do better with surgery and some do better without. What we don't know is which dogs fall into which category.

Acral Lick Granuloma

An acral lick granuloma is a sore on the dog's leg, usually caused by the dog incessantly licking at it. The reason for this licking is still a mystery. Some theories include trauma, nerve damage, boredom or bone disease, but no one seems to know for sure.

All types of medicines and bandages have been tried, but not one can really cure the problem.

Recently, antianxiety drugs and antidepressants have been tried, with limited success.

These sores seem to be more prevalent on yellow Labradors (and Golden Retrievers). My own yellow female has had one for over a year. She began licking when I was away for dog shows for several days, and now will not leave it alone. I'm thinking of trying those obsessive-compulsive disorder drugs to see if I can break the cycle. But they are a short-term solution, and should not be used long term.

Progressive Retinal Atrophy

Progressive retinal atrophy (PRA) is a degenerative disease of the retina that will eventually cause total blindness. There are two forms of PRA: early onset and late onset. Labradors are prone to late onset PRA, where there may not be signs of blindness and retinal degeneration until the dog is four to seven years old.

It affects both eyes at the same time. Night blindness is usually the first sign. You may notice that your dog's eyes appear greenish and reflective at night. This is because the retina is damaged and reflects back a larger amount of light than normal. You may also notice that your dog's eyes seem dilated all the time. This is the eye's natural response—it is allowing as much light as possible to reach the retina in the back of the eye.

There is no treatment for PRA. Fortunately, many dogs adjust well because the disease progresses slowly and they have time to learn to get around without their vision. Dogs are not at all self-conscious about being blind, and often adapt readily.

The Canine Eye Registration Foundation (CERF) will certify eyes as being clear of hereditary eye diseases, including PRA. Dogs need to be examined by a board-certified veterinary ophthalmologist, who then completes a form to be sent to CERF for certification. Every dog in a breeding program should be examined annually from two to ten years of age.

Fortunately, a new blood test to screen for carriers of PRA is almost ready to be marketed. Carriers are dogs that have a hidden gene for the disease, but are not affected themselves. If two carriers are bred, they can produce offspring that have the disease. The new blood test might be available by the time you read this book.

Cataracts

Cataracts are cloudy areas on the lens of the eye, and can be found in one or both eyes. They may be hereditary or not, and a veterinary ophthalmologist can sometimes tell the difference depending on the location, size and shape of the cataract and the age of the dog. Some cataracts can progress to cause partial or total blindness, while others never become a serious problem. Some can even disappear with time. Information on cataracts is reported on the CERF form.

Epilepsy

Labs do not have a particular predisposition to epilepsy, but since it is fairly common overall in dogs, it's worth mentioning. Epilepsy simply means a seizure disorder. Seizures can be very mild to very severe, and some can be life-threatening. A dog having a seizure may collapse, lose consciousness, become stiff, salivate, urinate and defecate. This can last from seconds to minutes, but if it persists for more than 10 to 15 minutes (called status epilepticus), you should call your veterinarian and bring your dog in *immediately*.

Idiopathic epilepsy, the most common form, is epilepsy that results from unknown causes, although heredity apparently plays a big role. Idiopathic epilepsy is usually first seen from six months to three years of age. Often the seizure occurs when the animal is resting or has just awakened. Other causes of seizures include toxins, biochemical imbalances in the body and tumors. Your vet may need to run tests to determine the underlying cause of the seizures.

Idiopathic epilepsy can be treated with many different drugs, the most common being phenobarbital. Even on phenobarbital, your dog may still experience some seizures, but they should be fewer and milder. Labs can lead a normal life with idiopathic epilepsy.

EMERGENCY CARE

Every dog owner should learn a few basic skills so they can assess their dog's health and know when to call the veterinarian. This section is certainly not meant to be a complete healthcare guide. In fact, it is a very good idea for you to buy a book that covers all types of emergency pet care. Another good idea is to have an emergency kit prepared in case you ever need it.

This dog has a yearly eye exam to rule out PRA and other abnormalities. The exam and the new blood test are important for any dog that is part of a breeding program. (Ed Katz)

It is extremely important to remember to muzzle your dog before handling it if it's seriously hurt. Any dog, even a Labrador, may bite if something hurts badly enough! If you don't have a muzzle, you can make one out of any long, thin material like cotton bandaging, stockings or a leash. Tie a loose knot in the material and loop it over the dog's mouth, then pull it tight. Now cross the material under the dog's jaw and tie the ends under the dog's ears behind its head. Remember, even *your* dog can bite when it's hurt!

Body Temperature

A dog's normal temperature can range from 101° to 102.5°. Minor variations are probably not important. Take your dog's temperature rectally using a mercury or digital thermometer. Lubricate the tip with petroleum jelly first, and wait at least one minute before removing the thermometer. If your dog's temperature is less than 100° or greater than 103°, it may be an emergency. Check with your veterinarian.

Vital Signs—Primary Assessment

Any time your dog is seriously ill or injured, you need to assess its condition. Practice on your dog now, while it's healthy, and you will know better when something is not right. Your dog's gums should be a nice pink color. When you press on them with your finger, they should turn white because you have squeezed the capillaries. After you release the pressure, it should take only one to two seconds for full color to return. This is called capillary refill time, or CRT. Pale gums or a prolonged CRT can indicate anemia or shock.

Heart rate in a normal, resting Labrador should be 80 to 120 beats per minute. You can place your hand on your dog's chest, just under its

BASIC PET FIRST AID KIT

Scissors	Gauze bandage roll
Thermometer	Adhesive tape
Vaseline	Pepto Bismol
Tweezers	Hydrogen peroxide
Tourniquet	Syrup of ipecac
Muzzle	Saline
Cotton	Eye wash

Your veterinarian's phone number
Emergency clinic phone number
National Poison Control Center for Animals: (800) 548-2423

elbow, or you can feel for the femoral pulse on the inside, middle of the thigh. A heart rate that is much higher or much lower than normal can indicate serious problems.

Respiration and breathing patterns should be observed. Normal respiration in a resting Labrador is 12 to 24 breaths per minute. If the rate is greatly increased, or if your dog is using its abdominal muscles to breathe, it may be an emergency.

Secondary Assessment

After an injury, always check your dog's vital signs first. Then check for other abnormalities. Look for bleeding, broken bones, swelling, lameness and other problems.

If your dog has a bleeding wound but doesn't seem too bad, take the time to clean it with hydrogen peroxide, an antiseptic or just plain water to remove any bacteria. Apply a topical antibiotic cream, such as bacitracin, and bandage the area. If your dog is bleeding more severely, you will need to apply a pressure bandage and get it to your veterinarian immediately.

If you notice any broken leg bones, try to make a splint out of anything you can find, and wrap it around the bone to stabilize it. A thick newspaper or magazine can even be used to wrap the leg, and wrap tape around that to hold it in place. Be creative, because it doesn't matter what a splint looks like. What is important is that it supports the broken bones!

If your dog has had an injury and can't walk or move, get a piece of plywood or a large towel or blanket, held taut, to move the dog, since it may have a spinal injury. Try to move the dog as little as possible, but get it to the vet immediately.

Insect Bites and Stings

A single insect bite or bee sting can cause a serious allergic reaction, which can progress to difficulty breathing, collapse and even death. The first indication that your Labrador is having a serious reaction may be swelling of the muzzle and face, or welts all over its body and sometimes the legs.

Minor reactions can usually be treated with over-the-counter antihistamines such as dyphenhydramine, but more serious reactions may need steroids and epinephrine as well, so contact your veterinarian to see what treatment he or she recommends.

Another problem that can arise from insect bites or any irritation to the skin is a hot spot. The irritated area becomes itchy and the dog chews or scratches at it until it becomes raw and oozing. If you don't break the itch cycle, these sores can become very bad, very fast. The best thing to do is clip or shave the hair around the area, wash it with an antibacterial soap and then pat it dry. Do your best to keep the dog from scratching or biting at it. Don't apply any ointments that will keep the area moist, such as bacitracin. Over-the-counter sprays to reduce the itch may help.

Poisoning

The most important thing to know about poisoning is what type of poison the dog ate or drank.

Antifreeze and rat poisons are the most common, but ordinary plants, indoors and out, can also cause serious problems.

Call your veterinarian before you rush your dog off to the clinic, because he or she may tell you to induce vomiting at home immediately. Vomiting can be induced with hydrogen peroxide, salt water or syrup of ipecac. When you take your dog to the vet, try to take the label or a sample of what the dog ingested. There is also a National Poison Control Center that you can call 24 hours a day for a small fee. The phone number is (800) 548-2423.

Choking

Signs of choking include drooling, pawing at the mouth and difficulty breathing. Open the dog's mouth and see if you can find any foreign objects such as sticks, bones, pieces of toys or food lodged in the mouth or throat. If you see something, you can use a pair of tweezers, pliers, a hemostat or your own fingers to try to pull it

Your dog depends on you, so make sure you know what to do in an emergency. (Ed Katz)

out. Be careful not to push it in further!

If you don't see anything or can't reach what you do see, lay the dog on its side on a hard surface and do a canine Heimlich maneuver by pressing quickly and firmly right behind the dog's rib cage. If this doesn't work, quickly find someone to get you to the vet while you continue to try to remove the object or expel it.

Heatstroke

Heatstroke is an absolute emergency. The signs include rapid but shallow breathing, increased heart rate and a 104° or higher temperature. Your dog needs to be cooled down immediately with cold water or ice packs. When its body temperature drops to 103° or lower, you can stop the cooling process but continue to monitor the dog's temperature and get it to your veterinarian immediately.

Prevention is the key with heatstroke. *Never* leave your dog for any period of time in a closed car in the heat. The temperature inside a car rises to an unsafe level in minutes. Also, if your dog is outdoors in the heat, be sure it has plenty of fresh water and shade. Do not overwork or play with it too hard in the heat because an exuberant dog like a Lab may not stop until it's too late.

Having mentioned all these things that could possibly be wrong with your Labrador, I want to emphasize that this is a pretty healthy breed! With good preventive care from you and your veterinarian, your Labrador should live 12 years. I've had many that made it to 14 and even 15.

BEST OF
OPPOSITE

CAPE
COD
KENNEL
CLUB

SUNDAY
SEPT. 14, 1997

(Chuck Tatham)

CHAPTER 9

Showing Your Dog

The dog show world is just that—a world all its own. Like the world of fashion or horse racing or the theater, it has its own rules, its own lingo, its own newspapers and magazines, its own luminaries. If you are involved in dog showing, chances are you have made many friends over the years, people from all walks of life. The common bond among all these people is a love of dogs and dog shows. We call it "being bitten by the bug."

Many people come and go from the show scene, but it seems that if they stay in it for more than 10 years, they are in it for life. Ten years seems to be the magic number to see if one can weather the ups, the downs and the heartaches of dogs, of which there can be many.

THE CHANGING SHOW WORLD

When I was growing up, dog shows were a family hobby. I have four younger sisters, and we traveled to dog shows on weekends with my parents. We all showed our dogs in the breed ring as well as in Junior Showmanship (where young people compete based on the way they present their dog). We had a motorhome and we traveled with the Metz family, who had eight kids and a trailer. There were lots of families that went to the shows that way. In the evening we had cookouts and played games. It was a terrific family sport, and we usually combined a trip to a show with an educational activity. If there was a museum or a historic landmark in the area, my mother would find it—often to our dismay. We really had some wonderful experiences.

Thinking back, though, when my family started showing things were a bit different. For one thing, there were more benched shows (shows where the dogs are required to be on display at the show all day). Spectators would not only be able to see the dogs compete in the ring, but they would have the opportunity to walk up and down through the benching area. Prospective puppy buyers could see different breeds and meet and talk to breeders. There were also outdoor benched shows as well as indoor shows. The thing that was wonderful about these shows was that people congregated at the benching area, before and after judging. We would all bring refreshments. We would socialize, celebrate, commiserate and "talk dogs" for hours. It was a lot of fun. Now people tend to show their dogs and then head off into their own little groups or just head for home. They miss a wonderful chance to exchange information and learn.

The Westminster Kennel Club Show, held every February at Madison Square Garden in New York City, is one of the few remaining benched shows on the East Coast. There is the huge Kennel Club of Detroit show, Golden Gate in San Francisco and a few others in other parts of the country, but only a handful. If you have a chance to attend one, it's definitely worth your time.

Another difference is that there are a lot more shows these days. Twenty or 25 years ago there were a few circuits (groups of dog shows arranged by dog clubs that coordinate five or six shows in a week in close proximity), and some three-show weekends, but by and large shows were Saturday and Sunday. Now almost every weekend is a three- or four-show weekend and there are a lot more

At a specialty show like this one put on annually by the Labrador Retriever Club of the Potomac, you'll see nothing but Labs and more Labs.

circuits. According to the American
Kennel Club, there are about 3,000 dog
shows a year across the country.

When you go to an all-breed show,
there may be about 25 Labs. But if a
breeder-judge (a breed expert) is judging,
you could see 70 or even 100 Labrador
Retrievers in the ring. There are also specialty shows, which are held for just one
breed. These usually last two days.
Specialties often include an obedience
trial and a hunt test for those who want
to compete in performance events as well
as conformation. These shows draw hundreds, and the Labrador Retriever Club of
the Potomac has drawn over 1,000 dogs
for its specialty.

The quality at a specialty show is usually very
good and the competition keen. There can be 60
6-to-9 Month puppy bitches or 60 or more Open
black bitches. (Six-to-9 Month and Open are dog
show classes—more about them in a moment.)
These are usually strong classes with a lot of depth
of quality. Watching classes like these being judged
by a good breeder-judge can be an excellent learning experience. Before anyone gets involved with
breeding I would strongly urge them to go to several specialties and immerse themselves in two days
of nothing but Labradors.

If you purchased your Labrador from a pet
store, your dog was not bred for conformation
competition. Puppies available at pet stores
come from commercial and backyard breeders.
Reputable breeders, breeding good-quality

A breeder can tell you if your pup is right for the ring. These breeders are
evaluating a litter at six weeks of age.

Labradors have a waiting list of people who want
their puppies. They never sell them to pet stores,
no matter what the store employees tell you.

However, if you have acquired your Labrador
from a pet store there are activities other than conformation shows that you can pursue. Your Lab
may be a nice, lovable, trainable dog and you may
want to get involved with obedience or agility
activities, or the other sports described in Chapter
10. If, however, you have purchased your Labrador
from a reputable breeder and the breeder told you
your puppy has the potential to compete at dog
shows, then why not go for it?

IT STARTS WITH SOCIALIZATION

Your dog's breeder will be able to guide you and
help you get involved in a puppy kindergarten or

puppy show handling class. (A good time to start is about 16 weeks of age, after the pup has completed its initial series of vaccinations.) A dog that is going to be shown needs lots of socialization with people and other dogs, so you'll have to introduce it to new and different things and encourage it to be brave. Dogs can't fake it. When they're happy it is very apparent, and when they're not it shows. When they're in the ring they've got to be happy, and that attitude is learned or encouraged at an early age.

Usually when I keep a puppy I let the kids play with it a lot from about eight weeks on. If I keep more than one from a litter, both pups need a lot of attention. I also try to play with the pup quite a bit and take it on short trips in the car. (There's always a clean crate in the back of the car for trips to the veterinarian. It's the safe way for dogs to travel, and if it is already in the car I'm more apt to use it.)

Show Training

Experience has taught me to not do too much show training early on because pups tend to quickly become bored with basic show stuff. What I do instead is a lot of off-leash (or what I call invisible leash) training. I go outside with the pup, armed with treats in my pocket, usually liver or cheese. After playing with a toy or a ball and giving lots of praise, I just stand in front of the puppy with the treats and encourage it to stand and look up at me. Every minute or so I give it a little bit of the treat. Next, I just have it trot alongside me as I would if the pup were on a leash, but without one.

There's none of that fighting, tugging and dragging that usually occurs when a puppy is first leashed.

When the pup is about 16 weeks old and we've been playing this way for a few weeks, with the pup happily coming along with me, I slip a soft slip lead or soft leather leash over the pup's head. If a puppy is already used to wearing a flat buckle collar, you can just clip a lightweight three- or four-foot leash to the collar. Most puppies nip at the leash a little or try to carry it in their mouths. This doesn't bother me, as long as they come along happily wagging their tails.

It is almost impossible to make a show dog out of one who decides to hate it at an early age. I swear that Labs are smart enough to know whether they like shows or not. If they go to enough of them and hang their heads down and

Early socialization is crucial for a future show dog.

Keep the early show lead training short and sweet.

don't wag their tails, they know you'll give up and leave them home to do something more enjoyable. I have had dogs like this. They're Ms. or Mr. personality plus at home. But take them to a show, put a show lead on them and walk into the ring and they act as if they've just finished running the Boston Marathon and can barely muster the energy to go around once for the judge. There's no way they can find the strength to wag their tails—they don't want to even look at the liver treats that they would otherwise devour.

Their plan works. I usually give up and leave them home, and they are delighted. I know they're smiling when I pull out of the driveway with their kennel mates for the next show. They're saying, "So long sucker." I truly believe that I started these puppies off wrong. Those that develop a love for showing and will stand there and wag their tails in 90-degree heat or freezing rain are the ones that learned to have fun with it at an early age. They're probably also the ones that got the right kind of attention in their early, formative months. (I have a friend who says it's all much simpler than that: The homebody dogs are the smart ones and the ones that wag their tails in 90-degree heat are the dumb ones. I don't subscribe to that theory.)

MATCH SHOWS

Match shows are the best place to get your pup's feet wet, and yours as well. A match is an informal type of show. You enter on the day of the match, and minimal training is needed. The atmosphere is usually fairly relaxed and schedules are somewhat flexible. Puppies usually have to be three months old. Classes are divided by sex and are offered for puppies three to six months of age, six to nine months of age and nine to twelve months of age. Classes—generally Novice and Open—are usually also offered for adults over one year.

The entry fee will be about five or six dollars. Some dogs may be pre-entered, but most entries are normally taken for a few hours before judging. Match shows are often judged by professional handlers or breeders aspiring to become approved judges. They are knowledgeable people who have been involved in dogs for many years. Often they are able to give you good tips on handling, and in breeds where it's necessary, grooming advice. No champion points are awarded, but prizes and ribbons are given out.

At a match show, as at a point show, the judge is looking for the dog that best conforms to the breed standard—that word picture of the ideal dog

Match shows are good practice, and good fun. Bring your puppy and your sense of humor.

that I described in Chapter 3. It's important to remember that the judge is not only comparing the dogs to one another, but is also comparing each to the Labrador Retriever standard.

Matches are great pre-point show experiences for pups, young dogs and new handlers. Just like point shows, they usually go on rain or shine, so be prepared for all kinds of weather. Your breeder will also let you know how to find out about match shows, and regular point shows when you're ready.

There are quite a few differences between matches and point shows, but you can get an idea of the basic ring procedure at a match. You will be given an armband with a number. The steward (the judge's helper in the ring) will call the numbers for each dog entered in each class. Puppy Dogs are judged first, Puppy Bitches second, then usually Best Puppy in Breed. After the puppies, Adult Dogs, Adult Bitches, then Best Adult in Breed. (In

dog show lingo, remember that males are referred to as dogs, females as bitches.)

You will be expected to pose or set up your puppy so it can be examined head to tail. The head examination includes having the teeth looked at, which takes some getting used to. You will be expected to gait the puppy. The judge may ask you to trot around in a circle with the whole class and then move individually.

At matches, judges understand that pups and young dogs are there for practice and training. Mistakes will be forgiven and second chances are usually allowed. Encourage your pup to behave, but don't get flustered if it doesn't. This is not Best in Show at Westminster. It is a match show; it's for practice and it should be fun.

If your pup or dog does well at match shows and your breeder, who should be one of your mentors, is encouraging you to go on, the breeder probably believes your dog has some potential and may have a chance to become a champion. Getting a championship can take a lot of time, money and traveling. There are several ways to go about this. You can try it yourself, you can hire a professional handler, or a combination of both.

ENTERING POINT SHOWS

Point shows are a totally different ball game from match shows. Unlike match shows, entries for an American Kennel Club licensed point show must be made in advance. A premium list is sent out to potential entrants about six weeks before the show. (If you want to receive the premium lists, you must find out the names of the superintendents that arrange shows in your area and ask to be put on their mailing list. You can get a list of show superintendents from the AKC.) A closing date is given on the entry form. It is usually about two and a half weeks before the show date. Most shows in my area close at noon on a Wednesday, about 16 days before the show weekend. After that time no additional entries can be made, so take the closing date seriously.

Entry blanks must be filled out carefully. You must provide the dog's official registered name, the names of the owners, the AKC registration number, the dog's date of birth, sire and dam's names,

Point shows are more serious, so make sure you and your dog are ready. (Lisa Weiss)

sex of the dog, breeder's name and the country where the dog is registered (imported dogs and dogs visiting from other countries may be shown at AKC events if the proper steps are followed). You must also state which class you want to enter.

The entry is sent to the superintendent with the entry fee, which is usually about $20. (When I started showing they were six to eight dollars!) Now entries can be faxed with charge card numbers or phoned in through entry services. These services often advertise their 800 numbers in dog magazines. There is a service charge, but it's convenient.

PICK A CLASS

There are more classes to enter at a point show. Unlike match shows, at a point show a puppy must be six months old by the day the show is held. Like match shows, there is some latitude for an unruly, unschooled puppy or Novice dog, but only a little. In the other classes most judges expect you and your dog to be familiar with ring procedure. The same classes are offered for both sexes.

The Puppy classes and the Junior class (which is open to young dogs 12 to 18 months old) are restricted by age. Sometimes the Puppy class is split into 6-to-9 Months and 9-to-12 Months. Sometimes it is not, but the premium list must state this.

In the Novice class, dogs must be six months or older and must not have won three first places (blue ribbons) in that class. The dog is also not eligible if it has won one first-place ribbon in any

Sometimes picking the right class is one of the hardest decisions you'll make. (Greg Goebel)

Bred-by-Exhibitor, American Bred or Open class. Of course, it can't have any championship points. The rules are somewhat confusing, and at all-breed shows the Novice class is not a very popular one. It is very rare that the point winner comes from the Novice class. When you enter this class you are basically saying (without actually saying it to the judge) that either your dog is green, you are green or you're both green, and you're really not ready for the tough competition. At a Labrador specialty however, where competition in most classes is keen, it is not unheard of for the point winner to come out of the Novice class. It doesn't happen often, but I have seen it.

The next class is Bred-by-Exhibitor. This class is for dogs six months or older who are not champions. The person showing the dog must be the owner or co-owner (or the spouse or child of the owner), as well as being one of the dog's breeders. This is a class where breeders can and should

proudly display animals from their breeding program. At specialty shows the Bred-by class is usually very strong, and often the point winner will come from this class. At all-breed shows the quality can and should be good in this class as well. Judges who are familiar with the breed usually give these entries a good look.

The American-Bred class is self-explanatory. Dogs entered in this class must have been bred and born in the United States. No imports or champions are eligible. Dogs must be six months of age or older. For the most part, this class is for dogs not quite ready for the Open class, and this is not usually a strong class at all-breed shows. It's not impossible for the point winner to come from this class, but it doesn't happen often. At a specialty show where there may be 30 dogs in American-Bred, there can be some quality animals entered and the point winner could very well be chosen from this class.

Finally, we have the Open class or classes. Open does mean *open to all*, and champions can be entered in the Open class. Usually after dogs earn the 15 points they need to become a champion they enter the Best of Breed competition. But if, for some reason, the owner wants to, a champion can continue to be shown in Open. However, it is not common.

Depending on the size of the show, the sponsor club may decide to divide the Open by color. So there could be an Open Black class, an Open Chocolate class and an Open Yellow class. The more mature, seasoned dogs are usually entered in the Open classes, and for the most part, the point winner comes out of one of the Open classes. But

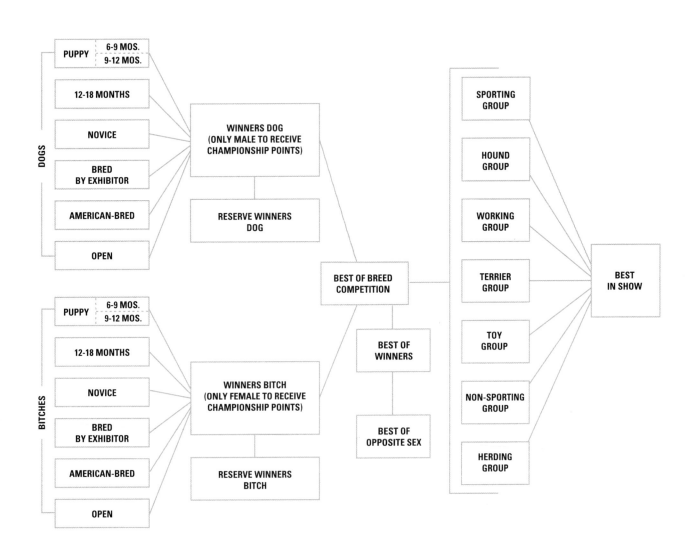

Breeding, training, care, grooming and the bond between you and your dog all come together in the dog show ring. The results can be spectacular. (Chenil Chablais)

by no means should this be a foregone conclusion. Any good judge should consider all the dogs equally, regardless of what class they were entered in.

The object is to win the class you compete in and get into the Winners class—which consists of the winners of every class. From the Winners, the judge will pick a Winners Dog and a Winners Bitch. These two are the only dogs that will win points toward a championship title.

When you're starting out, it's a good idea to ask your dog's breeder for advice about what class

your dog belongs in or is ready for. Don't enter your 10-month-old puppy in the Open class and be beaten by dogs that may not be better, but are more mature. It's not often that a puppy will win the Open class. However, a puppy that wins a nice Puppy class may be given serious consideration or even take Winners. The puppy's lack of maturity shouldn't be held against it in Winners, although it might be in the Open class.

ONCE YOU GET THERE

You should get to the show an hour or so early, so that you have time to exercise your dog a bit and let it relieve itself. It is frowned upon when dogs lift their legs or bitches squat to urinate when they're in the ring.

It's also your job to see to it that your dog gets to the ring on time. About 15 minutes or so before your breed is judged, you can pick up your armband. Then you should remain where you can hear the steward, because if your number is called and you are not there, the judge does not have to wait for you. Some judges will let you in the class late. Others, who don't have a lot of patience and have long forgotten what it is like to be a newcomer, will mark you absent if you are not there when you are called. The judge's decision in these matters is final, and in fairness, the judge does have an obligation to keep things going in an orderly fashion.

RING PROCEDURE

If you are not showing a 6-to-9 Month puppy, which is the first class to be judged, stand where

Win or lose, a day at the dog show should be fun for both you and your dog. Please don't let yourself forget that you love your dog no matter what happens in the ring. (Dominique DeVito)

you can watch the way the judge is running the ring. The procedure should be exactly the same for every dog in every class. This gives every dog an equal opportunity to perform. When the steward calls your class, it will usually be in numerical order, according to your armband number. It's fair that way and there is no one fighting to be first. It also makes it easier for spectators outside the ring to follow along with their catalogs.

Once the dogs and handlers line up according to armband number, the judge and steward check that the correct dogs are present and absentees are marked.

Now the judging begins. You will set your dog up (called *stacking*) and the judge will walk down the line and look at each one. First impressions are important, so have your dog looking the best you can. Next, the judge will usually ask the class to gait around the ring as a group, once or twice. This gives the judge the chance to see from the side how the dogs move. It also gives the dogs a chance to warm up and get their juices flowing.

Next, the judge will start examining the dogs one at a time. Most judges will instruct the rest of the class to relax or go under the tent if it is a very hot day. The dogs will then come out for examination in numerical order. Remember who was in front of you so you won't hold things up by making the judge ask, "Who's next?" You should have your dog stacked and ready for examination when the dog before you is done gaiting.

The judge will start at the dog's head. Then they will check the dog's bite and work their way down, usually checking shoulders and front assembly, amount of bone and coat. The judge will work their way to the hindquarters, checking the topline and the length of the dog in comparison to its height. They'll check the length of the tail and if it is properly set on (not too high, not too low). They'll check the rear angulation, the depth and the width of the thighs and muscle tone. Then the judge will usually step back and take in the total picture of the dog. This is most important! Does this dog make the correct picture? Will the words *type* and *balance* flash like blinking lights?

After the standing examination, the judge will ask you to move your dog. Usually this will be

This dog knows that Kathy keeps the treats in her pocket. It's a good way to make sure your dog's focus in the ring is where you want it to be. (Greg Goebel)

more than just how a dog puts down and picks up its feet. It is how the dog reaches with its front and drives with its rear. It is how it carries its topline as it is viewed from the side. The way it carries its head and its tail are also very important. Usually the head will drop slightly. The tail should be carried happily, wagging from side to side as it goes along. A dead tail (a tail carried too low, not wagging) or a tail carried up over the back (called a gay tail) will completely ruin the picture of the dog as it is gaiting.

There are some very important points to remember about ring procedure. Be considerate of your fellow exhibitors. Don't crowd or push—everyone will get a turn. Always have the dog on the inside of the ring. In other words, always have the dog between you and the judge so that you don't block the judge's view of the dog. Be prepared, have the right leash, a squeaky toy if your dog responds to one, and your bait to get and hold

down to the end of the ring and back in a straight line or down, across and back on the diagonal (like a triangle). To complete your dog's examination, the judge will send you around the ring and back to the end of the line. Then it's time for the next dog.

As a judge watches your dog move, they are looking for several things. Movement is much

Make sure you can hold the dog's attention, so your dog can look its best for the judge. (Chenil Chablais)

The judge must always pick the best dog on that day. But show dogs have good days and bad days. (Greg Goebel)

On *that day* can be a very important factor. Some dogs show better when it's hot outside. Some dogs just can't take the heat and look at you as if to say, "There's no way I'm going to wag my tail and look like I'm enjoying this torture!" A judge can have two or three fairly good specimens in the final lineup, but on that particular day one may be really shining and practically asking for the ribbon. It makes it easier to judge if there is one dog that really stands out and is head and shoulders above the rest. If there isn't such a dog, choosing a winner comes down to nit-picking and personal preference.

After the Winners Dog has been chosen, the steward looks to see which dog placed second in

the dog's attention (liver, cheese, hot dogs or whatever the dog likes as a treat).

THE BEST ON THAT DAY

After all the classes are judged, the first-place dogs from each class are called back to compete for Winners Dog and Winners Bitch. The judge will usually gait the dogs and go over them fairly quickly, as they have already been in the ring in their classes. Just as when the dogs were judged before, the judge must decide which dog comes closest to the standard for the breed. If there are two or three that come very close to the standard, the judge must decide which they think is the better dog *on that day.*

Waiting for the judge's decision can be an anxious moment. (Greg Goebel)

HOW A DOG BECOMES A CHAMPION

A dog needs 15 points to become a champion, and when that's accomplished we say the dog is *finished*. At any show, only one dog and one bitch (in each breed) will be awarded points toward their championships.

The number of points these dogs win is based on the number of dogs and bitches they defeat in competition. There is a point scale printed in the front of the catalog at every show. It is different for every breed and it can change from year to year. The point scale is reevaluated by the AKC every year based on the average number of dogs that are shown throughout the year. The country is also divided into regions, and the point scale varies from region to region. The point scale for all breeds is printed each May in the *AKC Gazette*, the official magazine of the American Kennel Club.

Depending on how many dogs are entered at a show, the Winners Dog or Bitch can receive anywhere from one to five points. A win of three, four or five points is called a *major*. To become a champion, a dog or bitch must win a minimum of two majors under two different judges and at least one point under a third judge. The rest of the points needed to bring the total to 15 may be won under those same three judges or several different judges. In other words, it would have to be the opinion of at least three judges that a particular dog is worthy of becoming a champion.

For example, a dog may win three 3-point majors under three different judges and three 2-point wins under three other judges, totaling 15 points. Once in a while a very good dog comes along and finishes with three 5-point major wins.

the class the Winners Dog's originally came from. That dog is then called back to compete for Reserve Winners Dog. In other words, if the Winners Dog was the first-place winner from the Open Black class, the second-place Open Black dog would be called back to compete with the remaining first-place winners for Reserve.

As in beauty pageants, if for some reason the Winners Dog is disqualified at a later date, the points would go to the Reserve Winner. Although this very rarely happens, I have seen a dog disqualified on a technicality. Suppose Winners Dog is awarded to a dog that won the Bred-by-Exhibitor class, but it is later brought to light that the dog's handler was not a breeder, co-breeder or family member. The points would be disallowed and the owner of the Reserve Winners Dog would be notified by the AKC that their dog was now the point winner from that particular show.

BEST OF BREED

The Winners Dog and Winners Bitch earn the privilege of competing for Best of Breed, a class that can only be entered ahead of time by a finished champion. They also compete for Best of

The glamorous win: Best of Breed at the Westminster Kennel Club Show. (Chuck Tatham)

Winners, an award given to either Winners Dog or Winners Bitch, and Best of Opposite Sex.

Best of Winners can be important because whichever dog gets Best may get more points. For example, let's say the Winners Dog only won two points (because he defeated seven dogs), but Winners Bitch won three points (because she defeated 23 bitches). If the judge decides the Winners Dog is a better specimen than the Winners Bitch and awards the dog Best of Winners, he'd get three points as well. The bitch would keep her three points and the dog would get three as well. If the judge went on to award the Winners Dog Best of Breed over five champions in the ring, the five champions would be added to the total number of dogs defeated, and that could mean even more points. So a two-point win can become a major if enough dogs are defeated.

Best of Breed is chosen from among the Winners Dog, Winners Bitch, and the champions that are entered that day. A dog or a bitch has an equal chance of winning the breed. Whichever sex wins, the judge will then choose the Best of Opposite Sex. Again, this can be important if the Best of Opposite hasn't finished yet.

This mother and son team (Ch. Tabatha's Windfall Abbey, WCX, JH, and Ch. Windfall's Black Bart, WC) took Best of Breed and Best of Opposite Sex at the same show. Wins like this highlight the consistent quality of a breeding program. (Eastwood)

If your bitch wins Winners Bitch and has defeated 18 bitches, and then is awarded Best of Opposite Sex over five bitch champions, that brings the number of bitches defeated to 23, and her two-point win could become a three-point major. If Winners Dog or Winners Bitch are awarded Best of Opposite Sex over champions, they can only add their same-sex competitors to their total. There are many possibilities and scenarios. That's what makes it all so exciting.

The system seems confusing and complicated at first, but after attending some shows and carefully observing how they work, it starts to make sense and becomes easier to follow. Pamphlets are also available from the AKC containing the rules governing point shows. At a show, for the most part, the professional handlers and experienced breeders can be relied on to coach newcomers. The judge also has a steward in the ring, and usually they try to be helpful and can answer questions. But remember that both the judge and the steward are very busy with the business of judging dogs.

The Best of Breed winner goes on to compete in the Sporting Group against the other Retrievers, Pointers, Setters and Spaniels that make up the Sporting Group. Then the breed winners in the other six groups—Hound, Working, Herding, Terrier, Non-Sporting and Toy—are judged. The winner of each of the groups goes on to compete for Best in Show—a very prestigious award not often attained by Labradors. It is hard for the Lab, even a really good one, to triumph over the flashy longhaired Setters and Afghan Hounds, the striking Poodles or the feisty Terriers.

JUDGING THE JUDGE

A judge's book has only numbers in it because the judges are not allowed to know the names of the dogs or the handlers they are looking at. You, however, should be keeping a book on the judges, and their names should be included.

I no longer have a little book, but I did when I started showing. I used + and - symbols—three - symbols and I didn't enter under that person again. My award system was not based on whether my dog won, but on whether I thought the judge was fair. Did they have a good understanding of Labradors? Could I follow the judging? All you can ask of a judge is that they be consistent. After watching a nice entry, you should know what kind of dogs the judge was looking for. I like to be able to say to myself, "The dog I brought today wasn't quite what the judge was looking for, but I have one at home that I believe is their type. Next time they judge, I'll enter that dog."

These are not decisions of good judge, bad judge. Rather, it is a matter of going to enough shows and watching someone judge a couple of times and then answering some important questions about that judge. If you don't win, ask yourself:

1. Is it political? Is the judge consistently putting up the same professional handler, no matter what dogs they show?

2. Is this a good judge who is consistent, but just doesn't like the type of dog or dogs I am showing?

3. Was my dog really better today than all the other dogs in its class?

Be honest with yourself. It is not always the judge's fault if your dog doesn't win. All too often I hear newcomers proclaiming a judge to be a jerk because they were sure they had the best dog and didn't win. You have to be able to separate your feelings for your dog from what is going on in the ring. You must be able to be objective when you are competing at a show.

MY FIRST SHOW

My first time in the ring was in 1968 at a match show. I won Best in Match with my yellow male Labrador, Buffy. Of course, I thought "Wow! This is easy." My second time in the ring my father entered me in the Open class at the Suffolk County Kennel Club show. I think he was trying to teach me something.

At this show there were lots of well-known handlers whose dogs have since gone down in history as great ones. One such handler was the famous Ken Golden, who showed exclusively for

Grace Lambert's Harrowby Kennels. The dog he
was showing in Best of Breed on this day was the
English import Ch. Sandylands Midas. He was also
showing a young dog, Harrowby Jim, in the Open
class. Everything I could have done wrong, I did.

I was right behind Ken (Mr. Golden to me at
that time), and there were about six other handlers
behind me. With only the one match under our
belts, Buffy and I were way out of our league.
Buffy kept inching up to sniff Ken's dog. The rest
of the time I had him set up facing the wrong
direction, so Buffy was tail to tail with Ken's dog
and nose to nose with the one behind us. Ken,
very nicely, kept telling me to move back and face
the other direction with the dog on my left. Buffy
kept trying to chase and catch up to Ken's dog
as we went around the ring, and again, he was
extremely patient with me. Of course he won, and
I didn't get a ribbon. Ken also won Best of Breed
that day with Ch. Sandylands Midas, who went on
to make breed history.

As I was walking away, Ken handed Midas to
someone and came after me. He said, "Hey, what's
your name?" I told him and he said, "You need
some lessons." He took me aside and worked with
me for about half an hour, drilling me in ring procedure and etiquette. He was honest with me and
said that my dog was not a great one, but that if I
wanted to be involved in this sport I should
become good at showing and make Buffy look his
best. He told me to watch the other dogs that
were out there and to decide where I wanted to
be in 10 years (by then I'd be 20).

I took his advice. I continued to show Buffy
and won lots of ribbons, but I never made him a

WHAT TO TAKE ALONG

When you are going off to a show, you will
find it helpful to have the following items:

• Bucket or bowl for water
• Bait (liver, cheese or hotdog treat given in
  the ring)
• Show leashes (I prefer a leather Resco or an
  English style slip lead. These can usually be
  purchased at the show or ordered through
  a catalog.)
• Crate (Where your dog can rest in the car, if
  the car is in the shade with all the windows
  open. The dog doesn't need to be walked
  around for six hours at the show.)
• Towel or chamois cloth (to shine the dog up
  a bit or wipe down the mud if it is raining)
• Hard bristle brush
• Roll of paper towels
• Can of mineral oil spray (to help shine the
  dog up)
• Bottle of SelfRinse (A shampoo that can
  be used without water for emergency
  cleanups. It takes off the silver that gets on
  yellow Labs from the crate.)
• A tack box is nice, but that can come later.

These things will get you started. As you
go along you'll learn all the tricks of the
trade. People are always coming up with new
ideas. Labrador show people, for the most
part, are a friendly group, like their dogs,
and are usually willing to pass tips along.

Fanciers help each other, practice together, and evaluate each other's dogs. (Diane Jones)

champion. After Buffy and Lobo, our first Labs (we used these two dogs to make up our kennel name, Lobuff), were killed in an accident, my parents bought our foundation bitch from Jan Churchill's Spenrock Kennels. The bitch was a daughter of the famous Ch. Spenrock's Banner, WC. We then got a male from the Metz' Waldschloss Kennel, a son of the national specialty winner, Ch. Lewisfield Gunslinger. Both Spenrock's Cognac and Gunslinger's Tawny Boy became champions and produced our first homebred champion, Ch. Lobuff Dandy Lion in 1971.

We became good friends with Ken Golden, and very occasionally throughout my teenage years I'd beat him. He'd always say, "Damn, why didn't I let you walk away that day?" However, I don't think he meant it. Ken was one of many wonderful people who helped us when we started. Over the years we've helped lots of other people get started. That's the only way the sport can continue. If you love your breed and the sport, you'll do the same.

(Susan Wing/K9Fotoz)

CHAPTER 10

Obedience Trials, Performance Events and Other Fun Things

The Labrador Retriever is an incredibly versatile dog. When you remember that this is a breed developed to hunt alongside a human companion, assisting at whatever task the hunter requires, you'll understand why Labs are happiest with a job to do and a person to do it with. There are formal hunting competitions you can train your Lab for, but if hunting is not your thing, there are many, many other activities, both fun and competitive, in which you can get involved.

OBEDIENCE TRIALS

Labs, with their intelligence, trainability and great desire to please, do well in formal obedience competitions, and obedience trials are a fun outgrowth of the kind of training you might do anyway, just to make your dog obedient and responsive. You can find an obedience training center in your area by contacting your veterinarian or the breeder who sold you your puppy. Local dog clubs may also offer obedience classes, or recommend good obedience instructors.

Obedience competition is divided into three levels. The first is Novice, a series of exercises designed to demonstrate your dog's trainability and value as a companion. The exercises are heeling on lead, stand for examination by the judge (with the dog off lead and you about six feet away), off-lead heeling, the recall (your dog is left on a sit-stay while you cross the ring and wait for the judge's instruction to call your dog), and two group exercises: the one-minute sit and the three-minute down, both done in the company of other dogs. If your dog earns more than half the points available for each exercise and gets a total of 170 or more points out of 200, it will be awarded a "leg" toward its Companion Dog title. To earn this title, the dog must earn three legs under three different judges. You can then proudly put the title CD after the dog's registered name.

If you want to go further, Open obedience is the next level of training. The Open exercises are more complicated than Novice, and focus on specific skills such as retrieving and jumping. The Open exercises include heeling off lead, drop on recall (in which your dog is called to you but must lie down on command), retrieve on the flat, retrieve over the high jump, the broad jump and the group exercises: a three-minute sit and a five-minute down with handlers out of sight. Earning three Open legs gives your dog the title Companion Dog Excellent, or CDX.

These dogs are practicing the group sit in an advanced obedience class. (Anna Clark)

The most advanced level of obedience competition is Utility, which demonstrates the dog's ability to learn and perform quite complicated tasks. The Utility class consists of five exercises. The first is the signal exercise. You will be asked to put your dog through a routine that includes heel, sit, stand, stay, down, come and finish or go to heel. Your dog already knows these from the first two levels of competition, but here's the catch: It is all done without verbal cues from you—hand signals only!

Scent discrimination is the next exercise. The dog must search out and retrieve a metal or leather article with your scent on it. The article will be placed among others that don't have your scent, and your dog must sniff and search until it finds the correct article, then retrieve and return the article to you. In the directed retrieve exercise, three white cotton gloves are placed at the far end of the ring—one in each corner and one in the middle. When the judge tells you which glove must be retrieved, you and your dog line up facing that glove and you give the command to retrieve. The dog must then retrieve the correct glove and deliver it to your hand. Does this sound tough? Not for your Labrador *Retriever!*

The moving stand and examination consists of heeling with your dog and asking it to stop and stand in place. The judge will then approach your dog and give it a thorough examination—much more thorough than the Novice stand exercise. Your dog must be steady and show no fear or resentment toward the stranger's handling.

Finally, the directed jumping exercise completes the Utility test. At your command, the dog must run out across the ring and sit facing you. There will be two jumps in the ring: a solid high jump and a bar jump. On the judge's instruction, you will send your dog over the indicated jump. The exercise is repeated with your dog taking the other jump. Three qualifying scores in Utility earns the title Utility Dog, or UD. It's the Ph.D. of dogdom!

Obedience competition does not have to end when a dog gets its UD. If qualifying scores are not enough to satisfy your competitive urge, you can try for first place in your class. The dog with the highest score of all three levels and the A and B divisions (classes are divided into A and B, depending on the handler's previous experience in Novice or whether a dog has earned a CDX or UD in Open and Utility) is awarded High in Trial. First and second placements in Open B and Utility B count toward points for an Obedience Trial Championship (OTCh). A dog that has earned the Utility Dog title and has a minimum of 100 points

in Open and Utility competition, with at least one win in both, becomes an OTCh.

If you're feeling a bit less competitive, another obedience title is Utility Dog Excellent (UDX). It recognizes consistency in qualifying in both Open and Utility. To be eligible, a dog must be a UD and then receive qualifying scores in both Open and Utility at the same trial on 10 different occasions.

FIELD TRIALS

Field trials are tests of a Labrador's skill at finding and retrieving game. The trials are quite complex, with long, multiple retrieves over all types of

Field trials are a test of a Lab's skill at finding and retrieving game—the work the breed was developed to do. (Winnie Limbourne)

terrain. Dogs compete against each other to earn points toward the titles Amateur Field Champion and Field Champion.

Field trials are dominated by professional trainers, and the training isn't something you do casually. This is highly competitive, very complex training, and it requires a big commitment of time and money. The type of Labrador that has evolved as a field trial dog is also quite different from the Lab you'll see in the show ring. Field-bred Labradors are generally taller, less stocky, faster and more animated than their more placid, show-bred cousins.

There are four divisions, or stakes, held at almost all field trials: Derby, Qualifying, Amateur All-Age and Open All-Age. Derby stakes are open to dogs under two years of age. Derby tests are meant to judge natural abilities, as opposed to skills a dog is trained to do. In all the tests, the dog must watch where the bird lands, and remember the spot—this is called *marking the fall*. The marking tests are usually a combination of singles, doubles and an occasional triple. A single is when one mark (bird) is thrown and the dog is sent to retrieve. A double is two marks thrown in succession before the dog is sent. The dog must then retrieve each fall, one at a time. A triple is when the dog sees three birds thrown in succession before being sent.

In a Derby, dogs are judged on their efficiency in finding the bird in a quick and stylish manner. The dog that takes the straightest line to the fall and finds the bird with the least amount of hunting is awarded first place. Placements are also

Competition is very demanding in field trials and training must begin early in a dog's life. (Anna Clark)

awarded for second through fourth. In addition, Judges Awards of Merit (JAMs) are given out to dogs that complete all of the series satisfactorily, but are not among the placements.

One of the goals for many Derby competitors is to make the National Derby List. This distinction is awarded to a dog that has earned ten or more points in Licensed Derby Stakes. A win is worth five points; second place earns three points; third place gets two points; and fourth place earns one point. The dog that earns the most points in a year is the National Derby Champion.

The Qualifying stake is the next level after Derby. In this stake, dogs are tested on a multiple land mark (a double or a triple) and a multiple water mark. In addition, there's a water blind and a land blind. A blind simulates a bird that has been shot but the dog does not see fall. The handler knows where this bird is, sends the dog and uses hand signals to direct the dog to the bird. A single blast of a whistle is used to indicate to the dog that it should stop and look at the handler for another signal.

Most dogs entered in the Qualifying stake are over the age of two, but have not placed in an All-Age stake. A dog that wins or places second in a Qualifying receives All-Age status.

The Amateur All-Age is the only stake restricted to amateur handlers. Some amateur stakes are limited to amateur handlers that also own the dog. The tests are extremely demanding, and include land and water triples and very difficult land and water blinds. Dogs earn points for first through fourth placements (first earns five points, second earns three points, third earns one point, fourth earns half a point). The title Amateur Field Champion (AFC) is awarded to the dog that accumulates a total of 15 points in Amateur stakes, including at least one win.

The Open All-Age stake is the most demanding and difficult offered. At many trials only qualified All-Age dogs are eligible to enter. In some parts of the country, Open stakes are almost totally dominated by professional handlers. Success at this level is very difficult for the amateur trainer and handler.

Marking tests usually consist of triples or even quadruples and the blinds are often incredibly difficult. Points are awarded in the same manner as the Amateur stakes. A Field Championship (FC) is earned by accumulating 10 points, of which 5 must be from a win. A dog handled by an amateur that earns 10 points in Open stakes is awarded the Amateur Field Champion (AFC) title, in addition to the FC.

HUNT TESTS

If you'd like to compete with your hunting companion in a sport that's a bit less intense, there are AKC hunt tests for all the retriever breeds and Irish Water Spaniels. These tests are more typical of an actual hunting situation, with retrieves limited to 100 yards. The dogs don't compete against each

Hunt tests like this one are a bit less competitive than field trials. (Bill Clark)

other, but only against the judges' interpretation of a written standard for correct responses to each situation. Dogs either pass and receive a qualifying score and credit toward a hunt test title, or fail and come back to try again.

Hunt test programs offer three levels of testing, based on the training level of the dog. The first level, which is called Junior in AKC tests, is designed for a young dog just starting out. In Junior tests, the dog is brought to the line (or starting place) on lead. It remains on lead, either sitting or standing, while a bird is thrown. The dog must watch where the bird lands and remember the spot—marking the fall. When the judge indicates that the dog should be sent, the handler releases it, and the dog must go to the mark and hunt for the bird. Once found, the bird is retrieved and brought to the handler, where it must be willingly delivered to hand.

At a Junior test, a dog can be worked on a leash.

Hunt test devotees say they're more like real hunting situations. (Susan Willumsen)

The Junior test consists of two land retrieves and two water retrieves. If each is performed to the satisfaction of the judges, the dog receives a leg (or, as some people say, a wing) toward its Junior Hunter title. Four qualifying legs are necessary to earn the title.

It has been my experience that Labradors love this activity, and are able to master it with very basic training. This is the kind of work your dog was born to do, and you'll both enjoy the time you'll spend together learning these exercises.

The next level of competition is the Senior Hunter title, which, like Open obedience, gets quite a bit more complicated. In a Senior test, the dog must mark several falls at the same time, remembering where the second bird fell after retrieving the first. Senior also requires the dog to do blind retrieves, where a bird is placed without the dog seeing it. The handler must direct the dog to the bird using hand signals and whistles, stopping it to receive new directions as the dog advances toward the area where the bird is.

A Senior dog works entirely off-lead, and watching a dog on the line mark a fall and wait to be sent is a thrilling study in desire and control. The dog must also honor—that is, sit quietly nearby while another retriever works. Four legs, or qualifying scores, are required to complete a Senior Hunter title.

The training gets more intense as you get to the higher levels in hunt tests. (Jan Grannemann)

The top level of hunt test competition is Master. A Master Hunter demonstrates the abilities of a polished hunting companion by performing tests similar to the Senior level, but with more complicated scenarios. It must be able to do triples, diversion marks and multiple blinds in conjunction with marks. Its performance must be nearly flawless, and faults that are overlooked at the lower levels are severely penalized or are cause for disqualification at this level.

Master-level tests include three separate tests of multiple marks on land, water and a land-water combination. The Master dog must also do a land blind and water blind, which is often closely associated with marks. A dog that qualifies at six tests (five scores if it previously earned a Senior title) becomes a Master Hunter (MH) in the AKC program. This level of performance requires a great deal of skill and patience on the part of the trainer-handler as well as the dog!

Devotees of retriever hunt tests believe these tests are more realistic than field trials, and demonstrate a dog's natural abilities. Many owner-handlers compete in hunt tests, and many top show dogs proudly sport hunting titles behind their names.

TRACKING DOGS

Another interesting activity for Labrador Retrievers and their owners is tracking. To earn a tracking title, a dog must demonstrate its ability to recognize and follow human scent. There are three levels of tracking proficiency recognized by the AKC, and a single passing score at a trial is required to earn any title. The titles are Tracking Dog (TD), Tracking Dog Excellent (TDX) and Variable Surface Tracker (VST). A dog that has earned all three titles is awarded the title Champion Tracker (CT).

The essential feature of all tracking tests is that the dog must follow the scent of a stranger and find the articles they have left on the track. The differences in what is expected at the three levels are based on the age, length and complexity of the track, and the number of articles that must be found.

At the TD level a track is no more than 30 minutes old and about 440 yards long, with two right-hand turns and one object to find. The TDX track is about two hours old, about 800 yards long, has cross tracks of other scents, four objects to find throughout the track and multiple turns. The terrain and conditions found on the TDX track vary quite a bit.

The VST track is 600 to 800 yards long, and from one and a half to three and a half hours old. It is laid in an urban environment. Tracks can be laid next to buildings, through or along fences and over any surface a person might go—within the safety limits of the dog. Turns are on different surfaces, with at least one on a surface that has no vegetation. The dog must find and retrieve four objects dropped on the track—one made of leather, one of plastic, one of metal and one of fabric. There is one starting flag at the beginning of the track, but no others.

At all levels, the handler walks the track with the dog in harness, but has no idea where the track goes and must totally trust their dog. Dogs may be

The Labrador Retriever, with its nose for hunting, is a natural at tracking as well.

spoken to and encouraged verbally at all tracking levels, and there are no time limits as long as the dog is working.

AGILE LABS

Agility competition is a relatively new addition to the sport of dogs. In this activity, a dog is asked to navigate an obstacle course not unlike a steeplechase course for horses. The course consists of jumps, ramps, see-saws, dog walks, tunnels, and lines of poles to weave in and out of. Scoring is based on the accuracy of the performance and the time it takes to complete the course. The dog doesn't work alone, but is accompanied by its handler running the course and giving verbal directions. For all their size and substance, Labradors enjoy agility, and some are *very* good at it!

Agility trials are divided into three levels, like obedience and hunt tests. The dog must receive qualifying scores of 85 or more in three tests to earn a title. The three levels, and

Agility competition capitalizes on the natural exuberance of dogs. (Bob & Emily Magnani)

their respective titles, are Novice Agility (NA), Open Agility (OA) and Agility Excellent (AX). A dog with an AX title that earns three more qualifying scores at this level earns the title of Master Agility Excellent (MX).

The differences in the three levels are the number of obstacles and their placement in relationship to each other. The course is set up by the judge and a maximum course time is set. The time is based on the length of the course and the number of obstacles. The handlers are allowed to view the course before the start of competition. Missing an obstacle, taking obstacles in the wrong order, missing a contact zone or exceeding the course time all incur penalties.

Agility is not a sport for very young or very old dogs. A dog should be fully mature physically (at least two years old) before it begins serious agility training. The stress encountered in this type of training can be extremely harmful to growing bones. A puppy can be introduced to certain pieces of equipment, such as the tunnel and the walks, with supervision. But any jumping should only be done with the jumps flat on the ground, so the puppy only associates the word "jump" with the act of going over an object.

Certain obedience skills are necessary in agility. A dog must be able to do sit-stays and down-stays for the pause table and to prevent it from jumping off of equipment. It must know "come" and be able to heel off leash.

CANINE GOOD CITIZENS

The American Kennel Club also offers the certification Canine Good Citizen, or CGC, to dogs that

CGC tests showcase the everyday good manners every dog should have. (John & Glenda Crook)

pass a single test demonstrating qualities that make it a desirable pet and member of the community. If you're not keen on competition, but do want to show off your dog's good manners, CGC is for you.

The CGC test includes 10 exercises, each of which is designed to highlight an aspect of the dog's good behavior. The tests include accepting the approach of a friendly stranger, sitting politely for petting, appearance and grooming, walking on a loose leash, walking through a crowd without undue distraction, sitting or lying down and staying in that position while the handler moves 20 feet away, coming when called from a distance of 10 feet, meeting another dog without overreacting, reaction to distractions, and supervised separation (leaving the dog in the care of another person while the handler disappears from view). This test is not a competition, and the exercises don't have to be performed with precision.

LAB THERAPY

Labradors also make excellent therapy dogs. Therapy dogs visit people in hospitals, nursing homes and residences, and bring the special love

AKC SPORTS

More information on all of these AKC activities is available from the American Kennel Club, 5580 Centerview Drive, Suite 200, Raleigh, NC 27606-3390. The phone number for the Performance Events department is (919) 854-0199. You can also visit the AKC Web site at www.akc.org. The Web site contains a wealth of information, including rules and regulations for all performance events.

A therapy dog can work magic. This is Ransom's Pockets of Graycroft, CDX, MH with his owner Anna Clark.

that only a dog has to give. A therapy dog may work its magic in various settings, but usually visits nursing homes and hospitals. The presence of a gentle dog can brighten the day for those away from their homes and in need of affection from a non-judgmental friend. The Labrador's patience and good nature make it an ideal dog to visit folks who crave attention and affection.

Of course, a therapy dog must be clean and well groomed, with basic good manners and just the right combination of gentleness and confidence. Many institutions also require some kind of certification that your dog is well trained and suitable for therapy work.

You'll find that your Labrador enjoys all kinds of activities, and that its desire to please makes it very trainable. So pick your area of interest and go for it! You and your dog will benefit greatly from the time and experiences you'll share.

(Roseberry)

CHAPTER 11

The Headliners

Every breed has its great breeders and its great dogs. The dogs are worth describing, because understanding where the breed has been helps us chart the best course for where it's going. Understanding the people involved is important, too, because what this whole sport really boils down to is people helping people. You can't just wake up one morning and decide you are going to be a top Labrador breeder. It's impossible to pull dogs and a breeding program out of thin air. It takes patience, time and help. One person's bloodlines are predicated on another's, and so on and so on.

Of course, it's impossible in a book like this to mention every person who has ever bred a great dog. There are so many wonderful people who have dedicated their lives to the betterment of this breed. I do not want to leave anyone out of this chapter, but I could fill a whole book just with the names of dogs and breeders. Some people and their stories will have to be saved for a *Who's Who in Labradors*. Here I'll introduce a few of the influential breeders and dogs whose efforts have benefited the Labrador Retriever.

BOB AND PEG

There were many great dogs that set the standard for Labs in America, but we might consider two English dogs to be the parents of the breed here: Dual Ch. Bramshaw Bob and Drinkstone Peg. Bramshaw Bob is behind many of the pedigrees in the great American dogs of today. And as I recounted in Chapter 2, Jay Carlisle imported Drinkstone Peg from England when she was already mated to

Bramshaw Bob. The litter that was born here went on to provide foundation stock for many American Labrador breeders getting started at the time.

One of the pups from that litter, Bancstone Bob of Wingan, went on to become Joan Read's first champion. Mrs. Read, who I introduced you to in Chapter 2, was a pioneer of the breed and helped a great many people get started in the dog fancy. Her kennel name was Chidley, and Chidley dogs can be found in the pedigrees of Kurt Unkelbach's Walden dogs, Barbara Barty-King's Aldenholme dogs and Mary Swan's Chebacco Labradors.

Remember I said all these lines ended up being connected somewhere? Barbara Barfield started her Scrimshaw lines by leasing a bitch from Aldenholme and breeding her to Swan's Ch. Chebacco Smokey Joe. That's how it works.

THE WEB OF INFLUENCE

The Whygin Labradors of the late Helen Whyte Ginnel (who was involved with English Setters in the 1930s) also go back to Chidley dogs. Helen's foundation bitch, Cedarhill Whygin (call name Dinah), was the dam, granddam and great-granddam of many champions. Sally McCarthy Munson's famous Shamrock Acres lines go back to the Whygin lines. Sally's 12-time all-breed Best in Show winner, Ch. Shamrock Acres Light Brigade, goes back to Dinah, and has sired 94 champions. Sally's Shamrock Acres dogs, in turn, were the foundation dogs for many other breeders, including Barbara Holl, who is still an active breeder and handler in the Midwest today.

Rupert Kennels, established by the late Dorothy Howe, also influenced the breed. Dorothy was an animal lover and had a farm in Vermont. She helped lots of people get off to a good start in Labradors using her stock as their foundation. Rupert dogs were seen in the show ring from the 1940s all the way through the 1980s.

Dorothy started with a bitch named Lena that went back to the import Dual Ch. Banchory Bolo. She bred Lena to a son of the famous Dual Ch. Shed of Arden, bred by New York Governor Averell Harriman, and got some excellent dogs. She also bred Lena to Dauntless of Deer Creek, and from this mating came Ch. Rupert Dahomey, Rupert Daphne and Ch. Rupert Desdemona. Dahomey is behind dogs in the Whygin, Shamrock Acres and Harrowby lines (Harrowby was founded by Grace Lambert).

Although Dorothy died in the late 1970s, Elinor Ayers of the Seaward Kennels (a friend and well-respected Newfoundland breeder; there's that Labrador–Newfoundland connection again!) kept the Rupert prefix going with Ch. Seaward's Adonis of Rupert and Ch. Seaward's Dr. Watson of Rupert. Adonis, or Donny as he was known, was ranked as one of the top 10 Labs shown in 1980 and 1981. He was always handled in the show ring by the well-known Newfoundland and Labrador handler Gerlinda Hockla.

Arden dogs also helped found the Franklin Labradors of Bernard and Madge Ziessow. Their first Labrador was Ch. Pitch of Franklin, a granddaughter of Dual Ch. Shed of Arden, Ch. Earlsmoor Moor of Arden and Ch. Buddha of Arden. All the Franklin dogs still go back to Pitch,

WHAT'S IN A NAME?

Purebred dogs usually have two names: a registered name and a call name. The registered name is a formal affair. It usually includes the name of the kennel that bred the dog. It will sometimes also have a word that designates the litter it was part of. For instance, in one litter the puppies might all get names that begin with the letter B, or names of flowers or spices or characters in a play.

The call name is the informal name the dog's owners use to call the dog to come join them on the couch.

This is Am./Mex. Ch. JanRod's Secret Agent, but his friends call him Spook. (Jan Grannemann)

and they had many top winners. The funny thing is, the Ziessows really wanted a Weimaraner. But a friend gave them Pitch to hunt with, and the rest is history. Imagine if the Ziessows had gotten that Weimaraner instead?

Franklin's pride and joy was Am./Can. Ch. Dark Star of Franklin, a top-winning Labrador in the Midwest for several years, a national specialty winner and the number one Sporting Dog in the United States in 1955. Another of their national specialty winners was Ch. Golden Chance of Franklin, a yellow bitch who was the granddaughter of Dark Star.

There was a group of breeders that had been involved in Labradors before the 1960s, or had established lines by then, and were able to help newcomers to the sport. They were Joan Read, Helen and Jim Warwick, George Bragaw, Ted and Joyce Squires (transplanted Yorkshire folk who owned Tudor Kennels), Mary Swan, Nancy and John Martin, and Janet Churchill. Marjorie Brainard's famous Briary dogs started with stock that was Sandylands and Lockerbie. All of these kennels are considered great because they consistently produced dogs that were of top quality in terms of their physical attributes, their health and their temperament. Their quality has been tested in the show ring, in the field and in the whelping box. It has also been tested by time because these bloodlines were used by serious breeders to establish their own kennels, which are now also producing top-quality dogs.

WHAT'S IN A PEDIGREE?

When you look at a dog's pedigree, it's nothing more than a bunch of names. It only has meaning if those names represent dogs you're familiar with—dogs of proven quality. That's why it's important to know the names of the great dogs of the 1960s and '70s. Many of these dogs can be found on pedigrees today, and some had a lasting influence on the breed. (You'll find several important pedigrees in Appendix E.)

Several of the American dogs that come to mind immediately are Ch. Lockerbie Sandylands Tarquin, a black male imported from Britain, and Ch. Lockerbie Kismet and Ch. Lockerbie Goldentone Jensen, both yellow males. All three were specialty winners and sired other specialty winners. Kismet was owned by Helen and Jim Warwick. Jensen was owned by the Warwicks but was sold to William Metz. Kismet and Jensen were both shown by Eric Thomee, a top sporting dog handler on the East Coast.

British imports Ch. Sam of Blaircourt, a black male, and Ch. Sandylands Midas, a yellow male, both did a lot of winning. They were owned by Grace Lambert and shown by the legendary Ken Golden. Ch. Lewisfield Gunslinger, a black male bred by Jim Lewis, owned by William Metz and shown by Eric Thomee, did a lot of winning, including a national specialty, and sired some wonderful dogs (among them was my dad's first champion, Gunslinger's Tawney Boy).

Sally McCarthy Munson had three Labs that were tops in the breed. Light Brigade was the first in 1968 (shown by Dick Cooper), Ch. Royal Oaks VIP O'Shamrock Acres was next in 1973 (handled by Stan Flowers), and finally Ch. Shamrock Acres Benjamin, CD, in 1974, shown by co-owner Dr. Richard Whitehill.

This is Ch. Royal Oaks VIP O'Shamrock Acres, another Shamrock Acres dog with winning ways. For you history buffs, the judge is William Kendrick and the handler is Stan Flowers.

Although there were many lovely bitches being shown and bred in the 1970s, one that stands out is the beautiful black bitch, International Ch. Spenrock Banner W.C., owned by Janet Churchill. Banner was a specialty winner, and also did very well at all-breed shows. She was often shown by Jan, but was also handled to some very impressive breed and Sporting Group wins by Bob Forsyth. (Bob later showed the British import Ch. Lawnwoods Hot Chocolate, one of the first chocolate Labs with a substantial number of breed, specialty and Group wins.)

Banner had five litters, and each one produced champions, stud dogs or foundation bitches for other breeders—many of whom are still active today. This is what makes Banner an important dog. Let's look at what happened to some of the pups in these litters.

Banner's first litter was sired by Ch. Sandylands Midas. It produced national specialty winner Ch. Spenrock San Souci, owned by John Valentine, an avid hunter who is still involved in hunting and show events. My own family's foundation bitch was Ch. Spenrock Cognac, a black puppy from Banner's second litter (the sire was Ch. Lockerbie Goldentone Jensen). Thirty years later, all my breeding today still goes back to Cognac.

Another bitch from that litter, Ch. Spenrock Bohemia Champagne, was the foundation bitch for breeder-judge Diane Pilbin's Chucklebrook Kennels. A litter brother, Ch. Spenrock Cardigan Bay, owned by Jan, did a lot of winning in the early 1970s and sired many wonderful dogs, including a beautiful yellow male who had some impressive wins in the late 1970s and early '80s. This dog was Am./Can. Ch. Agber's Daniel Aloysius, owned by Agnes Cartier and shown by Joy Quallenberg. Joy is one of the top Labrador handlers showing today.

From Banner's third litter, also sired by Ch. Lockerbie Goldentone Jensen, came Ch. Spenrock Topaz, the foundation bitch for George and Louise White and daughter Clair White-Petersen's Stonecrest Labradors. They, and other breeders, continue to spread Banner's legacy.

A kennel that did a lot winning in the 1960s, 1970s and on through the '80s was Springfield

Here's Ch. Spenrock Brown Bess with Jan Churchill, showing off her excellent type. (Gilbert Photo)

Farm Labradors, owned by Liz Clark, with the dogs shown by Constance Barton and Roy Holloway. Springfield Farm Labradors won Best of Breed at Labrador Retriever Club national specialty shows five times, which is quite an impressive record.

Some of the top Springfield dogs of the 1970s include Ch. Hillsboro Wizard of Oz and the British imports Ch. Kimvalley Crispin, Ch. Kimvalley Warrenton, Ch. Ardmargha Goldkrest of Syrancot, Ch. Sorn Sandpiper of Follytower and

At this show, Ch. Kimvalley Picklewitch took Best of Breed from the Veterans Class. (Shari Photo)

Ch. Poolstead Private Member. My favorite Springfield acquisition was the beautiful black bitch Eng./Am. Ch. Kimvalley Picklewitch (sired by Ch. Sandylands Mark), bred by Diana Beckett.

Later in the 1980s Connie Barton went to work for the American Kennel Club, and breeder Diana Beckett and her family came from England to manage Springfield Farm. She purchased Ch. Mardas Brandleshome Sam Song to be shown by Roy Holloway. Sam was the top-winning Labrador in the United States for two years in a row. He also placed second in the Sporting Group

at Westminster—a real honor and something Labs don't accomplish very often. In 1978 Diana entered Ch. Kimvalley Picklewitch at the national specialty and won Best of Breed (Diana's second national specialty win). Three years later she was entered in the Veterans Class, still possessing the grace and style she had as a young dog. Pickle won Best of Opposite sex over 221 other bitches.

Also showing some lovely dogs late in the 1970s and on into the '80s were Barry Rose and Roger Kottmeyer, using the kennel name Kernow. They imported some wonderful English dogs, including Sandylands Be Good. They also bought import Mansergh Old Geezer. When Diana Beckett went back to England, she worked for Barry and sent over some dogs for his breeding program.

It was about 1980 when we started regularly seeing Canadian breeders with some lovely dogs at shows in the United States. Some of the important kennel names are Shadowvale, Huntsdown, Ranbourne and Chablais. Am./Can. Chablais Myrtille and daughter Am./Can. Ch. Chablais Mia are two beautiful yellow bitches who have done a tremendous amount of winning here.

All of these people, and many others, have had a hand in shaping the breed into what it is today. We all must share the praise for the good and the blame for the problems—although luckily, the problems seem to be small and few.

THE TOP STUDS

Stud dogs that will be influential enough to leave their stamp on a breed are few and far between.

At one time or another every breeder looks into a whelping box of newborn puppies and wonders if such a dog could be in this litter.

Gwen Broadley of Sandylands Kennels in England has been blessed with several such dogs. Her top studs have had a tremendous influence on the breed, both in Britain and the United States. The Lockerbie and Briary dogs that are behind many of our show dogs today go back to Sandylands. And if you looked at a random sample of a dozen show dogs, I would be surprised if at least half of them didn't go back to a Sandylands dog somewhere in their pedigree.

Three of Gwen's dogs that I believe have had the most influence on the breed were Ch. Sandylands Mark (litter brother to Ch. Sandylands Midas, who was mated with Banner), Ch. Sandylands Tandy and Ch. Sandylands Tweed of Blaircourt. American breeders furiously sought to breed to Mark's sons and grandsons. Many sought out English breeders who could export Mark progeny.

Am./Can. Ch. Chablais Mia receiving one of her many Canadian rosettes. (Mikron Photos)

Ch. Ayr's Sea Mark is a grandson of Ch. Sandylands Mark, and shows his good breeding. (Klein)

Janet Churchill imported Ch. Spenrock Heatheredge Mariner, a black male sired by Mark out of Seashell of Heatheredge. He sired some very lovely dogs in all three colors. Two that showed excellent type were the chocolate bitch Ch. Spenrock Brown Bess and Ch. Lobuff's Seafaring Banner, both specialty winners.

A Mark grandson, Ch. Jayncourt Ajoco Justice, was imported by Richard Oster of Ajoco Kennels. He sold the black dog to Janet Farmilette and Jane Andersen. Justin (his call name) proved to be a top sire with lots of champion and specialty winning get (that's the fancy word for progeny or offspring) to his credit.

This lovely litter are all the grandpups of Ch. Jayncourt Ajoco Justice.

Helen Warwick imported Ch. Sandylands Markwell of Lockerbie, another black male who also produced nice puppies in all three colors. Markwell had a tremendous and long-lasting effect on the breed, bringing great quality to a number of lines. He was shown to some very impressive wins by Diane Jones and Helen, and was quite a handful but a wonderful dog. He won Best of Opposite Sex at the 1978 national specialty—the year his half-sister Ch. Kimvalley Picklewitch won Best of Breed. His legacy lives on, because there are still Markwell grandchildren and great-grandchildren being shown and bred.

As influential as the Sandylands dogs were, without a doubt the one stud dog that has had the most influence on Labrador Retrievers is Ken Hunter's Eng./Am. Ch. Receiver of Cranspire (you'll find a photo of him in Appendix E). Rever, as he was known, produced the top-winning puppy in Britain, Kimvalley Rags to Riches, as well as lots of other promising young-sters. When he immigrated, he was a very popular stud dog from the minute he landed on American soil. Rever lived with and was shown by Kendall Herr in Pennsylvania (although Kendall has since moved to Texas), so he was conveniently located for most breeders in the East.

Rever was bred to hundreds of Labrador bitches throughout all 50 states. Why was he so much in demand? He was a sweet and beautiful, deep-bodied dog, with a proper coat and super bone. He had a beautiful head, coal black pigment and a lovely expression.

Rever finished his American championship with three five-point majors, including Winners

This is a remarkable group of dogs. Ch. Jollymuff Fly Away is in the lead, followed by Ch. Jollymuff Barbry Ellen, Ch. Jollymuff Salina, Sandylands Margie of Lockerbie, Ch. Dickendalls Jollymuff Jane, Ch. Jollymuff Orange Blossom and last, but certainly not least, Ch. Sandylands Markwell of Lockerbie. (Diane Jones)

This is Ch. Aquarius Kismet's Legacy at Corey, a great grandson of Rever. (Ashbey Photography)

Dog at the prestigious Potomac specialty. His influence was such that when you spoke to another breeder in 1985 or 1986, you didn't even ask if they were breeding to Rever. Instead, you simply inquired, "When is your Rever litter due?" or "What do you have to breed to Rever?"

Kendall loved him dearly and did a wonderful job of sharing him with all of us. His name appears once or more in all the pedigrees of the dogs I have and love today. Because of the strict quarantine rules in Britain, Rever never returned to his birthplace. However, he did go to Europe, and proved to be a top stud dog there as well. He was loved everywhere he went, and lived out his life very happily in France.

The stud force Rever left behind is also unequaled. His son, Ch. Dickendall Ruffy, SH, is a beautiful black dog that also produces yellow pups. His offspring include two top-winning Labradors in the United States: Ch. Broadreach

Bocephus, SH, bred by Martha Lee Voshell and owned by Jim and Liz Bowron, who was number-one Lab in 1992 and was also a specialty and multiple Sporting Group winner; and Ch. Lobuff's Bare Necessities, CD, JH, the top dog in 1993 and '94, a multiple specialty winner, multiple Sporting Group winner and twice Best of Breed at Westminster. You'll notice both these dogs have hunting titles after their names as well, which means they had both the conformation and the instincts of the best Labrador Retrievers.

Ch. Lobuff's Bare Necessities, JH, CD, a son of Ruffy, has gone on to greatness himself. He's shown here with Lisa Weiss.

Ruffy sired many other champions and specialty winners, as well, but his biggest contribution to the breed was a son, Ch. Dickendall Arnold (his dam was Dickendall A-Ha). Next to Rever, this dog probably had the most profound and lasting impact on the breed in recent history. Arnold (named after Schwarzenegger), is a dominant black, which means he only produces black puppies. He has played a major role in improving type in the black dogs and bitches in this country, as well as in many others. When I read the results of show wins from Mexico, Canada or Finland, I am not at all surprised to see that the ribbons went to an Arnold son or daughter.

Arnold has not yet retired as a stud dog, and one of his sons is already making a name for himself. Ch. Tabatha's Drifter at Dickendall, JH, is another beautifully made black dog who carries the yellow gene. His dam is Ch. Tabatha's Valleywood Decoy, and he has produced some wonderful young dogs doing a lot of winning. In fact, Drifter is the sire of the 1998 Westminster Best of Breed winner, Ch. Linray's Over the Top. And two of Drifter's get (offspring) were Best in Sweepstakes

Ch. Dickendall Arnold played a major role in improving type in black Labs. (Kendall Herr)

This is Ch. Tabatha's Morning Chat, WC, a daughter of Drifter.
(Roseberry)

and Best of Opposite Sex in Sweepstakes at the Greater Boston Specialty in June 1998—littermates owned by Bob and Terri Shober.

With the technology now available to freeze and store sperm for later use, we'll be able to benefit from the superb genetic heritage of these dogs even after they have left us.

IN THE RING AND FIELD

Two other dogs of Kendall's breeding are also worth mentioning because they have made important contributions as stud dogs. They are Ch. Marshland Blitz (co-owned by Dennis Emken), and his son out of a Rever daughter, Ch. Graemoor Tim, JH (co-owned and always shown by Betty Graham). Tim is a multiple specialty

winner, as well as a Sporting Group winner and a Westminster Best of Breed winner.

These two dogs are especially impressive because they were not only beautiful to look at, with correct type and soundness, but were also able to demonstrate their working abilities (you'll find a picture of Tim in Appendix E). As I mentioned earlier, there was a time when show dogs did not hunt, and hunting dogs did not show. Now, more breeders than ever have become involved in breeding dual-, if not triple-purpose dogs.

There are many breeders showing their dogs at conformation events, and then going on to have their dogs earn their CD, CDX, UD, UDX, TD and even TDX. Other weekends these same dogs are traveling to hunt tests to qualify for their JH, SH or MH. (If all these initials are confusing, you'll find them explained in Chapter 10 and also in Appendix B.) These breeders are extremely dedicated and hardworking—these are not titles you earn in a couple of days or a couple of weeks. These titles require a lot of training, but most that are involved thoroughly enjoy it—as do their Labs.

From 1985 to 1997, 12 dogs gained their championships as well as Master Hunter titles. Some also earned obedience titles. Martha Lee Voshell and Sue Willumsen have each owned 2 of these 12 dogs. They are both dedicated and hardworking Labrador lovers. Martha Lee's dogs are Ch. Broadreach Trace of Grace, MH, a black

Ch. Broad Reach Gripper, CDX, MH, was sired by Dickendall Arnold, and is carrying on the tradition of dual-purpose Labs. (Martha Lee Voshell)

Martha Lee Voshell with FC Broad Reach Pebble, MH.

female sired by Ch. Marshland Blitz; and Ch. Broadreach Gripper, CDX, MH, a black female sired by Arnold. Martha Lee also just put a field championship on Broadreach Pebble, MH.

Sue's dogs are co-owned with Karen Kase: Ch. Willcare's Gypsy Chitina CD, MH, a yellow female; and Ch. Willcare's Gypsy Talkeetna, CD, MH, a yellow male.

Some other dogs who have proven their quality both in and out of the show ring include Ch. Devon's Rough Magic, TDX, MH, a lovely black bitch with titles in conformation, hunting and tracking. She is owned and trained by Sue Berman, and co-owned by Judy Race.

Am./Can. Ch. Plantiers Ruthless Ruthie, MH, is a chocolate bitch sired by specialty-winning British import Ch. Lindall Mastercraft. She is owned by Dick Plantier and bred by Carl and Nancy Brandow. Currently, a son of Ruthie's (sired

Ruthless Blazing Brentley, MH, CD, shown here with trainer Bill Clark, is following in his multitalented mother's paw prints. (Nancy Brandow)

Sue Berman and Ch. Devon's Rough Magic braved the cold for their TDX test.

Ch. Boradors Significant Brother, CD, is a beautiful black dog whose career has spanned eight years. (Sally Bell)

by Ch. Flying Clouds Tai-Pan) named Ruthless Blazing Brentley has completed his Master Hunter and Companion Dog titles and is just about to finish his championship.

Ch. Boradors Significant Brother, CD, has an obedience title and has also been winning in the show ring for eight years—a significant amount of time. He is co-owned by breeder Sally Bell and Jennifer Stotts, who has handled him to several specialty wins, a Judges Award of Merit at Westminster, Best Veteran obedience dog at the Potomac Specialty and Best of Breed at the Miami Valley Labrador Specialty.

Another triple-titled dog is Nancy Martin's Ch. Ayr's Real McCoy, CDX, JH (co-owned by Joann Summers). He's a son of Ch. Dickendall Ruffy, SH. Two more Dickendall bitches with

Junior Hunter titles belong to Faith Hyndman: Ch. Dickendall Buckstone Apple, JH, and Am./Can. Ch. Dickendall Moorwood Token, JH.

Marianne Foote has been breeding Labradors in California for a long time, and has always been involved with dual-purpose dogs. She also published a magazine in the 1970s called *Retriever International*, dedicated to promoting dual purpose retrievers of all kinds. To this day, if you need retriever information but are not sure how to get it, Marianne is the one to call. Her Winroc Yukon Dancer, UD, MH, is owned by Peggy Levikow. Dancer's sister, Winroc Barefoote Contessa, also has a JH. Then there's Winroc XLT Funnel Cloud, TDX, JH; Winroc XLT Onyx Injun, MH; and Ch. Winroc Goforit of Sundance, JH.

Winroc Yukon Dancer has earned advanced titles in obedience and hunt tests. (Vicky & Warren Cook)

Winroc XLT Funnel Cloud has made his mark in tracking and hunting. (Lee Foote)

How far can this go? Breeder, judge, owner and handler Cheryl Ostenson (a woman with four jobs) bred Ch. Chelons Tamarack Tundra Rose, UD, JH, TDX—a dog with four titles!

These breeders, and many others, are committed to having Labrador Retrievers who can do it all and still look the way Labradors should: powerful, strong, heavy-boned, double-coated dogs who look like the dogs the fisherman off the coast of Newfoundland would have been able to use.

FIELD TRIAL HEADLINERS

Most show people also do something else with their Labs. However, most people involved with field trials are involved exclusively with field trials. There are several reasons for this. The first is that it takes an enormous amount of time to train a dog for that kind of rigorous competition, and it doesn't leave a lot of time for anything else. Most field trainers keep two residences—a place to train in the south in the

NFC/AFC Lucayana's Fast Willie has had a stellar field career. (Laura Parrott)

winter, and a place up north to train in the summer. The competition is incredibly keen, and the dogs have to perform their absolute best. You don't get a Field Champion without a lot of sweat and hard work.

A dog with a very impressive field trial career is 1997 National Champion FC/AFC Lucayana's Fast Willie (his sire was FC/AFC/ CNAFC/CFC Aces High III and his dame was North Star's Alil' Woopi). Willie was bred by Linda Harger and is owned, trained and handled by Laura and John Parrott. He is one of the few retrievers to have won a National Championship and hold the title of High Point Derby Dog (an honor he earned in 1992). Willie is now eight years old.

In 1990, '91 and '93 the National Field Trial Championship was won by Candlewoods Tanks A Lot. Lottie, as she is called, is the only bitch to have won three National titles. She was bred by Mary Howley. Her sire is 1992 NFC and 1990 NAFC Candlewoods Super Tanker and her dam is Candlewoods Tiz Too. In 1996, NFC Storm's

Riptide Star became the first chocolate dog to win a National Field Trial Championship.

The field trial people I know are on the go all the time. It is a big commitment, especially if you are training and traveling with other people's dogs. Tanker, Lottie and Star, for example, were all trained by Mike and Cindy Lardy of Handjem Retrievers, who have residences in Wisconsin and Georgia.

Anna Clark is a field trainer who spends summers in Maine with her husband Bill and fellow Lab breeder and trainer Bernadette Brown, and then heads south in November to train where it's warmer. Anna trained and ran Baloo, a dog Emily and Lisa co-own, for his JH and CD. I went up to Maine for a day last summer, and was overwhelmed by the daily schedule! Anna had Baloo swim 10 miles a day behind a canoe that she was paddling. Of course, Baloo loved it, and our days in the backyard here on Long Island seem dull by comparison!

Baloo enjoys being thought of as a sporting dog. But he can and has done it all. (Viewpoint Photography)

TWO TYPES

Anna and Bernadette, as well as lots of other field trial enthusiasts, believe it is important to run dogs who are representative of the breed and can compete at conformation shows, as well. Unfortunately, not everyone feels this way. Most field trial breeders think performance is all that matters, and there are show breeders who concentrate solely on appearance. That is why we have two very different looking types of dogs today. It is not likely that field trial dogs will ever look like show dogs. The breeders just have different priorities. And maybe that's okay.

I do feel that through the efforts of many concerned show breeders we are working toward closing the gap, but we still have a long way to go. Hunt test, obedience and show fanciers are all working together to preserve this wonderful breed we all love so much.

If you are interested in getting involved with conformation shows, obedience, hunt tests or field trials, I recommend that you go to some of these events and seek out a reputable breeder in your area of interest. Then it would be wise to start looking at the pedigrees of that person's dogs. If that breeder doesn't have a dog available for you, perhaps someone with a similar or related breeding has a pup available or is planning a litter soon.

Don't be fooled just by ribbons and trophies. It's easy to be impressed by glitzy advertising and breeders who boast about big wins at little shows under judges who are not breed experts. You want to look for a breeder with a history and a solid line of sound dogs. There are plenty of those breeders out there; just look and you'll find one. Usually they are the ones who are not doing much boasting. The performance of their dogs speaks for them.

JanRod's Christopher Robin is a good example of the Lab's versatility. He's an American and Mexican show champion, and has CD, JH and TT titles. (Jan Grannemann)

CHAPTER 12

What You Should Know About Breeding

You've just spent a lot of money buying a well-bred, healthy Labrador puppy. Are you multiplying what you spent by the number of puppies the breeder had to sell? Are you thinking what a good source of income breeding dogs can be? Are you planning to have just one litter, for the children to learn about reproduction, or to use your male dog at stud to get a puppy back that's just like him? Breeding dogs is not like having a yard sale—something you do occasionally to pick up some extra cash and let the buyer beware. Dogs are living, breathing beings, and breeding is a very complicated affair.

WHAT CAN GO WRONG?

Let's consider some of the things that can happen when you breed puppies.

Scenario One: You bred a pet-quality bitch to another pet-quality dog. The puppies are sold, and your bank account is healthy. Then several people call to report that their puppies have been diagnosed with ectopic ureters and require surgery to remove a kidney. The unhappy buyers want you to replace the puppy or help pay for the surgery. What will you do?

Scenario Two: You sold a puppy six months ago to a young couple with three small children. But now they decide the puppy is too big and rambunctious, and the children have lost interest in him. They want to bring him back to you. What will you tell them?

Scenario Three: The puppy that you sold to the older couple down the block has crippling hip dysplasia at one year old. The veterinarian recommends euthanasia. The owners are heartbroken. Can you counsel them? And do you understand what this means for your breeding program?

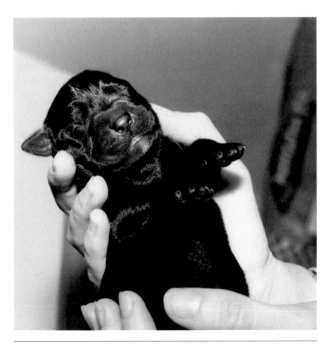

Breeding dogs is an awesome responsibility. What if the mother can't care for this three-day-old pup? Then it becomes your job. (K. Sneider)

WHO SHOULD BREED?

As you can guess, I consider breeding dogs an activity best left to those who have studied genetics, have experience in all aspects of training and care, and have engaged in breeding to produce quality animals and not just bank account deposits.

And speaking of bank accounts, let me tell you that serious breeders will all agree—breeding dogs *costs* money! On balance, the costs of feeding, veterinary care, exhibiting (a must, to prove the breeding worth of the dog), and the major expenses involved in breeding a litter outweigh the revenues from puppy sales.

If you've acquired your Labrador from a casual breeder, pet shop or dog pound, it goes without saying that you shouldn't breed. Sound breeding is based on a thorough understanding of the genetic background of the sire and dam, and you cannot research pedigrees of dogs acquired under those circumstances.

But even a well-bred puppy from a reputable source is not a ticket to the world of breeding. In fact, a serious breeder who values her dogs will actively discourage you from breeding. She knows how long it takes to gain the experience and knowledge necessary to make informed breeding decisions. In Chapter 4 we mentioned the many newspaper ads offering Labrador puppies for sale. These are the results of casual breeders, sometimes known as backyard breeders. For the most part, these are well-intentioned people who undertake breeding dogs without knowing enough to really do it right.

Breeding dogs costs a lot more than you might think. You need to be in it for love, not money. (Greg Goebel)

should not be based on a preliminary X-ray, as a dog's hips often change as they mature. It's better to wait until a dog is two years old for a health clearance.

Under the PennHIP system, offered through International Canine Genetics, a dog is X-rayed in different positions and actual angles are measured for the degree of laxity of the joint. Numbers are given for both hips, and are then interpreted on the basis of where the numbers fall within the range for Labrador Retrievers. PennHIP also rates osteoarthritis as none, mild, moderate and severe.

Elbow dysplasia is another concern evaluating soundness. This can be done at the same time as a hip X-ray. Elbows

IF YOU WANT TO GET STARTED

If you truly believe that you want to become involved in breeding, start by joining a local dog club and get involved in obedience training and conformation shows. Meet with and talk to breeders to educate yourself about dogs and pedigrees. Learn about health clearances for orthopedic and eye problems, and why all breeding stock must have them.

There is no reason to consider breeding a dog with hips that do not pass an Orthopedic Foundation for Animals (OFA) or PennHIP evaluation. Hip X-rays can be sent to OFA and receive a preliminary as early as six months of age, but an OFA number is not issued. Breeding

Serious breeders are also serious students of genetics. The inheritance of coat color is just one of the factors they must examine when considering a breeding.

There is no reason to breed any but the most physically and temperamentally sound dogs. (Carol Heidl)

receive either a pass or a fail rating, and dogs are eligible for official clearance at 24 months of age.

Any dog considered for breeding should also have its eyes examined by a board-certified ophthalmologist. All examinations are sent to the Canine Eye Registration Foundation (CERF). If you send the owner's copy of the ophthalmologist's report along with a minimal fee, you will receive a number that verifies your dog's eye report.

You can read more about health clearances in Chapter 6. But these clearances are only the beginning. Myriad aspects of a dog's health and temperament are controlled by a complex interaction of genes. While some health and temperament problems are easy to avoid through careful breeding, others are not. If you want to breed, you must be prepared to learn all you can about canine health and genetics, and then study the pedigrees of all the dogs you plan to breed. And you must remember that genetic combinations are, at best, only educated guesses. You never really know what you are going to get until the puppies are born.

You must also remember that you are responsible for the dogs you bring into the world—not just until they leave your care, but forever. That means finding the right home for each puppy, no matter how long it takes, and being prepared to take that dog back no matter what the reason, for as long as it lives.

If you still really want to be a breeder, find a mentor, one who has knowledge and a breeding philosophy to share with you, and listen, listen, listen.

You are responsible for all the lives you bring into the world. These pups are three weeks old. (Annie & Ron Cogo)

A breeder must be totally committed to raising the soundest, best puppies possible. The future of all Labs depends on it. (Lisa Weiss)

WHAT I'VE LEARNED AS A BREEDER

Being a breeder can be a joyful experience, but it can also be heartbreaking. Let me share a few of my more memorable experiences as a breeder with you. There was the time one of my bitches got past the kitchen gate and whelped a puppy on my best rug; do I need to tell you that the rug was ruined? There was another time I ended up with one live puppy, after I had shipped my bitch to the other side of the country for breeding. And I remember all the times my bitches have required cesarean sections to deliver their puppies, and the many times that I've sat with a bitch in labor *all night long* and had to go to work in the morning. And the times I've had to pay someone to come in and take care of my puppies when I needed to go away.

Do you know that breeding your bitch can result in mammary and uterine tumors? Do you know that a stud dog can become territorial and mark his belongings with urine? Do you know that an unspayed female can attract unwelcome neighborhood dogs to your doorstep? That bitches come into season every six months and bleed for three weeks? It's unhealthy and even cruel to breed a bitch at every season. Are you prepared to protect your bitch from every male dog in the neighborhood, and to protect your furniture and rugs from your bitch?

Do you know that unneutered males are susceptible to rectal and testicular tumors? That bitches bleed for days after delivering puppies?

These are just a few of the things you need to consider if you're serious about breeding!

As a breeder, I take my responsibilities seriously. I am ready to counsel puppy buyers on health and behavior problems. I would be willing to take any of my puppies back at any time in their lives, because I produced them and I am ultimately responsible for their welfare.

I know the correct way to socialize a litter and the correct time to let them go to new homes. If you don't have the knowledge and experience to do the same, you shouldn't think of bringing puppies into the world.

There's a lot of work involved in puppy care, and the mom can't do it all. Frequent weigh-ins are easy compared to the frequent cleanups! (Greg Goebel)

Unless you are ready to make a full-fledged commitment to learning about Labradors and bettering the breed, enjoy your dog as your pet and leave the breeding to those with the time and the knowledge to do what is best for the breed. It is often said that people stay in the dog show and breeding world for an average of ten years. Perhaps that is because there is so much disappointment and heartbreak along the way. Only those who are doggedly determined to learn and succeed will keep at it.

Breeding can be tough on your bitch. (Greg Goebel)

(Chenil Chablais)

Special Care for the Older Dog

I n what seems like the blink of an eye, your Labrador Retriever will be heading toward its senior years. The dog that has given you so many years of enjoyment will now need special care from you. The Labrador has an average life span of 13 years, although dogs can vary a lot from the average. That means your dog will be reaching middle age at about seven to nine years old.

In middle age, your dog's system begins to undergo the changes of the aging process. It's starting to slow down, and it doesn't function as efficiently as before. Musculo-skeletal changes, loss of visual and hearing acuity, and deterioration of the internal systems are some of the changes of aging that your dog will experience.

DIET AND WALKS

Dogs' nutritional needs change as they age. Your veterinarian can recommend any necessary diet changes, such as a senior formulation. But remember that not every dog needs a senior diet, especially dogs that are active into their later years. One way to lessen the strain on the dog's digestive system is to simply switch to two or possibly three smaller meals a day.

Dogs' systems change in many ways as they age, and special care may be needed. Aquarius Bunkerhill is 14 years old.

It was once thought that older dogs needed less protein, since they are less active; some people even believed the protein levels in adult maintenance foods would cause kidney failure in older dogs. But research has now proven that it is not protein that damages the kidneys, but phosphorus. Also, older dogs' digestive tracts do not function as well as they used to, so they actually require better quality proteins, not less protein.

Dog food manufacturers are currently addressing these needs, and several have reformulated their foods. One manufacturer has even made two geriatric formulas—one for normal weight dogs and one for overweight dogs. Ask your veterinarian, or call the dog food manufacturers for the latest information on their foods.

The routine for going out may also need adjustment, since the aging dog may no longer

have the same ability to control itself between walks. Occasional accidents are just that; please remember that a housebroken dog is ashamed of an accident, and don't make matters worse by scolding. If accidents are frequent, speak with your veterinarian about testing for urinary tract infections or metabolic imbalances that may be responsible for your dog's incontinence. Have the veterinarian examine your older dog more frequently, and bring a urine and fecal sample with you for analysis.

Spayed females sometimes leak urine, especially when asleep, because the lack of estrogen means they have less control over the urinary sphincter muscle. There are hormone supplements available that will control this problem. If you notice wet spots where your dog has been lying, suspect this condition and see your veterinarian.

Our Labs do their best to take care of us all their lives. But when they get older, it's our turn to take care of them.

An older dog can still be an active one. This is Am./Can. Ch. Campbellcroft's Angus, CD, WC, winning Best of Breed at the national specialty from the Veteran's Class, when he was 10 years old. (Marianne Foote)

EXERCISE

The older Labrador continues to need regular exercise, but use common sense and don't let your oldster overdo it. Your dog wants to please you, and will indulge in whatever form of exercise you choose, so it's up to you to select sensible activities.

Swimming is still good exercise for an older dog, but not when the water is too cold. (Olive & Joe Mainhardt)

A regular walk, for a reasonable distance, will be a welcome outing and a good source of controlled activity. Even if your dog loves a good swim, don't take it to the beach when the winter water temperature would keep you out! Arthritic changes are occurring, and those old joints don't need extremes of any kind.

And speaking of arthritis, there are several new medications and nutritional supplements that will help keep your dog comfortable. You'll find them discussed briefly in Chapter 6. Talk to your veterinarian about these products. Monitor your dog's weight, so you're not placing an extra burden on those aging joints. Obesity causes a variety of problems in older dogs, so don't let your old friend get fat.

Your old dog will still enjoy the company of your young friends. (Mollie Madden)

THE GROOMING ROUTINE

The elderly Labrador may need some changes in its grooming routine. Labradors are exceptionally low-maintenance types, but several things need your attention when your dog begins to age. Frequently inspect your dog's teeth for tartar buildup and gum inflammation. If you see either, let your veterinarian know so you can decide on a course of treatment. Left unchecked, gum disease can cause potentially fatal infections in other organs.

Your Labrador may also develop stains running down from the corners of its eyes. These are caused by blocked tear ducts. Gently wipe the stained area with a soft cotton ball moistened with warm water or a special preparation that will control staining.

It is especially important to keep your old dog's nails trimmed. With less activity, the nails may grow overly long. This causes the feet to splay, and affects the dog's ability to grip surfaces. The old dog's nails will be harder and more difficult to trim, but keep after them, or have them done by a groomer or veterinarian.

Brush your dog daily, both as a way to make your pet more comfortable and to express your continued love and concern for its welfare. Often, dogs smell a little "doggy" as they age, but this may well be due to problems with their teeth, ears, urinary tract or anal glands. Don't just assume your dog is meant to smell bad. Consult your veterinarian!

Baths should only be given indoors or when it is warm outdoors, and the dog should be thoroughly dried before going out in the cold. Taking

Your dog's eyes may stain a bit as it ages. That's Lisa with a very special friend, Am./Can. Ch. Lobuff's Sundown at Kerrymark.

Bumps and callouses are common in older dogs. (Martha Lee Voshell)

care to dry a dog thoroughly in cold weather is always important, but is even more so for the older dog. An older dog should never be left wet in an unheated area.

HEALTH CARE

As a dog approaches eight or nine years of age, a veterinary exam and blood screen should be done yearly. These routine tests can spot developing problems before they become critical. The functions of the kidneys and liver can be monitored, and any changes can be addressed with a combination of diet and medication.

Cysts and fatty tumors begin to show up with frequency as a dog ages, and these should be brought to the attention of a veterinarian. Most are benign, but they should always be observed for changes.

If your dog seems reluctant to leave familiar places, its eyesight may be failing.

Your dog may begin to develop cataracts and its vision may be impaired. Be alert to any reluctance to climb steps or go out at night, and discuss these behaviors with your veterinarian. In most cases, you can make small changes to your dog's routine that will make life more comfortable, such as scheduling walks when it's still light out, not moving the furniture or placing your dog's bed downstairs.

You may also notice that your dog's hearing seems to be decreasing. There is nothing to be done, except to show extra patience and consideration when your dog seems unresponsive.

ADDING A PUPPY

As your dog begins to age, you may decide to add a new puppy to your family. This can give the old-ster a new lease on life, or it can be a disaster. Dogs have their own ways of relating to each other, and not every dog wants to be friends with every other dog.

Be considerate of your old dog's position in your family, and don't try to thrust a new puppy into an old pet's territory without some preparation. The backyard and house are already your dog's territory, and he may not welcome an intruder! It is always best to introduce unfamiliar dogs on neutral territory. Don't have the puppy enter your home until your older dog has had the opportunity to inspect the newcomer from stem to stern, outside, perhaps on the front lawn.

When your dog has indicated acceptance of the puppy, bring them both in the house, but don't turn the puppy loose. The pup will have the rest of its life to explore, so don't risk upsetting your older dog at this point. You need to gradually acclimate the puppy to its new home, all the while continuing to give the old guy a full share of your attention. New puppies can be very compelling, and their needs can take up a lot of your time. But please don't leave your old friend on the sidelines. It's liable to resent the puppy. And your best friend of many years deserves better.

Sometimes an oldster will enjoy a younger companion. (Gloria Ennis)

Don't allow unsupervised play. A bouncy puppy can be mighty annoying to a senior citizen, so you need to be the referee during playtime. Even if your old dog *loves* the new arrival, the puppy shouldn't spend too much time with the oldster, or you'll have a pup that is bonded to another dog instead of to you.

Each dog needs a separate food bowl, and dogs should not eat in close proximity to one another. Food satisfies one of a dog's most basic instincts, and each should be allowed to eat without the other close at hand. You have to monitor the distribution of the toys, too. Like children, dogs always want the same toy at the same time!

THE HARDEST DECISION

You've done everything you can to make your dog's last years comfortable and dignified. But there will come a time when you have to decide whether the *quality* of your dog's life has deteriorated. I find that oftentimes people dread making the painful decision to euthanize a beloved pet. They go on, hoping perhaps that one day they'll wake up and find the dog has died in its sleep. In my opinion, this is unlikely to happen unless the dog is very ill and suffering.

Look at your dog as if it belonged to someone else, and try to be objective. Is the dog living, or just existing? Your veterinarian will be a good source of information as you make this difficult decision, but ultimately, the decision is yours.

I believe the last thing I owe my dogs is to be with them when the final moment comes. Euthanasia is very fast and painless—an overdose of barbiturates that puts the dog to sleep forever. Trust me, your dog will not suffer during the procedure, and your loving presence will comfort the dog as it gently departs this world. Do this as your last act of love for your best friend.

(*Winnie Limbourne*)

Dogs and the Law

We don't normally think of a puppy in legal terms, and certainly wouldn't expect to see lawyers involved in the process of buying one. Even so, the fairly simple decision to get a dog can raise a surprising number of legal issues the new dog owner should be aware of. You may find yourself presented with a sales contract when you buy a new puppy. Or your puppy may come home from the pet shop feeling a bit under the weather, and you think the store ought to pay the veterinary bills. Maybe Miss Gulch, your wicked neighbor, complains that the puppy barks too much, and threatens to take Toto away in a basket or to sue for disturbing the peace. What if your dog bites someone (or, as is more likely the case with a Labrador, the 80-pound "puppy" knocks a baby over while trying to lick it, and the baby gets hurt)? What if your dog is attacked by a loose neighborhood dog and you're saddled with big vet bills that the neighbor won't pay? Or maybe you've decided that Labrador quintuplets would make your family complete. Does your town have any restrictions about the number of dogs you may own?

As you can see, there are many ways dog owners can be involved with the law, and it's wise to be aware of them. The problem is that the legal issues of pet ownership are often local issues, and the laws vary from state to state and county to county. Therefore, the laws discussed in this chapter won't apply everywhere, and there are undoubtedly other laws in other states that will not be covered here. The purpose of this chapter is simply to make you aware of the legal issues that *can* arise when you buy and own a dog, and to help you find out where to look for the laws that may apply to your particular situation.

I'm going to concentrate on the laws that may affect your purchase of a puppy, because those issues seem to come up most often. But there are lots more legal questions that can come up. There are several books available that discuss the many, many legal issues dog ownership can involve. Check with your local public library or bookstore.

And here comes the legal disclaimer: This chapter is by no means complete, and is intended to provide only general guidance, not legal advice. If you have a specific legal problem, you should consult a lawyer. There are even a few around the country who specialize in dog law.

Your pal in the backyard can become the subject of some pretty hairy legal questions.

CONTRACTS

Many breeders will require a puppy buyer to sign a written contract, for a variety of reasons. One very good reason is that a written contract or bill of sale may be required by law in some states. The main advantage of a contract is that it can help avoid misunderstandings. If it is carefully written, it can also prevent disagreements and lawsuits.

At a minimum, any written contract for the sale of a puppy should identify the parties to the contract (the buyer and the seller, with their addresses and phone numbers), the date of purchase, the price being paid, and the "subject matter" of the contract. The subject matter is what the contract is about: In this case, it is about the sale of a dog. Some detail is helpful here. If it is important to you that the dog is a purebred, yellow, female Labrador Retriever that is eight weeks of age and has Romeo as her father and Juliet as her mother, for example, that is how the dog should be described in the contract. If you and the seller have agreed that the price you pay will include the puppy's first shot, or a week's supply of puppy food, or anything else, that should be in the contract as well.

You should be aware, however, that in some circumstances a contract can be enforced even if it is not in writing. In other words, sometimes oral promises can also be enforced in court. A little background about some very basic contract law may help you understand whether an oral promise can be enforced as a contract.

Contract law is often a mix between statutes and common law. A statute is a written law, voted upon by a legislative body (such as Congress or a state legislature), and then placed in a code that we can go to the library and read. The common law is law that is not voted upon by lawmakers, but that gradually develops out of the written decisions of judges deciding actual cases. There are certain common law rules that have developed over the years, but states often add to or even modify the common law by passing statutes.

There are two types of contracts: express and implied. An express contract is formed by language, whether it is written or oral. An example of an express written contract is a contract to buy a house: All of the terms of the contract are written down on paper and signed by both parties. An express oral contract is formed when a verbal promise is made. For example, suppose you leave your car at a repair shop because it's

The sales contract for your puppy may be your most important experience with dogs and the law. (Greg Goebel)

making a strange, scary noise, and you ask the shop to find out what's wrong. The shop calls you an hour later and says your brake pads are worn and need replacement. The repair shop tells you it will cost $75 and can be done that afternoon. You tell the shop owner to replace the pads. An enforceable contract has been formed, even though none of it is in writing. By contrast, an implied contract is one that is formed without language. How? By conduct. If you go to a gas station and fill your car with gas, there is an enforceable contract for the purchase of gas, despite the fact that you and the clerk have not even spoken.

Therefore, whether a valid contract exists may not depend on whether there is a formal, written agreement. Instead, it depends on a few common law rules. First, there must be an offer. To use the car example, the offer is presented when the repair shop says they will fix the car for $75. Then there must be acceptance of that offer—you have to say, "OK, fix the brakes." At that point, there is what lawyers call a "meeting of the minds." Finally, there must be something lawyers call "consideration." That is, the parties must strike a bargain—they must exchange something. In the car example, the parties are exchanging promises: The repair shop promises to fix the car, and you promise to pay $75.

The Uniform Commercial Code

So far I've discussed the common law rules for contracts, but as I mentioned earlier, statutes may also apply. The statute most likely to pertain to a contract for the sale of a puppy is the Uniform Commercial Code (UCC). The UCC is a model statute, written by a group of experts in commercial law. Almost all states have adopted the UCC, but most state legislatures made some changes to it before passing it in their state.

Article 2 of the UCC provides the rules for the sale of goods. Many of the cases interpreting Article 2 and the definition of the word "goods" have concluded that dogs are goods, and therefore their sale is regulated by the UCC. Although you and I both know that a dog can be a best friend and a close family member, in the eyes of the law it is property. And even though it sounds cold to an animal lover, dogs are goods under the UCC.

Another important word in the UCC is "merchant." If a seller is a merchant under the UCC's definition, additional rights and obligations arise. A merchant is a person who deals in goods of the kind involved in the transaction at issue, or who otherwise, by his occupation, holds himself out as having knowledge or skill peculiar to the goods involved in the transaction. Therefore, a neighbor whose dog accidentally got pregnant and who has

We all know that these are adorable 10-day-old puppies, but in the eyes of the law they are considered property. (Emily Magnani)

never before sold a puppy, and never intends to sell one again, is not a merchant. However, a breeder who has been breeding dogs and selling puppies for 20 years, and who represents himself to be knowledgeable about puppies, may very well be considered a merchant under the UCC. This is important, because if the seller is a merchant, a special kind of warranty arises.

The UCC provides that, with certain exceptions, contracts for the sale of goods for more than $500 must be in writing to be enforceable. Therefore, in general, if you have paid more than $500 for your puppy, you should see a written contract of some kind. It may not use the word "contract." It may just be a document that sets forth the terms of the agreement. In fact, some courts have said that two or more letters, when read together, can be a contract.

The UCC also gives certain kinds of warranties. An express warranty is created when the seller makes a statement of fact or a promise to the buyer, or gives a description of the goods, and this becomes part of the basis for the bargain—part of the very reason you bought the puppy from that person. For example, if the seller tells you that the dog is a purebred, registerable Labrador Retriever, and it turns out to be a Dachshund, you can sue for breach of an express warranty.

In fact, in New Jersey there is a separate state law that says if a pet dealer tells you the dog is eligible for AKC registration, but fails to give you the papers needed to register the dog within 120 days after the sale, then you are entitled to return the dog and get a full refund or keep the dog and get a partial refund of 75 percent of the purchase price. Buyers in New Jersey would not even have to sue under the UCC to get their money back.

Bear in mind that an express warranty under the UCC is created by a statement of fact, not by giving a mere opinion or by "sales talk." It can sometimes be hard to distinguish between statements of fact and sales puffery, and your best course of action is to make sure that if something is important to you, it is put in writing.

The UCC also creates several kinds of implied warranties. Implied warranties are warranties that are not spelled out, but which the law itself imposes upon the transaction. First, the mere sale of a puppy creates an implied warranty that the seller owns the puppy, has the legal right to sell it, and that no one else claims a legal interest in the puppy. This is called a warranty of title, and is not usually a problem.

Second, the UCC provides that when a merchant sells the goods, there is an implication of "merchantability"—which means the goods are fit for the ordinary purposes for which such goods are used. In the context of a dog sold as a pet, it means the dog is suitable as a pet. Therefore, if as soon as you get the dog home it tries to bite you every time it sees you, it is not fit for use as a pet and you would be able to sue for breach of warranty of merchantability and get your money back.

Finally, the UCC provides for a warranty of fitness for a particular purpose. This warranty will arise when any seller (not just a merchant) has a reason to know the particular purpose that the goods will be used for, and the buyer is relying upon the seller's skill to select suitable goods. For example, suppose you tell the breeder that you are unfamiliar with the world of dog shows, but you are buying this puppy in the hopes of owning your first show dog. You tell the breeder you want a puppy to show in conformation shows, and that you want the breeder to pick out a puppy that can be shown. The breeder picks the puppy out and tells you it can be shown. But if the puppy has only one testicle, it cannot be shown under AKC rules, and you may have a right to sue for breach of warranty of fitness for a particular purpose.

You should be aware that the last two warranties, the warranties of merchantability and fitness, can be disclaimed by the seller—that is, the seller can expressly state that they do not apply.

Sellers typically do that by using words such as "as is" or "with all faults," or by putting a provision in a written contract that conspicuously states that the warranties do not apply.

Contract Terms

Now that you are familiar with the very basics of the law of contracts, it may be helpful to know what kinds of things you may find in a contract for the sale of a puppy. As I said earlier, the contract will, at a minimum, be dated, identify the buyer and the seller, state the purchase price and identify what, specifically, is being sold. And now that you are familiar with the UCC, you know that there may be a disclaimer provision: language in the contract that says the warranties of fitness and/or merchantability do not apply. Or, it may simply say that the sale is "as is."

The contract may also state that it contains all of the terms the parties have agreed upon, or something to the effect that there are no other agreements between the parties except what is written in the contract. This is called a "merger" clause, and it can be very important. If the contract contains a merger clause, a court may very well say that you are prevented from presenting any evidence about any other terms you say were agreed upon. For example, suppose when you go to pick up your puppy, the breeder tells you it has worms. But the breeder ran out of worming medication, and tells you that if you take the puppy to your vet to get the deworming medication, the breeder will pay for it. You agree. However, the written contract you sign just before you leave says nothing about

that agreement, and contains a merger clause. If you need to sue the breeder to get a refund of the price you paid for the dewormer, you will not be able to claim in court that you and the breeder had this other agreement.

If you bought your puppy in another state, the contract may have a provision that determines which state's law will apply if there is ever a lawsuit. It may also say that if you ever want to sue the seller, you have to do it in the seller's state.

The contract may also say something about the registration of the dog. Many contracts will state that a puppy is sold with a Limited Registration. Under AKC rules, a Limited Registration means the dog will not be eligible to compete in AKC dog shows, and any puppies that dog produces will not be eligible for registration. A Limited Registration does not mean that the dog is inferior, but simply that it will make a good pet but not a good show dog. If you only want the dog as a companion, and intend to have it spayed or neutered (which, hopefully, you do!), a Limited Registration is just fine.

The contract may also contain the dog's health history, including a list of vaccinations it has had and any medications it has received. In some states, the seller is legally required to give you this information.

The contract should also cover the terms of any health guarantee the breeder gives. Some states have passed laws that provide for certain kinds of guarantees (more on that later in the chapter), but those laws don't always protect you. Your state may not have one, and even if it does, the law may only cover retail pet shops. Even if it covers private breeders, it still may only apply to breeders who sell lots of puppies in a year. If your breeder only sells a few puppies each year, the law may not apply.

Therefore, you should make sure you understand the terms of the health guarantee the breeder is offering. They should be clearly spelled out in the contract. How long does the guarantee last? Does it cover only certain diseases, or does it cover genetic defects as well? What must you do to invoke it? What kind of proof must you give the breeder that the puppy is sick? Must you give the puppy back in order to get a refund, or can you keep the puppy and just have the breeder pay certain costs? All of these points should be covered and explained to you.

LEMON LAWS

In addition to the UCC, some states have passed laws that specifically regulate the sale of dogs and cats. The purpose of these laws is to protect the buyer if a puppy is sick or otherwise unfit for sale. New York passed such a law, known as the Puppy Lemon Law, which I will use as an example. However, the provisions of these laws will be slightly different in different states.

New York's law applies to "pet dealers," which the law says is any person, firm, partnership or corporation that, in the ordinary course of business, sells more than nine dogs per year for profit to the

If your pup comes with a health guarantee from the breeder, make sure you understand all the terms. (Greg Goebel)

public. The definition of a pet dealer specifically states that it includes "breeders of animals who sell animals directly to a consumer." It does not include humane societies, whether or not they charge a fee for adoption.

Some states (Arkansas, for example) have drafted their laws so they do not apply to breeders, but only to retail pet stores. Others have different laws for different people: California has one law that applies to retail pet shops, and one that applies to breeders. However, California's law defines a breeder as someone who "has sold, transferred, or given away 50 or more dogs during the preceding calendar year that were bred and reared on the premises."

If a dispute arises about the puppy's health and the buyer wants to rely upon the Puppy Lemon Law, the buyer will need to show that the law applies. In New York, that means proving the seller sells more than nine puppies per year for profit. There is some room for disagreement here. Does the law apply to a breeder who sold only five puppies this year, but sold 15 last year? Unfortunately, no judge in New York has published a written decision that clarifies the rule.

Despite the uncertainty, the purpose of these laws is to give the buyer of a sick puppy some legal rights. A court is likely to interpret the law in a way that will best accomplish this purpose, and will try its best to protect the buyer.

Next, the buyer will have to show that the pet dealer sells the puppies for profit. A court will probably look at whether the seller's *purpose* is to make a profit, not whether the seller is, in fact, making a profit. If a pet dealer is selling the puppy for more than it costs to whelp and raise under normal circumstances, then a court is likely to conclude that there is a profit motive.

To comply with New York's law, a pet dealer must post a clearly visible notice telling the buyer about their rights under the law. The pet dealer must also give the buyer, at the time of sale, a written notice telling the buyer of his or her rights. The notice can be included in a written contract or an animal history certificate, or it may be placed in a separate document. The notice has to include the following information: a description of the dog (including the breed); the date of purchase; the name, address and phone number of the buyer; and the amount of the purchase.

The law gives a puppy buyer the following rights: If the buyer's veterinarian certifies that a puppy is "unfit for purchase due to illness, a congenital malformation which adversely affects the health of the animal, or the presence of symptoms of a contagious or infectious disease," then the buyer gets to choose one of three options. First, the buyer can return the dog and get a refund (including tax and reasonable vet costs directly related to the vet's certification); the refund must be made within 10 business days following receipt of a signed veterinarian's certification.

The second option is that the buyer can return the dog and get an exchange dog (of the buyer's choice) of equivalent value, plus reasonable costs directly related to the veterinarian's certification. The third option is that the buyer can keep the dog and be reimbursed, up to the purchase price paid for the dog, for reasonable services of a licensed veterinarian (of the buyer's choosing) to cure or try to cure the dog. The reimbursement must be made not later than 10 business days after receipt of a signed veterinarian's certification.

The New York law states that the buyer must get a vet's certification within 14 business days after the sale of the puppy, or after receipt of the written notice the pet dealer gives the buyer, whichever occurs last. Therefore, if the pet dealer doesn't give the notice for six months after he sells the puppy, the buyer has the six months plus 14 business days to get a vet's certification. Other states have different time periods within which the buyer must get a vet's certification. This is another good reason to take your new puppy to the vet shortly after you bring it home, even if the breeder's vet already gave the puppy a physical exam!

How many puppies you sell in a year determines if you are a dealer. But even then, it's not always clear. (Greg Goebel)

New York's law says that a dog is unfit for purchase when it has an illness, a congenital malformation that adversely affects its health, or the presence of symptoms of a contagious or infectious disease. In most states, including New York, the following are *not* grounds to say that a dog is unfit: intestinal parasites (unless the dog is clinically ill from the parasites) or an injury sustained or an illness contracted after the buyer takes possession of the dog. This is yet another reason to take your new puppy to the vet right away—it can prevent any claim by the seller that the puppy only got sick after you took it home.

The law also gives the pet dealer some rights. If the pet dealer disagrees with the vet's statement of unfitness, he or she can compel the buyer to produce the dog for an exam by the pet dealer's vet. This is true in most states. After that examination, if the pet dealer and the buyer can't reach an agreement, the buyer may sue the pet dealer to get the refund, exchange and/or reimbursement.

A pet dealer cannot use a contract to restrict the rights given to a buyer by law. In other words, any provision in a contract that is intended to waive the buyer's rights under New York's law is void and unenforceable. That is also true in other states. The purpose of this provision is to protect the consumer from "fine print" that might try to prevent the buyer from using the state law.

Finally, the law specifically states that it does not in any way limit the rights that are available to a consumer under any other law. It is in addition to those rights. Therefore, other laws may also apply: the common law of contracts, fraud and the warranties under the UCC, for example.

New York's Puppy Lemon Law is just one example, but it contains many provisions that are found in the laws of other states, as well. It does not, however, include one provision that is common in other states' laws. Many states have laws stating that if a puppy dies within a certain period after the sale, the buyer need not show the court that the puppy died of an illness or defect that existed at the time of the sale. Instead, the law assumes that the puppy had one; the pet dealer would have to show the court that it did not.

We mentioned in Chapter 8 that your breeder may be able to refer you to a veterinarian. But you should be aware that in some states, there may be a law that regulates even this. For example, the statute in New Jersey that regulates the sale of animals says it is a deceptive practice for a breeder to "refer, promote, suggest, recommend or advise that a consumer consult with, use, seek or obtain the services of a licensed veterinarian unless the consumer is provided with the names of not less than three licensed veterinarians, of whom only one may be the veterinarian" the breeder uses.

What Does All This Mean?

As you can see, there may be a lot more to buying a puppy than you realize. Hopefully, you will not have any problems with the process, and will just have a healthy puppy to share many years with. But there are a few lessons buried in all this legal talk. First, you should spend some time researching the breed, to see whether it is the right dog for you.

Next, you should spend some time researching the breeder. Check them out. Meet them, ask to see their adult dogs as well as their puppies, and spend some time asking questions. You will get a sense of the person you are dealing with. Do they seem honest and fair? Are their puppies raised in a clean, comfortable environment? Are the adult dogs well adjusted, friendly and happy? If you have a comfortable relationship with the breeder, you are less likely to have legal problems later on if the puppy does turn out to have some kind of illness, hereditary defect or injury.

Second, make sure all of the terms of your agreement are spelled out, preferably in writing. Make sure you have read and understand any contract you are asked to sign. If you are uncomfortable with anything in the contract, ask for an explanation. If you aren't satisfied with the contract after you've been given an explanation, explain your concerns to the breeder, and see if you can reach an understanding.

After you take your puppy home, take it to your own vet promptly for an exam. If everything is OK, call and let the breeder know. And if everything is not OK, let the breeder know that, as well.

Give the breeder the name and number of your vet, so they can get direct information. Follow up with a friendly letter, confirming what you've been told by the vet and what you've told the breeder, and keep a copy. The ultimate goal here is to avoid the increased tension that lawyers and threats involve. It's always best if you and the breeder can work things out amicably.

If you cannot work things out, however, you need to be prepared. Look up your state's law to see what your legal obligations are, just in case the breeder doesn't respond in a way that satisfies you. You certainly do not want to go in with both guns

right away, but you do need to know if your state has a lemon law, because there may be time limits involved. Chances are, if you've done your homework and checked out the breeder, you will be happy with the outcome.

KEEPING A DOG

The contract may be your only brush with the legalities of owning a dog. But there are lots of laws that can affect you throughout your dog's life, and it's important to know about them. Many of the laws that apply to your dog's daily life are local laws, enacted by the village, town or city in which you live. Therefore, it is impossible to tell you here what they may say. However, there are a few general areas that will probably affect you.

First, most localities require you to buy a license for your dog, and to keep it on your dog at all times. Keeping the license tag on your dog's collar will help identify the dog in case it ever gets lost (some dogs now sport a tattoo or computer microchip, as well). Getting a dog license usually involves paying a small fee (which may be slightly higher for unspayed or unneutered dogs) and proving that the dog is up-to-date with vaccines, especially rabies.

In addition, most areas have leash laws that make it illegal to just let your dogs run loose around the neighborhood. When the dog is off your property or in

Hopefully, you'll end up with a healthy puppy and you'll never have to worry about guarantees. Researching the puppy's parents and the breeder help ensure this will be the case. (Greg Goebel)

public places, the dog must be on a leash. While these laws certainly protect others, they protect you, as well. More and more courts hold dog owners strictly liable for the injuries caused by their dogs, and if your dog bites a person or another dog, things could get very expensive for you. It is to your advantage, therefore, to make sure that your dog is on a leash and under your control at all times.

Most villages and towns have ordinances that regulate noise levels in residential areas, and barking is often one of the noises regulated. It is very common for such laws to say that a dog barking for more than 10 or 15 minutes after a certain hour at night, or before a certain hour in the morning, is a violation of the law. If your dog is an offender, your neighbors will let you know!

The best course of action in this situation is to try to work the problem out amicably. See if you can identify the cause of the barking, and then remove it. For example, I had a neighbor complain many years ago that my dogs were barking every Monday and Thursday at five a.m. I discovered the problem was that the sanitation men were parking in front of my house at that hour, presumably beginning the day's route and having coffee. The solution was easy (though not cheap): a small stockade fence with a hedge out by the street, which blocked my dogs' view of them.

Some areas also have restrictions on the number of dogs you may keep. However, it is unlikely that this law will be enforced, unless your dogs become a problem. Towns simply do not have the staff to go door to door to check on how many dogs you

Most localities have laws that require you to keep your dog on a leash. (Carol Heidl)

own. But if your neighbors complain, you can actually be ordered by a court to get rid of some of your dogs. The lesson is: Be a good neighbor!

FINDING WHICH LAWS APPLY

One thing that can make the law difficult is that it is found in so many different places. Both statutes and common law can originate at the federal, state or local level. How do you know which laws apply to you and your dog?

Your local public library is a great starting point. Often, local libraries have copies of local

Some localities may try to restrict the number of dogs you can own.
(Greg Goebel)

and state statutes. These are typically found in the Reference section of the library.

Local town and municipal codes are the best starting point for finding laws regulating dogs. Very often, laws about barking, licensing dogs, kennels, leash laws and limits on the number of dogs you may own are enacted at the local level, by a village, town or county. They are often kept in a loose-leaf binder. If they are not available at the public library, try the town hall or the town attorney's office. Laws about vaccines and the sale of dogs are usually enacted at the state level, and will probably be available at the library.

Collections of statutes usually have an index, and finding the laws about dogs may be as simple as looking up the words "dogs," "pets" or "animals" in the index. If you know the citation of a specific law—the name and section number of

the law—a reference librarian will be able to help you find it quickly. Once you find a statute, you may notice that immediately after the statute, the book contains small summaries of court decisions that have interpreted that statute. These are called "annotations," and can be very helpful in understanding the statute.

Finding cases may involve driving a bit farther than a local public library, which probably won't have the volumes of books (called "reporters") in which court decisions are published. Instead, you should either check with your county courthouse to see if it has a law library that is open to the public (they often are), or a law school if you have one nearby. Although cases are not arranged in books by subject, as statutes are, there is a fairly simple way of finding cases about a particular subject. There are books called digests, which function almost in the same way as an index. You look up the words "dog," "pet" or "animal," for example, in the digest, and you may find a list of short summaries of cases about that topic.

In addition, a lot of information these days is readily available on the Internet—including some court decisions. Many state agencies, including those charged with the duty of regulating animals, now have Web sites that can be very informative. They may also have e-mail addresses where you can ask for more information.

The Labrador Retriever Club

E very breed has a national parent club. In our case, it is the Labrador Retriever Club, or LRC. The parent club is recognized by the AKC as the owner or custodian of the breed's standard. When a breed is seeking AKC recognition, it must have or form a parent club, and that club must apply to the AKC for membership.

The parent club also holds events for its breed, such as specialty shows and field trials. Judges' education seminars are usually offered at the national specialty show (as well as at regional shows), so that people who want to judge Labs can learn more about the breed.

If a breed develops an inherent problem, the parent club will also usually try to provide or raise funding for research and testing. Parent clubs usually try to offer referral services, as well, so that people looking for a well-bred puppy can find a breeder in their area.

Many clubs also offer rescue services and information for people looking to place or adopt a dog. Rescue groups sometimes go to pounds and shelters to look for lost or abandoned dogs, as well. Some parent clubs are better at this than others. Some of the breeds that have fewer dogs registered overall have an easier job of policing their breed and keeping their dogs out of shelters and laboratories. If tens of thousands of a particular breed are born every year, that job becomes bigger and more difficult. I believe the LRC tries to do its part in all those areas.

Most clubs have referral services to help buyers find a well-bred puppy.

WHEN IT ALL BEGAN

The history of the LRC fascinates me. Janet Churchill tells us in her book, *The New Labrador Retriever,* "In 1931, the American Kennel Club registered all retrieving breeds as one group under the title of Retrievers. Forty Retrievers were registered in 1931 without specifying a particular breed. By

1933 the Retriever breeds were separated and 84 Labradors were registered. From this humble beginning the Labrador Retriever has, at this writing, attained the number one spot in registrations of all breeds currently recognized by the American Kennel Club."

Nancy Martin, in *Legends in Labradors,* describes the first field trial held just for Labs:

The first Labrador Retriever Club (LRC) field trial was held at Glenmere, the estate of Robert Goelet in Chester, New York, on December 21, 1931. Colin MacFarlane was another of the great gamekeepers to have been brought over to raise birds and handle the dogs. He managed Glenmere, an 8,000-acre estate, a splendid place for a field trial, plenty of room, no parking problems. There were 29 starters. W. Averell Harriman and Mrs. Marshall Field were the big winning owners. There was a dress code at the trials. Tweed knickerbockers, ties and slouch hats were the outfit of the day for the men. Fur coats, stylish hats and long skirts were worn by the ladies. The night before was usually spent dining, drinking and wagering. As today, there was almost always calcutta betting on the open stake and it wasn't at all unusual for an owner to "buy" his or another's dog for $2,000 to $3,000. While the owners were enjoying the party, the trainers, handlers and dogs were no doubt trying to get a good night's sleep. Owners and trainers did not socialize with each other in the beginning, and owners rarely ran their own dogs. They had handlers to do that.

The first LRC specialty show was held in 1933 in New York City in a garage on 74th Street owned by Marshall Field. Joan Read, then still Joan

Redmond, had one of the 34 dogs entered that day. The show was superintended by George Foley. Foley was still superintending shows when I was a child. The F from Foley is the F in MB-F, the company that superintends most of the East Coast shows today.

Marshall Field judged the show. Boli of Blake, owned by Franklin P. Lord, was the Best of Breed winner, and a wonderful day was had by all. It was the beginning of modern Labrador history.

THE NATIONAL SPECIALTY

As I mentioned in Chapter 2, the club began on Long Island and the first shows and trials were held in the surrounding area. For many years the national specialty was held on the East Coast. As regional clubs began to form and become active, the national specialty started to rotate to different time zones to give more people a chance to attend and participate. Now, some years you have the convenience of being able to drive, and other years you have to fly or wait for a friend to call and tell you who won.

The national used to attract the biggest entry of Labs in the country, but now we have several regional clubs that host larger events. The Mid-Jersey, the Miami Valley Club in Ohio and the Huron River Club get entries of 500 or more. Usually the Potomac Labrador Retriever Club (held in Virginia for 19 years, and now held in Maryland for the past three years) pulls the biggest entry in the country with almost 1,000 Labrador Retrievers. It is an incredible couple of days!

AKC EQUIVALENTS

There are organizations other than the American Kennel Club that function as registering bodies and hold dog shows, such as the United Kennel Club, but the AKC is the most well-known in our country.

Most countries have their own equivalent of the AKC. In Canada it's the Canadian Kennel Club and in Britain it is The Kennel Club, or TKC. Much of Europe registers dogs and conducts competitions under the auspices of the Fédération Cynologique Internationale, or FCI. Quite a few rare breeds and breeds that are bred primarily in other countries and are not recognized by the AKC are FCI-registered.

One job of the parent club is to put on the national specialty show. At this national in 1989, Am./Can. Ch. Davoeg's Irish Gold, WC, was the big winner. (Patricia Weiss)

JOINING UP

It's not easy to join the LRC, or any parent club for any breed. You have to demonstrate a commitment to the breed, and club members must sponsor you. Membership is limited because club members decide important matters of policy, including the breed standard, and this requires breed expertise.

In a breed as numerous as Labradors, there are also other issues involved. The AKC registered 41,822 new litters of Labrador Retrievers in 1997, and 158,366 individual dogs. And that's just in one year! Because the breed is so versatile and capable, people want them to do many different jobs—jobs Labs do very well.

There are so many Labs in America that sometimes it's hard for the parent club to keep up with it all.

It can be really fun to join a local dog club that coincides with your particular interests. (Susan Willumsen)

With so many dogs doing so many things, it's not always easy for one parent club to keep up with the interests and activities of every constituency. In fact, it's almost impossible.

If I were in charge (I wish!), my solution would be to recognize two parent clubs: one to serve the people who love competing in field trials, and one to serve the conformation, hunt test and obedience folks. I think it's the best solution, considering how many people are involved in the breed.

The next best thing is to join a local club that coincides with your interests. Dog clubs don't just put on one or two dog shows a year. Today, they are apt to be the hub of a community's involvement with pets. Dog clubs conduct education seminars for dog owners at all levels, stage demonstrations of canine talent, offer training classes, organize classroom programs, lobby for positive canine legislation (and against negative laws) and much more. A dog club is a place to learn about

Labs, meet people with similar interests and keep you and your active dog busy.

There are many regional Labrador Retriever clubs (you'll find them listed in Appendix A). There are also all-breed clubs and clubs that focus on specific dog sports, such as agility, obedience or hunt tests.

To find dog clubs in your area, contact the AKC for a geographical list of its member clubs (the address is also in Appendix A). You can also check your local newspaper for listings of dog events sponsored by clubs. Then go and see if you'd like to join up.

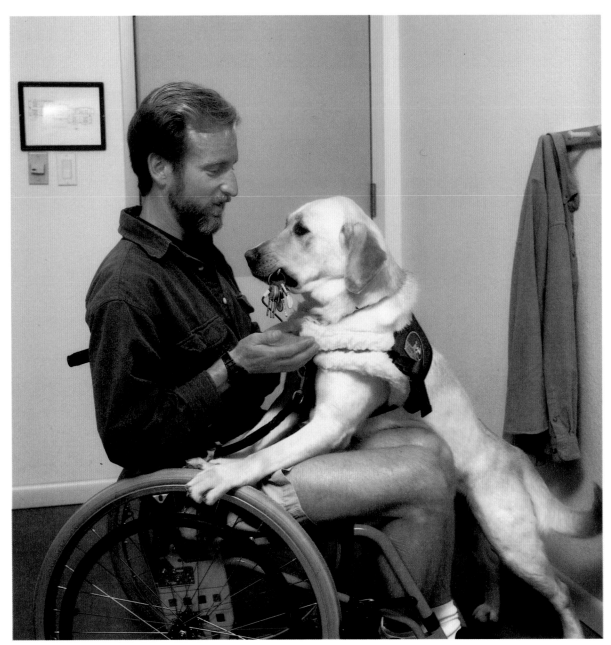

(Canine Companions for Independence)

CHAPTER 16

Labradors That Serve

The Labrador Retriever is indeed the dog that does it all. But this jack of all trades is also the master of many. With its love of work and desire to please, the Lab has made its mark in careers ranging from guiding the blind to detecting explosives and drugs.

GUIDING EYES

Although the German Shepherd Dog was originally used to guide the blind, the sturdy Labrador is now the most successful guide dog throughout the world. The British, who have a large guide dog program, were the first to try Labs. Now, every major group, in countries from the United States to Japan, has followed suit. When we visited Finland, we were pleased (but not surprised) to see the entire guide dog training kennel full of Labradors!

Guide work is different than some other forms of training, because no food is used to reward good behavior. The dog must do its job strictly out of the desire to please—and even though a Lab would try to stand on its head for a treat, it is also happy to work for the handler's praise and approval.

If you use public transportation in a big city, you will see Labradors patiently guiding their blind owners safely through the day's commute. The noise and activity don't faze them; in fact, they seem to thrive on the challenges of doing this important job. Healthy, easy to care for, instinctively protective but not overly so, the Labrador has endeared itself to guide dog owners the world over.

SERVICE FOR THE DISABLED

The idea that dogs could be used to help people with other kinds of disabilities came into being in the mid-1970s, pioneered by Canine Companions

The British were the first to use Labs as guide dogs for the blind, and this stamp honors the breed's years of service.

Frankie helps Steve Guerra get around everywhere in New York. (Guide Dog Foundation for the Blind)

for Independence. A service dog retrieves objects, turns on light switches, helps to pull a wheelchair, opens the refrigerator and performs a multitude of daily tasks for its disabled partner. These dogs know almost 100 commands!

The Labrador chosen for this special job must be very tractable and easy to control, but must also have the confidence to walk next to a moving wheelchair without worry. Thousands of disabled people have improved their quality of life with a Labrador helper to "sweat the small stuff" for them.

Both future guide dogs and service dogs are raised in foster homes. These puppy raisers are given guidance on how to begin the dog's socialization and training, so that they will succeed as adults. Puppy raisers are truly remarkable people. Imagine taking a small puppy, doing all of its early training, living through its difficult "teenage" months and then relinquishing it as a young adult. It's a special mission for special folks, but the reward of knowing that you were part of a process that makes life better for someone else is a powerful incentive. Many puppy raisers return one dog for formal training and take a new puppy in soon after. I think it's probably habit-forming!

If you think you'd like to be a puppy raiser, contact one of the organizations listed in Appendix A. They'd be glad to hear from you.

ACE DETECTORS

In the late 1970s, the New York City Police Department Bomb Squad, which had been using German Shepherds for bomb detection,

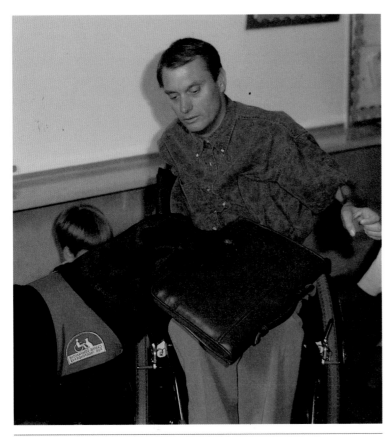

Labs can help people in wheelchairs in hundreds of ways. (Canine Companions for Independence)

dog's mind. Detector dogs are fed their daily ration by practicing their scenting skills, which keeps their training always fresh. No dog has ever been injured in this line of work.

When the creator of the bomb detection protocol retired from the NYPD, he theorized that a dog could also be taught to detect accelerants, such as gasoline, kerosene and lighter fluid. The federal Bureau of Alcohol, Tobacco and Firearms then established an accelerant detector program to help investigators determine if arson caused a fire. The dog is trained in the same way, with food rewards and daily lessons. The handler and dog search a fire scene, and the dog responds to minute traces of about 20 different accelerants by sitting and indicating the spot where it detects the scent. Samples can then be collected for analysis.

The dogs are more accurate than the most sophisticated equipment, and greatly reduce the time and effort needed to collect evidence of arson. On at least one occasion, an arson dog, while leaving its investigation, detected accelerant on an onlooker, sat, and helped to solve the crime by finding the perpetrator!

The Bureau of Alcohol, Tobacco and Firearms has also collaborated with the State Department to train bomb dogs and handlers for antiterrorist work in the Middle East and South America. Labradors work in Greece, Turkey, Cyprus, Chile

experimented with a guide dog dropout named Charlie. Since the training system was based on food rewards, Charlie the Labrador excelled, and another career opened up for the Lab.

Unaffected by noise or confusion, the single-minded Labrador does its job by sniffing for explosives and indicating their discovery by sitting down. The dog immediately receives a food reward, which links the scent and the reward in the

This is Phyllis Herrington, Consumer Outreach Coordinator at the Guide Dog Foundation for the Blind. Her dog, Hobson, is a grandson of top show dog Ch. Marshland Blitz. (Guide Dog Foundation for the Blind)

and Israel, protecting airports from terrorist attack. One Labrador found a cache of explosives buried deep underground, when electronic equipment couldn't detect its presence. The skies are definitely safer with these detectors on duty!

The most recent development in this field is the weapons detector dog. Charlie (yes, another

Charlie, also a guide dog with a career change) was trained using the same food reward system. He can detect ammunition from many different weapons, and works worldwide at events like the Olympics, the Super Bowl and visits by officials of foreign governments.

KEEPING OUT DRUGS

At airports and border crossings, you'll find Labradors working for the U.S. Customs Bureau as drug detectors. These dogs work in two ways. Some scan incoming baggage for traces of narcotics and paw at the source. This is called active alert. Passive alert dogs are walked through crowds at airports, and sit to indicate the scent. Customs dogs are rewarded by a game of tug-of-war with a towel. This high-energy play keeps the dog's excitement level up. The typical drug detector

The Lab's basic love of work and of people gives it amazing versatility as a service dog, and as a cherished companion. (Canine Companions for Independence)

This Lab detects explosives for the Greek government. He's a graduate of a training program sponsored by the Connecticut State Police.

CANINE CUSTOMS CARDS

To honor its drug detecting dogs, the U.S. Customs Service made up a set of All-Star trading cards. This one shows Nike, who has sniffed out almost $14 million in illegal drugs. Nike's most notable bust was finding 1,266 pounds of cocaine in three crates hidden in a truck.

dog is a high-energy extrovert, compared to its more sedate cousins doing bomb and arson work.

LABS TO THE RESCUE

Labradors are also used for search and rescue work, looking for lost people or survivors of disasters. Search and rescue dogs work very closely with their handlers (as do all service dogs), and these teams are highly trained specialists.

I believe the Labrador's amazing versatility is based on its inborn love of work and desire to be our partner in that work. New jobs for dogs, such as seizure alert dogs that can foretell an oncoming seizure before the handler is aware of it, are being developed all the time. And always at the forefront is the loveable, versatile Labrador Retriever.

Resources

NATIONAL CLUBS

The American Kennel Club
5580 Centerview Drive
Suite 200
Raleigh NC 27606-3390
(919) 233-9767
www.akc.org

The Labrador Retriever Club, Inc.
Christopher Wincek, Esq., Secretary
12471 Pond Road
Burton, OH 44201
thelabradorclub.com

REGIONAL LABRADOR RETRIEVER CLUBS

Central Ohio Labrador Retriever Club
Jan Eichensehr
5414 Vinewood Court
Columbus, OH 43229

Golden Gate Labrador Retriever Club
Georgia Burg
16306 Redwood Lodge Road
Los Gatos, CA 95030

Labrador Retriever Club of Southern California
Trudy Sonesen
25562 Toledo Way
Lake Forest, CA 92630

San Joaquin Valley Labrador Retriever Club
Laura Fletcher
144 Loma Vista
Modesto, CA 95354

Labrador Retriever Club of Greater Denver
Kris Beam
16588 Telluride Street
Brighton, CO 80601

Labrador Retriever Club of the Pioneer Valley
June Cook
51 Herrman Street, West
Springfield, MA 01089

Labrador Retriever Club of Central Connecticut
Julie Pease
95 Thankful Stow Road
Guilford, CT 06437

Labrador Retriever Club of Southern Connecticut
Ellen Plasil
5 Smoke Rise Ridge
Newtown, CT 06470

Labrador Retriever Club of Long Island
Jackie Savelli
24 Old Orchard Lane
Ridge, NY 11961

Labrador Retriever Club of Greater Atlanta
Greg and Tricia Lynch
565 Teresa Lane
Canton, GA 30115

Labrador Retriever Club of Hawaii
Marie Tanner
5-138 Kuahelani Avenue 120
Mililani, HI 96789

Hoosier Labrador Retriever Club
Debbie Brown
836 E. CR 500 N.
Pittsboro, IN 46167

Jersey Skylands Labrador Retriever Club
Donna Forte
2 Sharon Drive
Sparta, NJ 07871

Winnebago Labrador Retriever Club
Barbara J. Holl
1291 Joliet Street
Dyer, IN 46311

Shawnee Mission Labrador Retriever Club
Russ Swift
8956 Conser
Overland Park, KS 66212

Labrador Retriever Club of Greater Boston
Evelyn Cummings
401 Skitchewaug Trail
Springfield, VT 05156

Huron River Labrador Retriever Club
Lorry Wagner
9362 Hamburg Road
Brighton, MI 48116

Labrador Retriever Club of the Twin Cities
Linda Weikert
51767 Highway 57 Boulevard
Wanamingo, MN 55983

Mid-Jersey Labrador Retriever Club
Tony Ciprian
386 Stokes Road
Shamong, NJ 08088

Labrador Retriever Club of Albuquerque
Juxi Burr
4401 Yale Boulevard NE
Albuquerque, NM 87107

Iroquois Labrador Retriever Club
Ken Adams
935 Paul Road
Rochester, NY 14624

Labrador Retriever Club of the Piedmont
Colleen Kincaid
141 Lauren Court
Gastonia, NC 28056

Labrador Retriever Club of the Potomac
Sandy Schroeder
590 Treslow Glen Drive
Severna Park, MD 21146

Raleigh Durham Labrador Retriever Club
Tara Glodic
2700 McNeil Street
Raleigh, NC 27608

Miami Valley Labrador Retriever Club
Martha Couch
4010 Idlewild Road
Burlington, KY 41005

Rose City Labrador Retriever Club
Cindy Stuner
8555 N. Allegheny Avenue
Portland, OR 97203

Dallas Fort Worth Labrador Retriever Club
Marion Harris
1780 Chapman Court
Aledo, TX 76008

Puget Sound Labrador Retriever Club
Barb Ironside
4117 143rd Avenue SE
Snohomish, WA 98290

SERVICE DOG ORGANIZATIONS

Guide Dog Foundation for the Blind Inc.
371 E. Jericho Turnpike
Smithtown, NY 11787
(516) 265-2121
www.guidedog.org

Guide Dogs for the Blind
P.O. Box 151200
San Rafael, CA 94915
(415) 499-4000
www.guidedogs.com

International Guiding Eyes
13445 Glenoaks Boulevard
Sylmar, CA 91342
(818) 362-5834

Guide Dogs of the Desert
P.O. Box 1692
Palm Springs, CA 92263
(619) 329-6257
www.pubs-r-us.com/gdod/gdog.htm

Southeastern Guide Dogs
4210 77th Street East
Palmetto, FL 34221
(941) 729-5665
www.bhip.infi.net/~segd/segd.home

Leader Dogs
1039 South Rochester Road
Rochester, MI 48307
(810) 651-9011
www.leaderdog.org

The Seeing Eye
Washington Valley Road
Morristown, NJ 07963-4425
(973) 539-4425
www.seeingeye.org

Guiding Eyes for the Blind
611 Granite Springs Road
Yorktown Heights, NY 10598
(914) 245-4024
www.guiding-eyes.org

Pilot Dogs
625 West Town Street
Columbus, OH 432215-4496
(614) 221-6367

Canine Companions for Independence
P.O. Box 446
Santa Rosa, CA 95407-0446
(800) 572-2275
www.caninecompanions.org

Therapy Dogs International (TDI)
6 Hilltop Road
Mendham, NJ 07945

SPORT AND ACTIVITY GROUPS

U.S. Dog Agility Association
P.O. Box 850955
Richardson, TX 63125
(972) 231-9700
www.usdaa.com

North American Dog Agility Council
HCR 2, Box 277
St. Maries, ID 83861
www.teleport.com/~jhaglund/nadachom.htm

Agility Homepage
www.dogpatch.org/agility

HEALTH REGISTRIES

Orthopedic Foundation for Animals (OFA)
2300 Nifong Boulevard
University of Missouri
Columbia, MO 65211
(573) 442-0418
www.ofa.org

PennHip
International Canine Genetics
271 Great Valley Parkway
Malvern, PA 19355
(800) 248-8099

Canine Eye Registration Foundation (CERF)
South Campus Courts, Building C
Purdue University
West Lafayette, IN 47907
(317) 494-8179
www.vet.purdue.edu/~yshen/cerf.html

Titles a Labrador Retriever Can Earn

AMERICAN KENNEL CLUB TITLES

Conformation and Dual Titles

Championship titles always precede a dog's name.

Ch.	Conformation Champion
DC or Dual Ch.	Conformation and Field Champion
TC	Triple Champion (CH, FC and OTCh)
CT	Champion Tracker

Obedience Titles

CD   Companion Dog
CDX   Companion Dog Excellent
UD   Utility Dog
UDX   Utility Dog Excellent
OTCh   Obedience Trial Champion

Field Trial Titles

FC   Field Champion
AFC   Amateur Field Champion
FC/AFC FC and AFC

Hunting Titles

JH   Junior Hunter
SH   Senior Hunter
MH   Master Hunter

Tracking Titles

TD   Tracking Dog
TDX   Tracking Dog Excellent
VST   Variable Surface Tracking Dog

Combination Titles

UDT   Utilty Dog Tracker
UDTX   Utility Dog Tracker Excellent

Agility Titles

NA	Novice Agility
OA	Open Agility
AX	Agility Excellent
MX	Master Agility

Canine Good Citizen

Although CGC is an AKC program, the title is not officially recognized. While you may put it after the dog's name, it will not appear on an official AKC pedigree.

CGC	Canine Good Citizen

LABRADOR RETRIEVER CLUB TITLES

WC	Working Certificate
WCX	Working Certificate Excellent

NORTH AMERICAN DOG AGILITY COUNCIL TITLES

NAC	Novice Agility Certificate
OAC	Open Agility Certificate
EAC	Elite Agility Certificate
NATCh.	NADAC Agility Champion

Titles are also available for different classes, such as Gamblers and Jumpers. These would be NGC, OGC, EGC, and so on.

United States Dog Agility Association Titles

AD	Agility Dog
AAD	Advanced Agility Dog
MAD	Master Agility Dog
JM	Jumpers Master Dog
GN	Gamblers Master Dog
SM	Snooker Master Dog
RM	Relay Master Dog
VAD	Veteran Agility Dog
ADCh.	Agility Dog Champion

North American Flyball Association Titles

FD	Flyball Dog
FDX	Flyball Dog Excellent
FDCh.	Flyball Dog Champion
FM	Flyball Master
FMX	Flyball Master Excellent
FMCh.	Flyball Master Champion
FGDCh.	Flyball Grand Champion

Other Titles

TD	Therapy Dog
TDI	Therapy Dog International
TT	Temperament Test of the ATTS
SKC Ch.	States Kennel Club Champion
UCI Int. Ch.	International Champion, earned in the U.S.
Int. Ch.	International Champion

COMMON ABBREVIATIONS USED AT DOG EVENTS

BIS	Best in Show
BOB	Best of Breed
BOS	Best of Opposite Sex
BISS	Best in Specialty Sweepstakes
BOSS	Best of Opposite Sex Specialty Sweepstakes
WD	Winners Dog
WB	Winners Bitch
RWD	Reserve Winners Dog
RWB	Reserve Winners Bitch
BW	Best of Winners
JAM	Judge's Award of Merit (used in dog shows and field events)
Reserve JAM	JAM that is fifth place
HIT	High in Trial
HC	High Combined (from Open and Utility obedience classes)
OAA	Open All-Age Stake (field events)
AAA	Amateur All-Age stake (field events)
LAA	Limited All-Age stake (only Qualified All-Age dogs may compete)

You'll find your Lab will enjoy just about any sport you enjoy.

Ch. Tabatha's Windfall Abbey, WCX, JH

Recent National Specialty Winners

1997   **Fawnhaven's Sonny Boy,** owned by Fred and Linda Wakely, bred by Don and Barbara Ironside

1996   **Ch. Chablais Myrtille,** bred and owned by Jean-Louis Blais and Madeleine Charest

1995   **Ch. Hickory Ridge Gustav Mahler,** bred and owned by Robert T. LeBlanc and Arden LeBlanc

1994   **Campbellcroft P.B. Max, CD, JH,** owned by Peggie and W. E. Roberts and Virginia Campbell, bred by Donald and Virginia Campbell

1993   **Tabatha's Dazzle,** bred and owned by Carol Heidl

1992   **Ch. Breezy's Whirlwind, JH,** owned by Jackie McFarlane and Gordon Sousa, bred by Gordon Sousa

1991   **Ch. Chocorua's Seabreeze,** bred and owned by Marion Lyons

1990   **Ch. Chelon's Firestorm,** bred and owned by Cheryl and Lon Ostenson

1989   **Ch. Davoeg's Irish Gold, WC,** owned by Bob and Sylvia Shandley, bred by John Doherty

1988   **Ch. Tabatha's Windfall Abbey, WCX, JH,** owned by Annie and Ron Cogo, bred by Carol Heidl

1987   **Ch. Campbellcroft's Angus, CD,** bred and owned by Donald and Virginia Campbell

1986   **Ch. Ramblin's Amaretto, WC,** owned by Anne K. Jones, bred by M. Peckham and Georgia Gooch

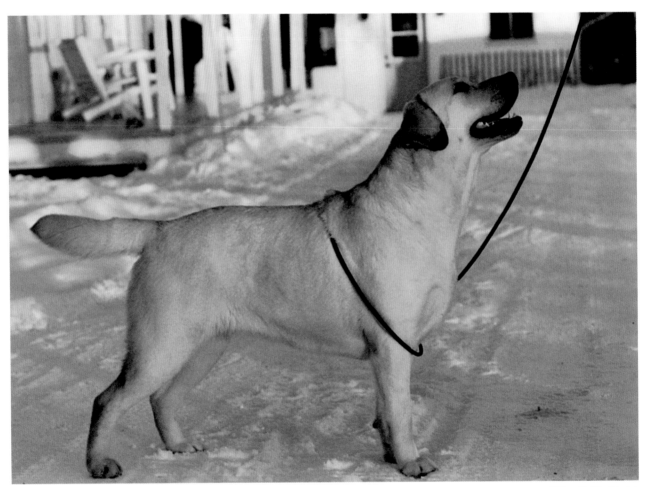

(Chenil Chablais)

APPENDIX D

The Labrador Retriever Standard Through History

It can be interesting to look at different standards that have been used for the same breed because changes in the standard often reflect changes in thinking about the breed. We'll start with two U.S. standards: The current one, and the standard that was in effect in the U.S. from 1957 until 1994. Then we'll look at two British standards. The one that was revised in 1988 is, I believe, the best. It is succinct and to the point, and gives a clear picture of the Labrador Retriever. It is also the standard used by most fanciers outside the United States. The final standard is the one drawn up in England in 1916—the first standard for the Labrador Retriever.

THE CURRENT U.S. STANDARD

GENERAL APPEARANCE—The Labrador Retriever is a strongly built, medium-sized, short-coupled, dog possessing a sound, athletic, well-balanced conformation that enables it to function as a retrieving gun dog; the substance and soundness to hunt waterfowl or upland game for long hours under difficult conditions; the character and quality to win in the show ring; and the temperament to be a family companion. Physical features and mental characteristics should denote a dog bred to perform as an efficient Retriever of game with a stable temperament suitable for a variety of pursuits beyond the hunting environment.

The most distinguishing characteristics of the Labrador Retriever are its short, dense, weather resistant coat; an "otter" tail; a clean-cut head with broad back skull and moderate stop; powerful jaws; and its "kind," friendly eyes, expressing character, intelligence and good temperament. Above all, a Labrador Retriever must be well balanced, enabling it to move in the show ring or work in the field with little or no effort. The typical Labrador possesses style and quality without over refinement, and substance without lumber or cloddiness. The Labrador is bred primarily as a working gun dog; structure and soundness are of great importance.

SIZE, PROPORTION AND SUBSTANCE

Size—The height at the withers for a dog is 22½ to 24½ inches; for a bitch it is 21½ to 23½ inches. Any variance greater than one-half inch above or below these heights is a *disqualification*. Approximate weight of dogs and bitches in working condition: dogs 65 to 80 pounds; bitches 55 to 70 pounds.

The minimum height ranges set forth in the paragraph above shall not apply to dogs or bitches under 12 months of age.

Proportion—Short-coupled; length from the point of the shoulder to the point of the rump is equal to or slightly longer than the distance from the withers to the ground. Distance from the elbow to the ground should be equal to one half of the height at the withers. The brisket should extend to the elbows, but not perceptibly deeper. The body must be of sufficient length to permit a straight, free and efficient stride; but the dog should never appear low and long or tall and leggy in outline.

Substance—Substance and bone proportionate to the overall dog. Light, "weedy" individuals are definitely incorrect; equally objectionable are cloddy lumbering specimens. Labrador Retrievers shall be shown in working condition well-muscled and without excess fat.

HEAD

Skull—The skull should be wide; well developed but without exaggeration. The skull and foreface should be on parallel planes and of approximately equal length. There should be a moderate stop—the brow slightly pronounced so that the skull is not absolutely in a straight line with the nose. The brow ridges aid in defining the stop. The head should be clean-cut and free from fleshy cheeks; the bony structure of the skull chiseled beneath the eye with no prominence in the cheek. The skull may show some median line; the occipital bone is not conspicuous in mature dogs. Lips should not be squared off or pendulous, but fall away in a curve toward the throat. A wedge-shape head, or a head long and narrow in muzzle and back skull is incorrect, as are massive, cheeky heads. The jaws are powerful and free from snipiness—the muzzle neither long and narrow nor short and stubby.

Nose—The nose should be wide and the nostrils well-developed. The nose should be black on black or yellow dogs, and brown on chocolates. Nose color fading to a lighter shade is not a fault. A thoroughly pink nose or one lacking in any pigment is a *disqualification*.

Teeth—The teeth should be strong and regular with a scissors bite; the lower teeth just behind, but touching the inner side of the upper incisors. A level bite is acceptable, but not desirable. Undershot, overshot, or misaligned teeth are *serious faults*. Full dentition is preferred. Missing molars or pre-molars are *serious faults*.

Ears—The ears should hang moderately close to the head, set rather far back, and somewhat low on the skull; slightly above eye level. Ears should not be large and heavy, but in proportion with the skull and reach to the inside of the eye when pulled forward.

Eyes—Kind, friendly eyes imparting good temperament, intelligence and alertness are a hallmark of the breed. They should be of medium size, set well apart, and neither protruding nor deep set. Eye color should be brown in black and yellow Labradors, and brown or hazel in chocolates. Black, or yellow eyes give a harsh expression and are undesirable. Small eyes, set close together or round prominent eyes are not typical of the breed. Eye rims are black in black and yellow Labradors; and brown in chocolates. Eye rims without pigmentation is a *disqualification*.

NECK, TOPLINE AND BODY

Neck—The neck should be of proper length to allow the dog to retrieve game easily. It should be muscular and free from throatiness. The neck should rise strongly from the shoulders with a moderate arch. A short, thick neck or a "ewe" neck is incorrect.

Topline—The back is strong and the topline is level from the withers to the croup when standing or moving. However, the loin should show evidence of flexibility for athletic endeavor.

Body—The Labrador should be short-coupled, with good spring of ribs tapering to a moderately wide chest. The Labrador should not be narrow chested; giving the appearance of hollowness between the front legs, nor should it have a wide spreading, bulldog-like front. Correct chest conformation will result in tapering between the front legs that allows unrestricted forelimb movement. Chest breadth that is either too wide or too narrow for efficient movement and stamina is incorrect. Slab-sided individuals are not typical of the breed; equally objectionable are rotund or barrel chested specimens. The underline is almost straight, with little or no tuck-up in mature animals. Loins should be short, wide and strong; extending to well developed, powerful hindquarters. When viewed from the side, the Labrador Retriever shows a well-developed, but not exaggerated forechest.

Tail—The tail is a distinguishing feature of the breed. It should be very thick at the base, gradually tapering toward the tip, of medium length, and extending no longer than to the hock. The tail should be free from feathering and clothed thickly all around with the Labrador's short, dense coat, thus having that peculiar rounded appearance that has been described as the "otter" tail. The tail should follow the topline in repose or when in motion. It may be carried gaily, but should not curl over the back. Extremely short tails or long, thin tails are *serious faults*. The tail completes the balance of the Labrador by giving it a flowing line from the top of the head to the tip of the tail. Docking or otherwise altering the length or natural carriage of the tail is a *disqualification*.

FOREQUARTERS—Forequarters should be muscular, well coordinated and balanced with the hindquarters.

Shoulders—The shoulders are well laid-back, long and sloping, forming an angle with the upper arm of approximately 90 degrees that permits the dog to move his forelegs in an easy manner with strong forward reach. Ideally, the length of the shoulder blade should equal the length of the upper arm. Straight shoulder blades, short upper arms or heavily muscled or loaded shoulders, all restricting free movement, are incorrect.

Front Legs—When viewed from the front, the legs should be straight with good strong bone. Too much bone is as undesirable as too little bone, and short legged, heavy boned individuals are not typical of the breed. Viewed from the side, the elbows should be directly under the withers, and the front legs should be perpendicular to the ground and well under the body. The elbows should be close to the ribs without looseness. Tied-in elbows or being "out at the elbows" interfere with free movement and are *serious faults*. Pasterns should be strong and short and should slope slightly from the perpendicular line of the leg. Feet are strong and compact, with well-arched toes and well-developed pads. Dew claws may be removed. Splayed feet, hare feet, knuckling over, or feet turning in or out are *serious faults*.

HINDQUARTERS—The Labrador's hindquarters are broad, muscular and well-developed from the hip to the hock with well-turned stifles and strong short hocks. Viewed from the rear, the hind legs are straight and parallel. Viewed from the side, the angulation of the rear legs is in balance with the front. The hind legs are strongly boned, muscled with moderate angulation at the stifle, and powerful, clearly defined thighs. The stifle is strong and there is no slippage of the patellae while in motion or when standing. The hock joints are strong, well let down and do not slip or hyper-extend while in motion or when standing. Angulation of both stifle and hock joint is such as to achieve the optimal balance of drive and traction. When standing the rear toes are only slightly behind the point of the rump. Over angulation produces a sloping topline not typical of the breed. Feet are strong and compact, with well-arched toes and well-developed pads. Cow-hocks, spread hocks, sickle hocks and over-angulation are serious structural defects and are to be *faulted*.

COAT—The coat is a distinctive feature of the Labrador Retriever. It should be short, straight and very dense, giving a fairly hard feeling to the hand. The Labrador should have a soft, weather-resistant undercoat that provides protection from water, cold and all types of ground cover. A slight wave down the back is permissible. Woolly coats, soft silky coats, and sparse slick coats are not typical of the breed, and should be severely penalized.

COLOR—The Labrador Retriever coat colors are black, yellow and chocolate. Any other color or a combination of colors is a *disqualification*. A small white spot on the chest is permissible, but not desirable. White hairs from aging or scarring are not to be misinterpreted as brindling. *Black*—Blacks are all black. A black with brindle markings or a black with tan markings is a *disqualification*. *Yellow*—Yellows may range in color from fox-red to light cream, with variations in shading on the ears, back, and underparts of the dog. *Chocolate*—Chocolates can vary in shade from light to dark chocolate. Chocolate with brindle or tan markings is a *disqualification*.

MOVEMENT—Movement of the Labrador Retriever should be free and effortless. When watching a dog move toward oneself, there should be no sign of elbows out. Rather, the elbows should be held neatly to the body with the legs not too close together. Moving straight forward without pacing or weaving, the legs should form straight lines, with all parts moving in the same plane. Upon viewing the dog from the rear, one should have the impression that the hind legs move as nearly as possible in a parallel line with the front legs. The hocks should do their full share of the work, flexing well, giving the appearance of power and strength. When viewed from the side, the shoulders should move freely and effortlessly, and the foreleg should reach forward close to the ground with extension. A short, choppy movement or high knee action indicates a straight shoulder; paddling indicates long, weak pasterns; and a short, stilted rear gait indicates a straight rear assembly; all are serious faults. Movement faults interfering with performance including weaving; side-winding; crossing over; high knee action; paddling; and short, choppy movement, should be severely penalized.

TEMPERAMENT—True Labrador Retriever temperament is as much a hallmark of the breed as the "otter" tail. The ideal disposition is one of a kindly, outgoing, tractable nature; eager to please and non-aggressive towards man or animal. The Labrador has much that appeals to people; his gentle ways, intelligence and adaptability make him an ideal dog. Aggressiveness towards humans or other animals, or any evidence of shyness in an adult should be *severely penalized.*

DISQUALIFICATIONS

1. *Any deviation from the height prescribed in the Standard.*

2. *A thoroughly pink nose or one lacking in any pigment.*

3. *Eye rims without pigment.*

4. *Docking or otherwise altering the length or natural carriage of the tail.*

5. *Any other color or a combination of colors other than black, yellow or chocolate as described in the Standard.*

U.S. STANDARD, 1957 TO 1994

General Appearance
The general appearance of the Labrador Retriever should be that of a strongly built, short coupled, very active dog. He should be fairly wide over the loins, and strong and muscular in the hindquarters. The coat should be close, short, dense and free from feather.

Head
The skull should be wide, giving brain room: There should be a slight stop, i.e., the brow should be slightly pronounced, so that the skull is not absolutely in a straight line with the nose. The head should be clean-cut and free from fleshy cheeks. The jaws should be long and powerful and free from snipiness; the nose should be wide and the nostrils well developed. Teeth should be strong and regular, with a level mouth. The ears should hang moderately close to the head, rather far back, should be set somewhat low and not be large and heavy. The eyes should be of medium size, expressing great intelligence and good temper, and can be brown, yellow or black, but brown and black is preferred.

Neck and Chest
The neck should be medium length, powerful and not throaty. The shoulders should be long and sloping. The chest must be of good width and depth, the ribs well sprung and the loins wide and strong, stifles well turned, and the hindquarters well developed and of great power.

Legs and Feet
The legs must be straight from the shoulder to the ground, and the feet compact with toes well arched, and pads well developed, the hocks should be well

bent, and the dog must neither be cowhocked nor be too wide behind; in fact, he must stand and move true all round on legs and feet. Legs should be of medium length, showing good bone and muscle, but not so short as to be out of balance with the rest of the body. In fact, a dog well balanced in all points is preferable to one with outstanding good qualities and defects.

Tail

The tail is a distinctive feature of the breed; it should be very thick towards the base, gradually tapering towards the tip, of medium length, should be free from any feathering, and should be clothed thickly all round with the Labrador's short, thick, dense coat, thus giving the peculiar "rounded" appearance which has been described as the "otter" tail. The tail may be carried gaily but should not curl over the back.

Coat

The coat is another very distinctive feature; it should be short, very dense and without wave, and should give a fairly hard feeling to the hand.

Color

The colors are black, yellow, and chocolate and are evaluated as follows:

(a) *Blacks:* All black, with a small white spot on chest permissible.

(b) *Yellows:* Yellows may vary in color from fox-red to light cream with variations in the shading of the coat on the ears, the underparts of the dog, or beneath the tail. A small white spot on chest is permissible. Eye

coloring and expression should be the same as that of the blacks, with black or dark brown eye rims. The nose should also be black or dark brown, although "fading" to pink in winter weather is not serious. A "Dudley" nose (pink without pigmentation) should be penalized.

(c) *Chocolates:* Shades ranging from light sedge to chocolate. A small white spot on the chest is permissible. Eyes to be light brown to clear yellow. Nose and eye-rim pigmentation dark brown or liver colored. "Fading" to pink in winter weather not serious. "Dudley" nose should be penalized.

Movement

Movement should be free and effortless. The forelegs should be strong, straight and true, and correctly placed. Watching a dog move towards one, there should be no signs of elbows being out in front, but neatly held to the body with legs not too close together, and moving straight forward without pacing or weaving. Upon viewing the dog from the rear, one should get the impression that the hind legs, which should be well muscled and not cowhocked, move as nearly parallel as possible, with hocks doing their full share of work and flexing well, thus giving the appearance of power and strength.

Approximate Weights of dogs and bitches in working condition: Dogs, 60 to 75 pounds; bitches, 55 to 70 pounds.

Height at Shoulders: Dogs, 22 ½ inches to 24 ½ inches; bitches, 21½ to 23½ inches.

CURRENT BRITISH STANDARD

General Appearance
Strongly built, short coupled, very active; broad in skull; broad and deep through chest and ribs; broad and strong over loins and hindquarters.

Characteristics
Good tempered, very agile. Excellent nose, soft mouth; keen love of water. Adaptable, devoted companion.

Temperament
Intelligent, keen, and biddable, with a strong will to please. Kindly nature, with no trace of aggression or undue shyness.

Head and Skull
Skull broad with defined stop; clean cut without fleshy cheeks. Jaws of medium length, powerful, not snipey. Nose wide, nostrils well developed.

Eyes
Medium size, expressing intelligence and good temper; brown or hazel.

Ears
Not large or heavy, hanging close to head and set rather far back.

Mouth
Jaws and teeth strong, with a perfect, regular, and complete scissor bite, i.e., the upper teeth closely overlapping the lower teeth and set square to the jaws.

Neck
Clean, strong, powerful, set into well-placed shoulders.

Forequarters
Shoulders long and sloping. Forelegs well-boned and straight from elbow to ground when viewed from either front or side.

Body
Chest of good width and depth, with well-sprung barrel ribs. Level topline. Loins wide, short coupled and strong.

Hindquarters
Well-developed, not sloping to tail; well turned stifle. Hocks well let down, cow-hocks highly undesirable.

Gait/Movement
Free, covering adequate ground; straight and true in front and rear.

Coat
Distinctive feature, short dense without wave or feathering, giving fairly hard feel to the touch; weather resistant undercoat.

Colour
Wholly black, yellow or liver/chocolate. Yellows range from light cream to red fox. Small white spot on chest permissible.

Size
Ideal height at withers: Dogs 56–57 cms (22–22½ ins). Bitches 54–56 cms (21½–22 ins).

Faults
Any departure from the foregoing points should be considered a fault and seriousness with which the fault should be regarded should be in exact proportion to its degree.

Note

Male animals should have two apparently normal testicles fully descended into the scrotum.

THE 1916 ENGLISH STANDARD

General Description

The general appearance of the Labrador should be that of a strongly-built, short-coupled, very active dog. Compared with the Wavy or Flat-Coated Retriever he should be wider in head, wider through the chest and ribs, wider and stronger over the loins and hindquarters. The coat should be close, short, dense and free from feather.

Detailed Description

Head

The skull should be wide, giving brain room: there should be a slight "stop," i.e., the brow should be slightly pronounced so that the skull is absolutely in a straight line with the nose. The head should be clean cut and free from fleshy cheeks. The jaws should be long and powerful and quite free from snipiness or exaggeration in length; the nose should be wide and the nostrils well developed. The ears should hang moderately close to the head, rather far back, and should be set somewhat low and not be large and heavy. The eyes should be of medium size, expressing great intelligence and good temper, and can be brown, yellow, or black.

Neck and Chest

The neck should be long and powerful and the shoulders long and sloping. The chest must be of good width and depth, the ribs well sprung and the loin wide and strong, stifles well turned and the hindquarters well developed and great power.

Legs and Feet

The legs must be straight from the shoulder to ground, and the feet compact with toes well arched and pads well developed; the hocks should be well bent and the dog must neither be cow-hocked nor move too wide behind; in fact, he must stand and move true all round on legs and feet.

Tail

The tail is a distinctive feature of the breed; it should be very thick towards the base, gradually tapering towards the tip, of medium length, should be practically free from any feathering, but should be clothed thickly all around with the Labrador's short, dense, thick coat, thus giving that peculiar "rounded" appearance which has been described as the "otter" tail. The tail may be carried gaily, but should not curl too far over the back.

Coat

The coat is another very distinctive feature; it should be short, very dense, and without wave and should give a fairly hard feeling to the hand.

Colour

The colour is generally black, free from any rustiness and any white markings except possibly a small spot on the chest. Other whole colours are permissible.

Important Pedigrees

S tudying pedigrees can tell you a lot about a dog. For example, if a sire or dam produces a great many champions, it will subsequently be found in the pedigrees of many top dogs. And the ability to produce excellent specimens of the breed is what makes a dog truly great—it is far more important than wins in the show ring.

In the pedigrees of these dogs, you will find the names of the great dogs that came before them. They, in turn, will turn up in the pedigrees of their many excellent offspring.

Studying pedigrees also helps you understand how a breeder shapes a breeding program, using certain bloodlines to his or her best advantage. And it helps you see how bloodlines intersect, and what the result was. Look closely here and you will see the same kennel names popping up again and again.

Pedigrees read from left to right; the farther to the right you go, the farther back in time. The sire's name always appears above the dam's, so from top to bottom you'll see dog, bitch, dog, bitch. When you see a letter in parentheses after a dog's name, it denotes the color: Y for yellow, B for black and C for chocolate. This helps breeders study the inheritance of color.

Receiver of Cranspire (Kendall Herr)

AM./ENG. CH. RECEIVER OF CRANSPIRE (Y)

Dutch Ch. Cranspire Skytrain (Y)

- Cambremer Petrocelli (Y)
  - Eng. Ch. Poolstead Problem (Y)
    - Aust./Eng. Ch. Sandylands My Lad (Y)
      - Eng. Ch. Sandylands Mark
      - Sandylands Good Gracious
    - Poolstead Pussy Willow (Y)
      - Eng. Ch. Cornlands Kimvalley Crofter
      - Eng. Ch. Poolstead Kinley Willow
  - Braunspath Simona of Cambremer (Y)
    - Eng. Ch. Longley Count-On (Y)
      - Sandylands Charlie Boy
      - Sandylands Go Lightly of Longley
    - Polyester of Sixhills (Y)
      - Eng. Ch. Sandylands Tandy
      - Lawnwoods Fancy Free

- Poolstead Purpose of Cranspire (Y)
  - Elvelege Turmeric (Y)
    - Sandylands Jayncourt Tally-Ho (Y)
      - Eng. Ch. Sandylands Tandy
      - Jayncourt Star-Misty
    - Merriveen Matilda (Y)
      - Eng. Ch. Timspring Little Tuc
      - Merry Joy Spring Rapture
  - Eng. Ch. Poolstead Purdey (Y)
    - Eng. Ch. Sandylands Mark (B)
      - Eng. Ch. Reanacre Mallardhurn Thunder
      - Eng. Ch. Sandylands Truth
    - Eng. Ch. Poolstead Popularity (Y)
      - Eng. Ch. Sandylands Tandy
      - Poolstead Pussy Willow

Polly's Pride of Genisval (Y)

- Eng. Ch. Newinn Kestrel (Y)
  - Eng. Ch. Keysun Teko of Blondella (B)
    - Eng. Ch. Sandylands Mark (B)
      - Eng. Ch. Reanacre Mallardhurn Thunder
      - Eng. Ch. Sandylands Truth
    - Keysun June Rose (Y)
      - Eng. Ch. Kingsbury Nokeener Moonstar
      - Keysun Sweet and Lovely
  - Newinn Fleur (Y)
    - Eng. Ch. Poolstead Problem (Y)
      - Aust./Eng. Ch. Sandylands My Lad
      - Poolstead Pussy Willow
    - Newinn Angelina (Y)
      - Eng. Ch. Sandylands Tandy
      - Newinn Sandylands Catrina

- Heatherbourne Genista (Y)
  - Heatherbourne Silver Crown (Y)
    - Sandylands Charlie Boy (Y)
      - Cliveruth Harvester
      - Eng. Ch. Sandylands Katrina of Keithray
    - Eng. Ch. Heatherbourne Harefield Silver Penny (Y)
      - Eng. Ch. Candlemas Rookwood Silver Moonlight
      - Harefield Honey of Nijusa
  - Grace of Heatherbourne (Y)
    - Eng. Ch. Heatherbourne Laughing Cavalier (Y)
      - Eng. Ch. Gay Piccolo of Lawnwood
      - Eng. Ch. Poolstead Personality of Lawnwood
    - Parklyn Josie (Y)
      - Eng. Ch. Sandylands Garry
      - Parklyn Julia

Dickendall Arnold at 9½ (Kendall Herr)

Dickendall's Ruffy (Richard Herr)

CH. DICKENDALL ARNOLD

			Eng. Ch. Poolstead Problem
		Cambremer Petrocelli	**Braunspath Simona of**
	Dutch Ch. Cranspire		**Cambremer**
	Skytrain (Y)	**Poolstead Purpose of**	**Elvelege Turmeric**
Am./Eng. Ch. Receiver of		**Cranspire**	**Eng. Ch. Poolstead Purdey**
Cranspire (Y)			**Eng. Ch. Keysun Teko of**
		Eng. Ch. Newinn Kestrel	**Blondella**
	Polly's Pride of Genisval (Y)		**Newinn Fleur**
Ch. Dickendall's Ruffy,		**Heatherbourne Genista**	**Heatherbourne Silver Crown**
WC, SH (B)			**Grace of Heatherbourne**
		Eng. Ch. Mansergh Moose	**Ch. Dale of Tarmac**
	Ch. Eireannach Black		**Musquash of Mansergh**
	Coachman (B)	**Powhatan Sable**	**Powhatan Chief**
Ch. Moorwood Jewel (B)			**Powhatan Corn**
		Ch. Somersett Cider of	**Eng. Ch. Sandylands Blaze**
		Kimvalley	**Portia of Kimvalley**
	Ch. Beaver's Lavinia of		**Am./Can. Ch. Shamrock Acres**
	Moorwood, WC (Y)	**Ch. The Black Baroness**	**Top Brass**
			Heidi of Huntington
		Ch. Eireannach Black	**Ch. Mansergh Moose**
	Ch. Allegheny's Eclipse (B)	**Coachman**	**Powhatan Sable**
		Ch. Allegheny's Bezique	**Ch. Sandylands Mark**
Ch. Marshland Blitz (B)			**Ellerthwaite Jay**
		Ch. Elysium's Thunderstorm	**Sandylands Stormy Weather**
	Ch. Marshland Paisley		**Briary Banbury Belle**
	Broone (Y)	**Hawkett Paisley Amb'r**	**Ardmargha Samson**
		Breeze	**Ch. Paisley's Apricot Delight**
Dickendall's A-Ha (B)		**Ch. Lockerbie Brian**	**Ch. Lockerbie Kismet**
	Ch. Briary Bracken (Y)	**Boru, WC**	**Lockerbie Tackety Boots**
		Ch. Lockerbie Shillelagh	**Ch. Lockerbie Sandylands**
			Tarquin
Dickendall's Rose Royce (B)			**Princess Marlow**
		Rosedale Beau	**Am./Eng. Ch. Sandylands Midas**
	Raisin Cain of Woodbrook,		**Harrowby Polly**
	CD (B)	**Ch. Spenrock Spun Candy**	**Am./Eng. Ch. Sandylands Midas**
			Int. Ch. Spenrock's Banner

Sandylands Markwell of Lockerbie (Diane Jones)

CH. SANDYLANDS MARKWELL OF LOCKERBIE (B)

Eng. Ch. Sandylands Mark (B)	**Eng. Ch. Reanacre Mallardhurn Thunder**	**Eng. Ch. Sandylands Tweed of Blaircourt**	Eng. Ch. Ruler of Blaircourt
			Eng. Ch. Tessa of Blaircourt
		Mallardhurn Pat	Eng. Ch. Polleton Lieutenant
			Gunsmith Susette
	Eng. Ch. Sandylands Truth	**Aus. Ch. Sandylands Tan**	Eng. Ch. Sandylands Tweed of Blaircourt
			Sandylands Annabel
		Sandylands Shadow	Am./Eng./Can. Ch. Sam of Blaircourt
			Diant Pride
Eng. Ch. Sandylands Waghorn Honesty (Y)	**Eng. Ch. Sandylands Tandy**	**Aus. Ch. Sandylands Tan**	Eng. Ch. Sandylands Tweed of Blaircourt
			Sandylands Annabel
		Sandylands Shadow	Am./Eng./Can. Ch. Sam of Blaircourt
			Diant Pride
	Eng. Ch. Sandylands Honour	**Aus. Ch. Pinchbeck Nokeener Harvest Home**	Cliveruth Harvester
			Nokeener Novelblack
		Eng. Ch. Sandylands Truth	Aus. Ch. Sandylands Tan
			Sandylands Shadow

Graemoor Tim (Graham)

CH. GRAEMOOR TIM, CD, JH (B)

Ch. Marshland Blitz (B)

- **Ch. Allegheny's Eclipse (B)**
  - **Ch. Eireannach Black Coachman (B)**
    - Ch. Mansergh Moose (B)
    - Powhatan Sable (Y)
  - **Ch. Allegheny's Bezique (B)**
    - Eng. Ch. Sandylands Mark (B)
    - Ellerthwaite Jay (B)
- **Ch. Marshland Paisley Broone (Y)**
  - **Ch. Elysium's Thunderstorm (B)**
    - Sandylands Stormy Weather (B)
    - Briary Banbury Belle (Y)
  - **Hawkett Paisley Amb'r Breeze (Y)**
    - Ardmargha Samson (Y)
    - Ch. Paisley's Apricot Delight

Ch. Graemoor Tanqueray (Y)

- **Am./Eng. Ch. Receiver of Cranspire (Y)**
  - **Dutch Ch. Cranspire Skytrain (Y)**
    - Cambremer Petrocelli (Y)
    - Poolstead Purpose of Cranspire (Y)
  - **Polly's Pride of Genisval (Y)**
    - Eng. Ch. Newinn Kestrel (Y)
    - Heatherbourne Genista (Y)
- **Ch. Graemoor Cymbidium (Y)**
  - **Ch. Allegheny's Eclipse (B)**
    - Ch. Eireannach Black Coachman (B)
    - Ch. Allegheny Bezique (B)
  - **Ch. Sandylands Radiance (Y)**
    - Eng. Ch. Sandylands My Rainbeau (Y)
    - Eng. Ch. Sandylands Sparkle

Jayncourt Ajoco Justice (Janet Farmillette)

CH. JAYNCOURT AJOCO JUSTICE (B)

Ch. Ballyduff Marketeer (B)

- **Eng. Ch. Sandylands Mark (B)**
  - **Ch. Reanacre Mallardhurn Thunder**
    - Ch. Sandylands Tweed of Blaircourt
    - Mallardhurn Pat
  - **Ch. Sandylands Truth**
    - Aus. Ch. Sandylands Tan
    - Sandylands Shadow
- **Eng. Ch. Ballyduff Marina (Y)**
  - **Int. Ch. Ballyduff Seaman**
    - Ch. Ballyduff Hollybranch of Keithray
    - Cookridge Negra
  - **Electron of Ardmargha**
    - Ch. Sandylands Tandy
    - Hollybarn Ebony of Ardmargha

Jayncourt Star Performer (Y)

- **Eng. Ch. Sandylands Garry (Y)**
  - **Sandylands General**
    - Ch. Garvel of Garshangan
    - Sandylands Annabel
  - **Sandylands Memory**
    - Ch. Reanacre Mallardhurn Thunder
    - Ch. Sandylands Truth
- **Jayncourt Star Attraction (Y)**
  - **Sandylands Charlie Boy**
    - Cliveruth Harvester
    - Ch. Sandylands Katrina of Keithray
  - **Jayncourt Lucky Charmer**
    - Ch. Sandylands Mark
    - Jayncourt Michelle

Tabatha's Drifter at Dickendall (Richard Herr)

CH. TABATHA'S DRIFTER AT DICKENDALL, JH (B)

Ch. Dickendall Arnold (B)	**Ch. Dickendall's Ruffy, WC, SH (B)**	**Am./Eng. Ch. Receiver of Cranspire (Y)**	Dutch Ch. Cranspire Skytrain (Y) — Cambremer Petrocelli / Poolstead Purpose of Cranspire
			Polly's Pride of Genisval (Y) — Eng. Ch. Newinn Kestrel / Heatherbourne Genista
		Ch. Moorwood Jewel (B)	Ch. Eireannach Black Coachman (B) — Eng. Ch. Mansergh Moose / Powhatan Sable
			Ch. Beaver's Lavinia of Moorwood, WC (Y) — Ch. Somersett Cider of Kimvalley / Ch. The Black Baroness
	Dickendall's A-Ha (B)	**Ch. Marshland Blitz (B)**	Ch. Allegheny's Eclipse (B) — Ch. Eireannach Black Coachman / Ch. Allegheny's Bezique
			Ch. Marshland Paisley Broone (Y) — Ch. Elysium's Thunderstorm / Hawkett Paisley Amb'r Breeze
		Dickendall's Rose Royce (B)	Ch. Briary Bracken (Y) — Ch. Lockerbie Brian Boru, WC / Ch. Lockerbie Shillelagh
			Raisin Cain of Woodbrook, CD (B) — Rosedale Beau / Ch. Spenrock Spun Candy
Ch. Tabatha's Valleywood Decoy, WC (Y)	**Ch. Driftwood's Celebration (Y)**	**Ch. Sandylands Markwell of Lockerbie (B)**	Eng. Ch. Sandylands Mark (B) — Eng. Ch. Reanacre Mallardhurn Thunder / Eng. Ch. Sandylands Truth
			Eng. Ch. Sandylands Waghorn Honesty (Y) — Eng. Ch. Sandylands Tandy / Eng. Ch. Sandylands Honour
		Ch. Driftwood's Limited Edition (Y)	Ch. Mijan's Corrigan (Y) — Anderscroft Stalayna Sioux / Ch. Driftwood's Honeysuckle
			Ch. Driftwood's Gypsy — Ch. Lockerbie Kismet / Driftwood's Seabee
	Ch. Valleywood's Kannonball Kate (Y)	**Ch. Jayncourt Ajoco Justice (B)**	Eng. Ch. Ballyduff Marketeer (B) — Eng. Ch. Sandylands Mark / Eng. Ch. Ballyduff Marina
			Eng. Ch. Jayncourt Star Performer (Y) — Eng. Ch. Sandylands Garry / Jayncourt Star Attraction
		Ch. Ballyduff Lark (B)	Eng. Ch. Timspring Sirius (B) — Am./Eng. Ch. Ballyduff Seaman / Timspring Myrtle
			Spark of Ballyduff (B) — Eng. Ch. Ballyduff Marketeer / Sparkle of Tuddenham

Lobuff's Bare Necessities with Bethany Agresta (Booth Photography)

CH. LOBUFF'S BARE NECESSITIES, CD, JH (B)

Ch. Dickendall's Ruffy, SH (B)

- **Am./Eng. Ch. Receiver of Cranspire (Y)**
  - **Dutch Ch. Cranspire Skytrain (Y)**
    - Cambremer Petrocelli (Y)
    - Poolstead Purpose of Cranspire (Y)
  - **Polly's Pride of Genisval (Y)**
    - Eng. Ch. Newinn Kestrel (Y)
    - Heatherbourne Genista (Y)
- **Ch. Moorwood Jewel (B)**
  - **Ch. Eireannach Black Coachman (B)**
    - Ch. Mansergh Moose (B)
    - Powhatan Sable (Y)
  - **Ch. Beaver's Lavinia of Moorwood (Y)**
    - Ch. Somersett Cider of Kimvalley (Y)
    - Ch. The Black Baroness (B)

Second Sight Brandie (B)

- **Ch. J.Sun Farms Cedarhill Cadet (Y)**
  - **Ch. Heatherbourne Clansman (Y)**
    - Eng. Ch. Heatherbourne Court Jester (Y)
    - Heatherbourne Party Spirit
  - **Ch. Graemoor J.Sun Farms Sassy**
    - Ch. Allegheny's Eclipse (B)
    - Ch. Sandylands Radiance (Y)
- **Second Sight Onyx (B)**
  - **Ch. Northwood Sandman (Y)**
    - Ch. Sandylands Markwell of Lockerbie (B)
    - Ch. Finchingfield Fantasia (Y)
  - **Second Sight Eloise**
    - Ch. Lobuff's Seafaring Banner (B)
    - Tudor Belle Savage

(Winnie Limbourne)

Bibliography

General Information

Books

Check www.amazon.com for a list of out-of-print Labrador books that might be available.

Brown, Julie. *Julie Brown's Directory to Labrador Retriever Pedigrees.* Melrose Park, PA: 1971–1998.

Churchill, Janet I. *The New Labrador Retriever.* New York: Howell Book House, 1995.

Wiles-Fone, Heather, ed. *The Ultimate Labrador Retriever.* New York: Howell Book House, 1997.

Martin, Nancy A. *The Versatile Labrador Retriever.* Wilsonville, OR: Doral, 1994.

Coode, Carole. *Labrador Retrievers Today.* New York: Howell Book House, 1993.

Warwick, Helen. *The New Complete Labrador Retriever.* New York: Howell Book House, 1986.

McCarty, Diane. *Labrador Retrievers.* Neptune City, NJ: T.F.H. Publications, 1995.

Agresta, Lisa Weiss. *The Labrador Retriever, An Owner's Guide to a Happy, Healthy Pet.* New York: Howell Book House, 1995.

Martin, Nancy. *Legends in Labradors.* Spring House PA, 1980.

Howe, Dorothy. *This is the Labrador Retriever.* Neptune City, NJ: T.F.H. Publications, 1985.

Beckett, Diana. *Pet Owner's Guide to the Labrador Retriever.* New York: Howell Book House, 1994.

Roslin-Williams, Mary. *All About the Labrador.* London, U.K.: Pelham Press, 1983.

Ziessow, Bernard W., ed. *The Official Book of the Labrador Retriever.* Neptune City, NJ: T.F.H. Publications, 1995.

Web Sites

The Labrador Retriever Home Page
  www.k9web.com/breeds/l/labrador/

The Labrador Retriever Club Inc. Home Page
  www.thelabradorclub.com

Magazines

The Labrador Quarterly. Hoflin Publishing, Inc. 4401 Zephyr Street, Wheat Ridge, CO.

The International Labrador Digest. P.O. Box 17158, Fayetteville, NC.

RETRIEVER TRAINING

Free, James Lamb. *Training Your Retriever* (7th Edition). New York: Putnam, 1980.

Quinn, Tom. *The Working Retriever.* New York: Dutton, 1983.

Walters, D. L. and Ann. *Training Retrievers to Handle.* LaCyne, KS, 1979.

George, Bobby N., Jr. *Training Retrievers: The Cotton Pershall Method.* Travers City, MI: Countrysport, 1990.

Wolters, Richard A. *Water Dog.* New York: Dutton, 1984.

Index